THE QUEEN UNDERNEATH

STACEY FILAK

PAGE STREET
PUBLISHING CO.

PAGE STREET
PUBLISHING CO.

Copyright © 2018 Stacey Filak

First published in 2018 by
Page Street Publishing Co.
27 Congress Street, Suite 105
Salem, MA 01970
www.pagestreetpublishing.com

Distributed by Macmillan, sales in Canada by The Canadian Manda Group.

22   21   20   19   18   1   2   3   4   5

ISBN-13: 978-1-62414-560-5
ISBN-10: 1-62414-560-4

Library of Congress Control Number: 2017915452

Cover and book design by Rosie Gutmann for Page Street Publishing Co.

Printed and bound in the United States

To Don and Esther Martin,
who were the first to believe;
and for Clay, who taught me to believe.

CONTENTS

To die: to sleep;
No more; and by a sleep to say we end
The heart-ache and the thousand natural shocks
That flesh is heir to, 'tis a consummation
Devoutly to be wish'd. To die, to sleep;
To sleep: perchance to dream: ay, there's the rub;
For in the sleep of death what dreams may come
When we have shuffled off this mortal coil,
Must give us pause.

　　　　—William Shakespeare, Hamlet

PART ONE

THIS MORTAL COIL

CHAPTER ONE

THE BLACK CHAMBER

Gemma hurried through the tunnels of Under, avoiding piles that might be rubbish and could be worse. She patted the satchel that hung at her side, grateful for the heft of the clean pair of boots within. It would not do to meet the King of Above for the first time with some urchin's shit on her feet. These tunnels led to the Golden Door. And though Melnora had brought her there countless times, the queen had never taken her through.

Tonight would be different. Melnora, Queen of Under, lay dying in Guildhouse. Just half an hour ago, her good eye had stared vacantly at Gemma, one side of her face sagging and paralyzed, her tongue stilled. It was the way of things—a master was supposed to pass on her apron to her apprentice, even if the apprentice was to be queen—but Gemma realized, only now, that she might not be ready. Perhaps, she never would be.

When the summons had come, little more than an hour after the palsy that had shaken Melnora, Gemma had felt the worst sort of cowardice. She had been nearly overwhelmed by the desire to run—to flee Yigris and leave the Guild without a leader. Temptation had made her limbs quake with adrenaline as she'd dressed in lightweight pants and a silken tunic for the clandestine meeting. But despite her raging desire to disappear, Gemma now found herself in the tunnels, known only to the Guild and to a few of the King of Above's most trusted advisors. The flush of her exertions painted her cheeks pink as she rushed toward the Golden Door. But her legs were steadfast despite the drumming of anxiety in her heart. The torch in her hand illuminated the rough-hewn walls, and she saw that she was nearing the Black Corridor, where the walls changed in the last stretch before the Golden Door that attached the tunnels Under to the palace Above. The first King of Above had required that the neutral meeting spot be up to the standards he was used to in his palace, but the Queen of Under was used to the dank tunnels and a less luxurious life. They could have met in a whorehouse, a tavern, or on the docks for all the Under cared.

She stopped and drew a breath to calm herself. She was the head of the Shadow Guild now. This was the first of many meetings that she would take with the King of Above. Though she'd not been born the heir of Under, she'd spent half a decade training for this moment. Melnora had put more than a few strong men and women to the knife for questioning Gemma's ability to lead, and now, Gemma would find out if Melnora's trust had been well placed. Everything—her entire life—had led her here. If Abram, King of Above, refused her, then Yigris would face a civil war that could prove as dangerous and devastating as the

Mage War that had led to the creation of Above and Under in the first place.

She drew herself to her full height, taller than many men, and wiped her sweat-dampened palms on her breeches before smoothing her tunic and patting at her short, spiky hair. She inspected her boots, which were blessedly clean, then took off her pack and placed it at her feet. It bore the mark of the Queen of Under. She smiled down at the black crest embossed into the red leather, a stylized seabird with a rat in its beak. In the dark of Yigris, it was good to be queen.

The Black Corridor was different from the rest of the tunnels she had left behind. Here, the shining stone was cleanly hewn and polished, a work of art that only emphasized the hodgepodge of debris and rubble she'd just passed through in the abandoned gold mines beneath the city. Lanterns, kept alight by the King of Above's mage women, illuminated the hallway. A hundred paces beyond, she could see the glimmer of the Golden Door. Its knocker was made of onyx and ruby, and its knob was a diamond the size of her palm. The thief in her saw both sides of the tempting treasure—the gnawing desire for such glorious wealth, and the obvious trap.

She sidled toward the door and mentally retraced the steps that Melnora had drilled into her. Dozens and dozens of times, her queen had shown her the intricate workings that separated Under from Above. At least ten times Gemma had disarmed the devices, but the door was ever changing. This was the final test. The gateway to her new life.

As she neared the door, her senses—so keenly honed to this

very work—reached out, observing it in every way she could. She smelled the dank of Under behind her, but it was mostly masked by the scented oily haze of the lanterns, which seemed to drift unnaturally upward.

Placing her hands on the barren space to the left of the knob and the right of the hinges, she felt the tingle of magery. The door should have been cool to the touch, but instead it hummed with warmth.

She could feel the vibrations of the mages' tests. One ripple. Two. Three. She smiled as if she'd been given a gift. Once, when she'd accompanied Melnora, there had been eleven traps set.

She scanned the glimmering door, searching out the nastiness that lay in wait for her if she were to be too hasty. Two wide-set hinges showed that the door opened toward her. Glancing downward, she ran her gaze along the floor.

"Ahhhh," she clicked her tongue. A slender line of light ran from one side of the wall to the other just six inches behind her feet. If she were to step back to allow the door to open, she'd interrupt the beam, and Aegos only knew what horrors would await her. Minding each step, she moved to the wall and bent low. A tiny, perfectly square niche held a brilliantly glowing gem. A mage mark scrawled upon it beamed brightly across to the other side of the corridor. She couldn't read the mark—it was written in the secret language of the Vagan mage women—but she recognized it by its swirls and flourishes.

Opposite, she found a tiny mirror that bounced the reflection back. She eyed it warily, knowing that her only option was to disarm it from this end. To touch magic without permission could mean death—or worse. She inhaled, gathering the cool, damp air into her lungs. Then she squatted and slid a finger into the groove that began just below the mirror. She clasped the fragile piece of glass between her pointer finger and thumb, then worked it free of its grooves, holding it in line with the gem. Taking painstaking low-to-the-ground steps, she moved the mirror toward the gem, shortening, but intensifying the beam as she went. A rivulet of sweat ran down her back, and she silently cursed the silk of her tunic, which would be ruined now. Step after slow, muscle-grinding step, she moved the mirror closer to the gem until the beam was glowing with such intensity that she had to close her eyes.

The door was designed so that, in theory, only the Queen of Under, leader of thieves and assassins, would be deft enough to disarm its traps. Gemma slid the mirror into its niche without looking. In that moment, she was calm. Melnora believed that she was capable of this. She would survive to meet the king. She felt the mirror click into place, opened her eyes and was amazed at the blank, featureless wall before her. She drew a trembling breath then stood up, a wide grin spreading across her face.

"That's one."

She turned back to the door and studied it. The butterflies that had filled her belly just moments before had settled, and her muscles grew taut with anticipation. She was made for work like this. Her gaze drifted along the door's surface, searching for the next of the mage women's machinations. Each channel and crevice held the potential for death, each piece of filigreed decoration could be hiding agony. She searched the midsection, so close to where she had recently placed her hands, then moved on, eying the knob warily. She could see herself reflected in its multitude of facets. Her red-gold hair stood out wildly, above eyes that seemed odd and alien in the diamond's angles. Seeing nothing, she moved on to the next, more painstaking part of detection. She placed two fingers—infinitesimally gentle—against the knob and began to feel her way along it. There had to be a mechanism, and so long as her movements remained slow and light, she could detect it with her sense of touch without setting it off.

Slowing her breathing to allow herself to hear even the faintest of clicks, she slid her fingers along the top of the doorknob, then along the iron shaft that connected it to the plate that buttressed the gleaming door. She felt for the slightest rise or depression, searching for any anomaly. Just as her fingertips brushed the burnished gold of the doorplate, she heard a soft click, and a tingle went through her. Before she even had time to yank her fingers back, another click, louder and closer, sounded. Her skin broke out in gooseflesh as she fell backward, her heart catching in her throat.

"Holy Aegos," she groaned as her ass hit the stone floor. She waited, expecting a poisoned dart or the fiery throes of a vicious death mark, but neither came. Instead, the door clicked once more and then swung open.

Standing in the doorway was a tall, dark-skinned young man with long curly hair and an expression of utter surprise on his face. Prince Tollan, royal heir, looked down at her. Behind him loomed the stooped figure of a woman. Long white hair hung in tangles hiding most of her face, which was devoid of emotion.

"Where's Melnora?"

The rising note of panic in Prince Tollan's voice made Gemma think, just briefly, that perhaps he was as unsure of his footing as she was. She stood and straightened her tunic, then took one step toward him and knelt on the floor. She forced herself not to think of the mirror-and-gem trap that she had just disarmed, right where she now knelt.

"I . . . I am sorry, Your Highness," she stammered, averting her gaze, as she pretended to grapple with the proper way to greet the royal heir. "My queen has taken ill. She was summoned to your father. I am Gemma Antos. I am to be Queen of Under when she is gone."

The prince's face fell, his gray eyes growing dark. "I am sorry to be the one to tell you, this, then," he said as he reached down, grabbing her arm and pulling her into the room after him, "but Melnora was not summoned by my father." The Golden Door slammed behind her, and all the air rushed out of Gemma's lungs as she gaped at his hand holding her arm. This was not the way this meeting was supposed to go at all.

"I summoned Melnora," the prince said gruffly. "King Abram is dead." He swallowed, looking as stunned by the words as she was.

Gemma met his gaze, disbelief and distaste mingling on her tongue like sour milk.

He must have realized that he still held a stern grip on her upper arm. "Oh, I . . ." He released her, staring down at his own hand as if it disturbed him. "Sorry."

The elderly woman shuffled her feet behind him, and he spun. "Oh, yes. Hannai, go back to your room."

The woman, who Gemma realized must be one of the king's mage women, stared up at the prince with eerie, watery eyes. Her eyebrow fluttered as if she were about to voice some displeasure, but then she turned and walked slowly away. The door clicked shut behind her, and the prince turned back to Gemma. His hands were trembling, and he clasped them in front of him to hide it.

Goddess, he's a mess. "I am sorry to hear of your loss, Your . . . Your Grace," she said, purposefully stumbling over the proper way to address him. Her bottom lip trembled slightly. "Please forgive me, Your Grace. I am . . . distraught over Melnora's illness, and I was unprepared for—"

"It's all right," he said, "I'm a bit of a—"

The door that led deeper into the palace burst open. The younger prince, Iven, who Gemma recalled as little more than a boy at the last royal parade, stormed into the room brandishing a bloody sword. He was followed by a pale-faced young woman and two elderly mage women.

"Stop!" Iven bellowed at the top of his lungs. "You, Tollan Daghan, are under arrest for regicide and patricide." There was a dangerous glint in his eyes.

Prince Tollan stared at his brother, eyes wide and mouth open and closing like a fish on the beach. When he spoke, his voice quavered. "No! Father collapsed, and I was called to his rooms. He died in his bed."

"Yes, at the point of your blade!" Iven waved the sword.

"I didn't!" Tears sprung to the elder prince's eyes.

Gemma had seen enough to know that this family argument was one she had no interest in witnessing. She glanced at the mage women, whose eyes stared blankly out of emotionless faces. A chill ran down her spine. The young woman beside Prince Iven smiled smugly. Mind racing ahead, Gemma made a decision. The royal family could tear itself apart later—Melnora was lying on her deathbed. She turned to go, then turned back, sighing over her own sentimentality. Tollan Daghan didn't look like he'd fare well in this fight.

"Come on, Your Highness," she grabbed his arm. "Time to go. This is one ball you were not invited to." She pulled him backward, slamming the Golden Door shut behind them. Several mage marks flared upon its surface and the walls of the Black Corridor, resetting themselves.

She grinned at him. "We've got a few minutes' head start." Scooping up her satchel, she pulled him along, past the elegant Black Corridor and into the chilly debris-strewn tunnel. They ran, making turn after turn as she counted in her head and ignored his panting. The darkness was complete, but Gemma knew her way. Tollan tripped repeatedly, but she caught him. His breath was coming in gasps when she finally pulled to a halt.

"So, about that whole assassination thing..." she said, unable to keep the sarcasm out of her words.

"I didn't do it. I swear," he said while wheezing.

"That's what they all say," she said, then realized that he might not be able to tell that she was joking. "What did happen to the king?"

Tollan coughed and she could hear tears in his voice as he said, "He was in meetings for most of the morning. After luncheon, he said he had a headache and went to his chambers. He . . . he had some kind of a fit that left him dead on one side of his body." She could feel the movement of the air around him as he slid to the floor. His words came out in choked sobs. "He . . . he fell asleep and . . . "

Gemma's heart began to pound as she realized how similar his story was to what had happened to Melnora. "Did he fall into a slumber and could not be awakened?" she continued.

"He did," Tollan croaked. "And then . . . he died."

Fear and rage raced through her veins. "How long?" she snapped. "How long did the slumber last?"

Tollan's voice was a small moth of a thing. "Hours," he whispered. "Only a few hours."

"Shit. Prickling, shitting Void," Gemma snarled. Pieces of a puzzle were fitting themselves together neatly in her mind, forming a picture that terrified her.

"What? Are you all right?"

"Of course I'm not all right! Are you? Your father is dead, and for all I know, Melnora's gone now, too. The physician said she wouldn't last the night. And I just helped you escape royal justice. Oh, balls." She slapped her palms against the tunnel walls.

"I didn't do it." He sounded pitiful and pathetic.

"We've been over that. You're not a half-wit, are you? I need to know if you're up for the challenge, here."

"No, I . . . What challenge?"

"Obviously, you're telling the truth. The mage women marked you as king, right?"

"Yes." He gasped as her fingers slid beneath his tunic, touching the skin of his back.

She could feel the rough skin around the mark, the flesh branded with magic. "Sorry, big guy. I just had to be sure."

"It's . . . it's fine. What am I going to do?"

"Who can you trust back at the palace?"

All the air in Tollan's lungs poured out in a rush. "There's no one. There's only you."

Gemma stopped walking. She could hear the clop of horses' hooves and people talking nearby. She ignored the fear that was trying to seep its way into her chest. "Hey," she said, punching him lightly on the shoulder. "You're doing just fine, then."

CHAPTER TWO

SIX-MAST INN

Gemma pushed aside the thin wooden panel that hid the entrance to the underground tunnels from the storeroom of the Six-Mast Inn. "Welcome to Dockside."

Tollan blinked, his eyes watery. "Where are we?"

Gemma grinned. "You're in the pantry of the most famous whorehouse in Yigris, my friend."

Tollan's jaw fell open, and he took a step backward as if the very air around him might tarnish his skin. "Oh, goddess."

"We're here to keep you hidden until we figure out what's going on. I've got things that need doing, and you need to loosen your laces before your brain explodes."

"What? I'll do no such thing!" Tollan barked.

"It's an expression, for goddess's sake. You're wound as tightly as a clock. But I can see that you're not interested in spending time with the ladies, so I'll just pay for a room."

"Who else would I possibly want to spend time with?"

Tollan said indignantly.

Gemma arched an eyebrow at him. "Let's not get our smallclothes tied in knots, Tollan. I'll get you a room so you can rest before you get the vapors."

She strode through the pantry, trusting that Tollan would rather follow her than be left alone. "I need a brief audience with Madam Yimur," Gemma said to the serving girl they passed in the hallway.

The maid curtsied. "Of course, Miss Gemma. Follow me."

"Come here often?" Tollan looked ashen.

Gemma stopped and stared at him. "Occasionally. Why?"

"Even the help knows your name."

She glared at him. "Does everyone in the palace know your name?"

He nodded.

"You're in my kingdom, now. Get used to it."

The new King of Above kept quiet after that as they wound their way through the back hallways of the Six-Mast and came to a stop at the office door of Madam Yimur, Under's mistress of whores.

Her thin smile betrayed no true emotion as she opened the door. "Miss Gemma. What a surprise." She glanced at Tollan and smoothed her gown as she eyed his well-dressed figure. "What can the Six-Mast do for you?"

Gemma laughed as Tollan blushed. He lowered his gaze and began to stammer, but Gemma interrupted him. "Yimur, I need a favor. Prince Tollan needs a place to hide for a few hours, and I need you to keep him here, no questions asked."

Yimur's smile turned into a frown. "Prince? Trouble, then?"

"The deepest. There'll be a call to Guildhall soon, and I wouldn't be surprised if there was word from Above, as well."

As if on cue, a knock sounded on the door. "Enter," Yimur commanded.

"Pardon me, madam," a young man said. "The bells at the palace and Canticle Center are ringing. The King of Above is dead."

"Thank you, Bellamy," Yimur mumbled, waving him away. She turned her attention back to Gemma. "What sort of storm have you brought to my house, Gemma?"

"The worst kind, I'm afraid."

When Yimur had situated Tollan in a poshly decorated room, Gemma turned to leave. "I've got a few things to address, and then I'll be back. A fancy princeling like you doesn't have any noblemen he can call on in a pinch?"

Tollan, who looked as if he were in shock, suddenly shook himself awake. "Yes. I mean . . . no. There's Wince . . . Wincel Quintella. Probably my only friend."

"He's in the palace?"

"No. He's . . . his father is weapons master. He lives on Steel Street, I think."

"You've never been there?"

He shook his head.

"Would your brother think to look for him?"

"No. I don't think so. I honestly doubt Iven even knows Wince exists."

Gemma grinned. "Excellent. Yimur will help disguise you, and a runner will deliver a message to Wince. You'll need all the friends you can get."

Tollan blushed and stammered his way through the costuming like a storm-spooked horse. Knowing he was making a fool of himself did nothing to soften the rough edges of his anxiety. When Yimur's dresser, Zin, spread out an assortment of clothes on the bed and told him to remove his finery, Tollan's heart raced and his fingers trembled as he undid his shirt buttons.

"Now, then," Zin said, maple eyes dancing. "Out of your breeches."

Tollan felt his skin go warm, but he undid his laces. Zin, whose black, curly hair was trimmed extremely close to his scalp, ran his hand across his head and said, "I'm sorry, but you're too clean. We need to get you dirty."

The level of shame and embarrassment that Tollan felt as he swelled within his smallclothes was almost equal to the sudden ache of desire that left his mouth dry, but some ridiculous sense of pride and privilege kept him from turning his back to the man.

Zin smiled kindly at him. "You flatter me, Your Grace, but I've got orders from the madam, and not enough time to do the thing proper."

Tollan followed the man's instructions in shamed silence, running in place until his hair clung to his sweat-dampened face. He couldn't bring himself to look at Zin, couldn't bear to look at himself in the mirror, even after the man helped him into rough brown-wool breeches and a stained and worn cotton shirt, along with a pair of work boots. Zin tied Tollan's hair back in a single plait, then smeared gum paste along his chin line to affix a false beard like something in a mummer's show. He pulled a seaman's cap low over Tollan's brow, and then he added a padded black eye patch over Tollan's left eye.

"I look a fool," Tollan said. "Anyone will see the farce."

"No, Your Grace," Zin said, bending down and straightening the eye patch. "You look the part. All you have to do is believe it yourself."

When Zin had gone, Tollan finally managed to catch his breath. An hour in Under, and he was behaving just like his father had always said the "degenerate, depraved animals" did down here. But he couldn't disregard the kindness Zin had shown him. No man in Above would have treated his awkwardness so gently.

Tollan grinned rakishly at himself in the looking glass but immediately regretted it. His teeth were too pretty to be a sailor's. Best if he kept his mouth shut.

CHAPTER THREE

GUILDHOUSE

A fter sending the runner off to Steel Street, Gemma went back to her own room at Guildhouse. She sagged into a chair. Who had murdered King Abram and tried to murder Melnora? She would bet her very best blade Tollan Daghan had nothing to do with it. And yet, it also didn't have the feel of Under. If a Guild assassin came for you, it was brutal and bloody, but it was fast. Melnora was suffering. That wasn't the way of the Under.

Gemma stood and paced the room, remembering when she'd been even less than an urchin begging for bits and cutting a purse now and then to get by. One day she'd cut the wrong strings and found herself in the grip of a snapping, pointed-toothed Balklander named Fin who dragged her kicking and hissing to Melnora for judgment. By then, Gemma had spent three years in orphanages and missions until she'd finally set out on her own. At the ripe age of thirteen, she'd thought she had

Yigris by the balls. She couldn't help but smile at the memory despite the thickness in her throat.

"Come here, child," Melnora had said, crooking her finger.

Gemma had trembled, chewing her lip as big fat tears washed away the grime on her face. "I'm s-sorry, milady," she'd choked, "I didn't mean to steal your man's purse. I just . . . I was so hungry, and I . . ." She let out a long, dramatic sob. It was much the same scared-little-girl act that she'd put on for Tollan in the Black Chamber.

Melnora, however, had tipped her head to the side, dark eyes pensive. She'd held out her hand to one of the serving men, who'd plopped a scalding wet rag into her palm, and grabbed Gemma's chin, clasping tightly as she scrubbed away the filth from her face.

Gemma could still feel the stinging heat of the water and smell the clean scent of chamomile soap.

Melnora had held Gemma at arm's length, her gaze appraising. Finally, she'd said, "Have you been paying your dues, child?"

Gemma had simply stared, sniveling.

"I thought not. Every thief in this city belongs to me, child." She'd stared at Gemma, eyes hard. "It seems that you owe me some money."

Gemma knew noble folk would never let a filthy street rat get away with their precious coin. She dug her fingernails into her palm to bring tears to her eyes and wailed, "Are you going to strap me, mistress?"

Melnora chuckled. "Now, what good would that do anyone? You owe me money, and you need to learn a trade. You're too old to be begging like an urchin. And if you've an inkling to play the helpless victim, you're going to have to get much, much better than you are now."

For all of Gemma's faults, stupidity wasn't one of them, and she looked Melnora in the eye. "What do you want me to do?"

Minutes later, she'd been put into a warm bath and left to soak until the water turned gray with her filth. Then, Melnora's maid, Lian, had scrubbed her until she was shiny and pink. She trimmed Gemma's hair and nails and gave her clean clothes to wear. Then she was led to the dinner table, where Melnora, Fin and several other Guild members were waiting for her.

The table made Gemma's eyes go wide. Roasted fowl, rare, dripping roast beef, large bowls of potatoes and beans and crusty loaves of bread with butter slathered on. Each Guild member had a large glass of wine poured before them, and as Gemma sat down, Melnora nodded to the attendants, who began to serve the meal. It was only then, as slices of roast beef were being laid upon plates, red juices pooling against the white of whipped potatoes, that Gemma realized she had no plate. Saliva filled her mouth and hot, stinging tears threatened her eyes, but she sat, back straight, chin thrust outward and watched the others eat. A lad of about her own age smiled apologetically, while a second, hard-eyed young man ate his food with relish, grinning wolfishly when their eyes met. The meal was a hell she'd not yet experienced.

When the others had been excused, Melnora looked at her. "You're not peasant-born. I can tell. Give me your story."

Gemma had scowled as she told Melnora of her childhood spent in the house of a minor nobleman, Lord Ghantos. When Gemma was seven, Lord Ghantos had died and her mother, who had been his favorite mistress, had tried to make a living as a laundress. But her skills had never been of a domestic sort, and she'd taken ill and died when Gemma was eight. "I can read and do sums and I know when to say 'isn't', and when to say 'ain't', if that's what you mean, Your Grace."

Melnora smiled, broadly this time. "And you've got a good deal of pride, haven't you, child? In Under, the queen is addressed as Regency. *Any fool can be born to a position of control and claim it is the goddess's will. Down here, we believe that a ruler must lead."*

Gemma had simply stared at her.

"You're going to work off the money that you owe the Guild. Six months as my chambermaid. Then we'll see where your place in Under should be."

Gemma nodded as if she were consenting to the situation even though she saw no other choice. No amount of time would ever diminish the memory of the smile that Melnora had graced her with as she rang a small bell. A servant entered the room with a plate laden with food, which he placed before Gemma. Hands clenched tightly in her lap, Gemma felt actual drool begin to slip out from between her lips.

"Eat," Melnora said.

Doing her level best to maintain her dignity, Gemma snatched up a fork and knife and dove in.

"I, too, was born of noble blood yet never had my place among the court," Melnora said. "That makes us kin, of a sort, you and I. You please me, with your sharp chin and your eyes that see too much. Learn our ways. Find your calling. There are positions within the Guild that can make you a very powerful woman, Gemma." She leaned over, whispering conspiratorially. "Some say that we're more powerful than the King of Above, himself."

Gemma had nearly choked on her roast beef. "I'd like to be as rich as the king!" she said, "With rings on each finger and fat that hangs from his belly like he's with child."

"If that is what you wish, and you are willing to work hard, then it can be yours." Melnora's eyes danced in the light of the torches that lit

the dining room. "But I imagine we will find other things that please you just as well."

And for five years, they had. When her six months as chambermaid were finished, Melnora had offered her the status of ward heir and had adopted her into her household. Gemma was placed on a three-member team—one thief, one assassin and one paramour—who lived together, planned together and trained together. It was the only team overseen by the queen herself, who made sure they were following Guild laws and not bringing dishonor to Under.

Even then, Devery had been a skilled assassin. At eighteen, he was dead quick, cold as a midwinter outhouse, and sharp as the daggers he doted on. Elam, the fifteen-year-old paramour, was as warm and open as Devery was closed. He welcomed Gemma into their little apartment with a loaf of sweet bread and a hug. And though he was often out meeting patrons, he came home every night and snuggled into bed with her. Elam was the first friend she ever had.

Days and weeks and months and years blended together as the three of them honed their crafts. They spent a great deal of time with Melnora and Fin learning the intricacies of Under and secrets that the rest of the Guild had never been granted access to. Gemma had never wanted for anything, except perhaps sleep, and she had grown to adore Melnora as only an abandoned child could.

And now, though Gemma wanted desperately to throw herself into bed and pull the covers over her head, she knew that Melnora had taught her better than that. The Guild must never be without a leader.

She pulled the rope beside her bed and within seconds Lian entered, her eyes red rimmed. The tight bun that kept her graying locks tied up was slipping, stray curls hung loose around her face.

"Yes, Miss?" Her eyes did not meet Gemma's, and once more Gemma thought her heart would crack in two.

"I need you to send out the children. Have them spread the word as far as possible. We meet at Guildhall in an hour."

A quiet sob leaked out from between the maid's lips. "As you say, Miss . . . Regency." It was the change in title that suddenly made Gemma realize how well and truly pricked she was.

Gemma forced herself to go through the motions of dressing for the occasion: tight black pants, knee-high black leather boots, a black silk shirt and a red velvet vest that came down over her hips with the queen's mark embroidered on one breast and the Guild's shadowed ring on the other. Gemma loved the crest of the Guild and what it represented—a gold ring, the symbol of Yigrisian commerce, caught in a looming shadow. The darkness of Under always protected the coin.

She washed the redness of her grief away from her face and darkened her lids the way Melnora had taught her. "It gives you more age, girl, more authority," she'd said, and Gemma was grateful for that lesson—and every lesson—just now. She put silver rings in her ears and slid a large gold ring inset with an opal onto her right pointer finger. She ran trembling fingers through her hair, though it did little to calm its wayward nature. Then she slid her knives into the sheaths at her wrists, ankles and waist.

There was a knock on her door, the comforting sound of a huge hand pounding as gently as it could. The owner of that knock was a man of restraint and kindness, and Gemma's heart broke for him and what he must be going through.

"Come in, Fin."

The Balklander entered, his beady eyes bloodshot. "Need an escort, Gem?" he grunted, running a gray hand over his bald head.

She wrapped her arms around his waist, and he gripped her in a bear hug, his back quaking with sobs. If anyone alive had loved Melnora more than Gemma, it was Fin. He'd been the Queen of Under's unlikely lover for more than twenty years.

"You don't have to go, Fin. You know what I have to say. If you want to stay with her ..."

"I can't watch her die, Gem. She's gone now, and she ain't coming back. She'd want me to help you do this thing that needs doing."

Gemma looked up into his oddly unwrinkled face. Sometimes it was easy to see why the Balklanders were said to have been bred from sharks, with their pointed teeth and smooth ashen skin, but looking up into Fin's eyes, Gemma could feel his heart breaking. She stood on her tiptoes and kissed him lightly on the cheek. "Thanks, Fin."

She glanced around, surveying her room. When she returned, she would be a different person. The old Gemma would never walk through these doors again. She made her way to the door, gesturing for the old Balklander to walk out before her. "I have to go say goodbye."

In Melnora's room, Lian stood to leave when she saw them enter, but Gemma motioned her back to her chair. Fin stood by the door, his eyes hooded. The shadows under his eyes and his unwillingness to stay and watch her final moments told Gemma that he'd already said whatever he needed to say to Melnora.

Gemma was struck by how lifeless Melnora already seemed. Her beautiful mahogany skin was ashen, her black hair—laced with silver—had lost all its luster. Her breathing rattled, like rocks tumbling in her chest. Gemma bit her lip to keep from crying.

She bent over and whispered in her benefactor's ear. "I've got to go keep your folks in line, now. Thank you . . . for everything . . ." A slow sob ripped its way out of her. "I love you, Mother." The words were ragged and clumsy—and Gemma cursed herself for never having said them before. "I'll take care of things, here. Sleep well, and give Aegos the Void."

CHAPTER FOUR

GUILDHALL

G emma did her best to remember to breathe. The seats had filled up, and still members flooded through the great doorways that led to the spoked half wheel of the underground amphitheater. The room was divided into five sections—representatives from the thieves, the pirates, the sex workers, the assassins and the mercenaries filled the seats, while the urchins were crammed together like rats on the floor just below where she stood, jostling and jarring one another to secure the best view.

She could tell which of the urchins had already distinguished themselves as leaders. A tall, slender boy of about twelve with a shock of ragged black hair was given a wide berth. So was Katya, a younger girl with long brown hair marked by a strand of pure white near her temple. Gemma winked at the dirty-faced girl, who grinned broadly, then turned to punch a bigger boy who had bumped her in the shoulder. He twisted around, snarling—until he saw Katya's face. He bobbed his head in apology and scooted away.

Gemma had made a special effort to get to know the girl, and she found that Katya was light-fingered, charismatic and quick-thinking. Gemma believed that one day she could stand on the dais in Gemma's place should Gemma fail to produce an heir of her own.

Fin stepped out from the shadows. "All right, you animals!" he bellowed. "Gemma's got the floor, now. Give her your prickling respect." He flashed pointed teeth in her direction, despite the hollowness in his eyes.

Immediately, a hush fell over the crowd. Gemma estimated that as many as six hundred had crammed into Guildhall—a full quarter of the membership. Clearing her throat, she stepped forward, holding before her the enormous tome that contained the Guild's bylaws. "You know what it says here." She paused, drawing in a deep breath. "Melnora is dying. She was stabbed three hours ago."

Of course, this was complete horseshit—and she looked around to see if anyone seemed to know she was laying a false trail. She forced herself to meet the eyes of the leaders: Riquin, the oddly bearded head of the pirates; Yimur, ironically flat-chested mistress of whores; Gellen, straight-arrow captain of the sellswords; Dalia, one-eyed leader of thieves; and Devery, the cold-as-ice master assassin. Her stomach flipped when she saw him. He was supposed to be on Far Coast on assignment for Melnora. These leaders had reported directly to Melnora, and now they would come to Gemma for favors, coin, guidance and leadership. Though the youngest was a handful of years older than Gemma and some were Melnora's age, Gemma would be their mother.

Every thief in Yigris belongs to me now.

She steeled herself, meeting the master assassin's cold, calculating eyes and holding his gaze longer than any other's. She wanted to let the Guild believe that even if he and his ilk were responsible for the strange attacks on Melnora and Abram, that she was not afraid of him. Devery glanced away first, his pale face coloring slightly.

"I pray to Aegos we will meet back here in a few days and I will tell you the queen lives. But until then"—she thrust the book forward—"Melnora has named me heir in the absence of a true child of her blood and bone."

Gemma nodded to Fin to take the book, and she drew the knife at her waist. Holding her hand up, she slid the blade along her palm, drawing a shallow line of crimson. "I bleed for the Shadow Guild. I lay my life down for the well-being of my brothers and sisters. I accept the weight of this duty upon my shoulders. Anyone who does not accept my leadership should draw blades against me now." She stood back, waiting to see if they would come.

Slowly, she realized no one rose from their seats. She began to breathe easier as she stared out at the sea of faces. Blood dripped from her hand onto the wooden dais, leaving her stain next to the stains of those who'd come before her and naming her Queen of Under.

"Above suffers today, too, and I do not know what the goddess has planned for Yigris. But I will do whatever it takes to see that our way of life is not altered. I will not let their poison contaminate our Under. You have the promise of your queen."

As quickly as the meeting had begun, it ended, and Guild members spilled out into the tunnels. Fin clapped her on the shoulder as she wrapped her hand in a clean cloth. "You did good, Gem," he said, his big hand ruffling her hair the way it had when she was a kid.

Gemma nodded. Melnora's greatest fear had been that someone would use her passing to undermine the Guild, and though she should have been elated that no one had challenged her, Gemma felt it hard to breathe through her guilt. Her heart hurt for Melnora and Fin, and Gemma would have given up all the power in the world to have her queen back. Sighing, she looked up and saw Devery pushing his way through the crowd.

Fin thrust his chin toward the master assassin. "You want me to keep him away?"

"I'm good. I've got some other people I need to see tonight. Check on Melnora. Give her my love."

When Fin was gone and the crowd had thinned, Devery finally reached her. "Regency," he said, his voice little more than a whisper.

She met his eyes steadily, though her heart was pounding. "Walk with me. I've got places I still need to be." She turned her back on him. She knew that all eyes were still on her, that the Guild wanted to see how she would handle these first moments, so she put her back to the assassin, letting those still in the hall see that she was brave enough to do so, and made her way to the door at the back of the dais, toward the bowels of Guildhall. She listened to the absence of sound from his footsteps, not for the first time both horrified and amazed by the master assassin's ability to be utterly undetectable.

She opened the door into a darkened hallway and felt—rather than heard—him slip in behind her. As she turned to him, his unnaturally dexterous hands slipped beneath her vest and unbuttoned her shirt. Her breath caught as she leaned in to kiss him. "I didn't know you were back yet." She felt the heat of his mouth against her throat and was met by silence as his lips found her breasts. She pressed herself against the wall as his fingers smoothly undid the laces of her breeches and found their way between her legs. "Dev," she moaned, "I don't know if . . ."

Her nipple audibly popped out of his mouth as he pulled away from her. She had to stop herself from pushing his hand immediately back to where it had been. "Gem," he whispered, mouth pressing against her ear, "I've been gone three months. I want . . . I need to . . ."

She could feel his urgency as he pressed against her, the thin material of their clothes seeming like a futile barrier to desire. *Aegos, I want him to bend me over and prick me right here, but . . .* She drew herself straight, her own body requiring as much if not more restraint than his. "I promise, I'll make it up to you," she said, running a finger down the bulging front of his breeches. "But I have a meeting with the King of Above. I'm sorry, love."

He kissed her, groaning against her mouth. "Don't go. Don't waste your time on the Above. I can think of much more entertaining ways of wasting your time."

The hint of mischief in his voice sent shivers up her spine.

"I have to go," she said, sighing. "An assassin got Abram, too, Dev. Everything's all cocked up. I need to see it straight."

Devery leaned away from her. "Truly? Goddess."

"I assume you haven't heard anything?" she asked, straightening her shirt and tightening her laces.

He shook his head. "It wasn't the Under. I can tell you that."

"I might be late," she said, pulling her vest down over her ass, "but you can wait for me in the home tunnel if you want." He leaned against her, and she kissed him lightly on the forehead. "I'd be glad if you did."

"Wouldn't miss it," he said. "I am secretly in love with the Queen of Under now."

She wanted to curl up in his arms, and if she didn't force herself to go, that was exactly what she would do. "There's something I want to tell you later."

He kissed her deep and long before he said, "Why not tell me now?" His hand wandered up the buttons of her shirt as he leaned in to kiss her once more.

"Not in the dark." She laughed, biting his lip. Though she could have easily been convinced to stay here and spend the evening with him, she knew what she had to do. She'd already decided on the disguise she'd wear when she went to the Six-Mast to meet with Tollan. Until she knew who was really behind the attacks on Melnora and Abram, she had to take every precaution. "Want to help me get dressed?"

"I believe we have established that is exactly the opposite of what I want to do."

CHAPTER FIVE

SIX-MAST INN

Wince was led through a labyrinth of hallways by a curvy young woman in an apron and little else. Despite the scenery, he couldn't help but wonder why he was meeting his best friend, who should be in the palace being crowned king, at this moment, in the most infamous whorehouse in Yigris. Somehow, he knew it wasn't good, but he couldn't put all the pieces together. His mind slipped backward as memories rose to the surface like air bubbles from the deep.

Tollan had burst into the stables, eager for some sword work, but Wince blurted, "What does 'in perpetuity' mean?"

"Goddess, Wince!" Tollan had stammered, slamming the door shut behind him and staring at the slim black-and-red leather volume Wince had swiped from under Tollan's tutor's nose. "You're not supposed to read that! Nobody's supposed to read that!"

"What do you mean? You and Master Yubron have been reading it for weeks."

"Yes, but . . . but it's only for Daghans. It's a secret." Tollan lowered his voice and then glanced over his shoulder as if half expecting his father to be standing there. "If anyone finds out, you'll be strapped for sure."

"They can't do that. My father's the weapons master. He would . . ." But his voice trailed off. The king could do anything he wanted.

"Just give it to me, Wince. I'll put it back and no one will know. I won't tell."

"I know you won't tell, Toll. But what does it mean?"

For an instant, Tollan seemed to war with himself but then a proud grin spread across his face. "It means that my father's in charge of the good people, and his cousin's in charge of the bad ones. But they work together to keep Yigris safe, so we've got enough gold. It means that someday, I'll be in charge of the Above, and no thief or pirate can say or do anything against me because my family's in charge of them, too. In perpetuity." He winked at Wince. "That means forever."

Wince stared at him openmouthed. "Do you think you'll actually meet a real thief?"

Tollan nodded. "There's a thief queen. She's House Daghan, too, and when I'm king, she and I will make deals and bargains."

Wince stared off for a long moment. Then he grinned at Tollan. "Do you think she's pretty?"

"This is the room of Mr. Hu Tratala." The girl broke into his reverie. "He is a fine, upstanding gentleman, not a rogue like you," she winked playfully at him as his gaze slipped down then immediately bounced back up to her face. She curtsied and pinched his backside as she walked past him.

It was downright scandalous . . . but that didn't stop him from swelling within his small clothes and fantasizing about what a woman like that might be willing to do. There were no women like this in Above. There were dowdy mistresses and young women with their hair curled too tight. Of course, it wasn't seemly for a woman to behave so saltily. It was the man's place to express desire, to control the relationship. The world where he lived was rigid and cold, but from what he'd seen of the Under thus far, this was exactly the kind of adventure Wincel Quintella could get used to.

When Tollan opened the door to his room at the Six-Mast, Wince couldn't help but let out a harsh bark of laughter.

"What?" Tollan grunted. "Is the eye patch too much?"

"Nah. I mean..." Wince choked on another laugh, and then he smiled. "I'm just teasing, Toll. Ah, prick." He glanced away. "I'm sorry about your father."

Tollan nodded. "Thank you. I've got a bit to tell you."

As Wince followed him into the bedroom, Tollan briefly considered doing a jaunty pirate's jig or knocking Wince's trick knee out of place the way he had when they were kids. But they were grown men now, and no comedic device was going to lessen the strain of this night.

"This is as good a time as any, Toll. Tell me what's going on. Why are we doing"—he waved in the direction of Tollan's costume—"whatever the prick this is?"

Tollan sighed, leaning in as close as he could to his friend. "It's a lot to tell. My father was murdered. We believe that the same assassin attacked the Queen of Under today, too. We're waiting to meet with the new queen, and we can't meet in the Black Chamber because," he gulped, "because Iven's accused me of the murder."

Wince stared at him, speechless.

Tollan continued, "Right now, I can't go back to the palace because I don't know what Iven's thinking. If he truly believes I've killed our father, he'll have the guards out searching for me. I could be tried for treason. I have no choice but to put my trust in the Under, and in Gemma Antos, the new Queen of Under. It rankles. This isn't how any of this was supposed to happen. "

"Have you lost your damn mind?" Wince's eyes went wide. "What makes you think *she* didn't have them killed?"

Tollan smiled. He knew he could count on Wince not to treat him like the king. He wanted to reach out and hug his friend, though he restrained himself. "I can't believe that any woman who's capable of being Queen of Under is going to blatantly assassinate the King of Above and the Queen of Under in the same manner on the same day. Gemma must be too smart to do such a stupid thing." But the truth was Tollan had no choice but to trust Gemma. He had nowhere else to go.

Wince raised an eyebrow. "You've already met this new queen? Maybe she's going to show up here and finish the job?"

"Aegos. If she wanted to kill me, she could have done it this afternoon. I was alone with her in the Black Chamber. There wasn't a person who could have stopped her. This is why the pact works. Because the Above trust the Under, and vice versa."

"Yeah, but, she isn't . . ." Wince was treading on unsteady

ground. He wasn't technically supposed to know about the family connection between the rulers of Above and Under, or that Melnora had been barren.

"And why here? Why is the King of Above sitting in a gold-painted room in a whorehouse?" Wince gestured around them with distaste.

Tollan chuckled. "I get the feeling I'm the black sheep of the family. I don't think I'd have fit in very well at her meeting with murderers and thieves. She'll be here to meet us soon."

Wince rolled his eyes, clearly displeased by the circumstances. "I just . . . I don't like some thief queen holding your fate in her hands."

"Melnora trusted her. She raised her and named her heir. That has to be good enough for me."

Wince lifted his hands in mock surrender. "All right, Your Grace. I understand. So, this new queen? Is she pretty?"

When Tollan opened the door for Gemma, she was done up like a diamond-ringed whore. She wore a clinging dress of nearly sheer gold cloth, which lifted her breasts to obscene heights. Her face was painted with shimmering gold powder, and brilliant splashes of color highlighted her lips and cheekbones. Long, coppery curls trailed down her back as she walked through the door to Tollan's room. Had Tollan not been expecting her, he wouldn't have recognized her.

"Lord Tratala," she murmured, curtsying deeply.

Tollan understood immediately, as this was a game he knew the rules to. In Above, they shared fake pleasantries like the clap. "Darling," he said, using his best phony Farcastian accent, all nasal twang and soft vowels. "This is my associate, Master Wincel Quintella. I have utter faith in his integrity and—" he paused, accentuating the word as if it meant something lascivious—"discretion."

Gemma sighed, whispering for his ears alone, "Thank Aegos. This prickling wig was about to drive me mad!" She pulled it off and tossed it onto the bed, running a bejeweled hand through her hair, then turned to grin at Wince. "I am most grateful to make your acquaintance, Master Quintella."

"And I, yours, Miss . . ." He trailed off, his green eyes wandering down her gold-drenched body. Tollan felt his own face grow red with embarrassment for his friend.

"Ah, yes. Discretion," Gemma said, still in the voice of a courtesan—breathy and feigning desire. She lifted two fingers in an obscene gesture that nearly made Tollan choke with laughter. Wince's eyebrows climbed to his hairline.

Tollan continued in his accent, "You're not here to do the pricking, Wince. See to the door."

Gemma laughed and said, "I don't mind if he joins us. That is, if you don't, sir." Wince's eyes grew wide.

"Oh, how very . . . titillating, my dear." Tollan nodded to Wince, who opened the door, checked to be sure that no one was listening and then pulled it closed and threw the lock.

When Tollan glanced back at Gemma, she was sitting cross-legged on the bed, showing enough stocking to be salacious and grinning broadly. At mid-thigh on each leg she wore a leather sheath that held a wickedly sharp dagger. In her lap was a leather-bound book full of blank pages and two charcoal pencils. Licking her lips, she bent over the book and wrote: *Sorry. I forgot there'd be two of you. I didn't bring enough pencils.*

Wince moved closer, seemingly unable to drag his attention from Gemma's ample bosom, but she didn't seem to notice. Tollan flicked his friend on the ear, drawing a hostile glare followed by an embarrassed shrug.

Gemma handed Tollan the book and a pencil, and he scrawled quickly: *Don't worry. Wince is a simpleton—can't write worth shit.*

Wince grabbed the book, and wrote carefully: *Prick you, Toll. I write fine.*

Both of them looked up as Gemma moaned loudly. "Oh, Hu." She grinned, winking at them and pointing at the door. She cupped her hand to her ear as if she were eavesdropping.

Wince looked at Tollan, eyes gone wide once more.

As Gemma wrote, she interjected the silence with whimpers and moans, and once, a high-pitched giggle. Then she held the book out to Tollan.

Until we know who killed your father and attacked Melnora, we have to assume we're being watched. Don't let your guard down.

After Tollan read the note, he wrote: *I'm hoping you know who might be behind it all. Crime isn't my area of expertise.* He was having a hard time concentrating with her moaning and Wince's increasingly heavy breathing.

Gemma looked up at him, eyebrow raised as if to say, *oh,*

really? She made a stuttering, breathy sound—a mix between a squeal and a moan of ecstasy.

A similar sound escaped from Wince, and Tollan couldn't be sure if he was playacting or not.

Gemma wrote for several long minutes, pausing only to bounce, groan or moan. Her face had gone pink with exertion. The gold shimmer had begun to disappear in spots where sweat trickled down her face. *Melnora is still hanging on but just barely. We've had no official word from Above, which means your brother is playing things close to his vest. He should have summoned the queen by now. But there have been reports of royal guards in Shadowtown, Merchant Row and Whitebeach going door to door, hunting traitors. It won't be long before they get to Dockside. Until they get here.*

Tollan took the book and wrote: *Iven doesn't know how to summon the Queen of Under. That information is guarded from all save the heir.*

Gemma scoffed, meeting Tollan's gaze for a long moment before writing: *Seriously? You have no third in case of a situation like this? How the Void do you people even function up there, let alone keep control for a hundred fifty years? Whatever he knows or doesn't know, the soldiers are searching 'in the name of King Iven.' It sure looks like your brother is making a grab for your throne.*

She stretched out and nudged Tollan gently in the ribs with her foot, making it impossible for him to dwell on her revelation. He grunted, and she nodded encouragingly. She moaned, feigning sexual delight, and he felt his mouth fall open as understanding dawned on him. She wanted him to play along, to contribute to the charade she was already playing in. He groaned loudly and awkwardly, elbowing Wince to join in. Red-faced, Wince panted loudly, averting his gaze. Gemma bounced harder on the bed until her ass left the mattress. "Oh, oh!"

Gemma's face was lit with what he thought was a genuine smile. It appeared to Tollan that she was having a grand time playing Tease the Nobleman.

Dampness ran down Tollan's neck, and his plait had come undone during the bouncing. His hair hung tangled and wild around his face. Wince was panting and ruddy—and as near to exuberant laughter as Tollan was willing to let him get—when a loud knock sounded on the door.

Gemma flicked the page over and scrawled hurriedly: *It could be the soldiers. Take off your clothes and make it look real. Now!*

In an instant, she had shimmied out of her gown and stood bare save her stockings. With a flick of her wrists, she unhooked the knife sheaths and tossed them on the bed alongside the book and pencils, which she covered with her discarded gown.

Tollan unbuttoned his shirt and tried not to look at her as she pinched her breasts, leaving red marks on her skin. But he couldn't ignore her when she grabbed his right hand and slapped her ass cheek with it. A raised, red handprint rose before his eyes, and his hand stung from the impact.

She was gesturing wildly at Wince when the pounding came again. Her dexterous fingers unlaced Tollan's breeches in an instant. She glared at Wince, then gestured at Tollan's boots. As if in a dream, Tollan cast off his boots and shimmied out of his pants, while Gemma tugged at his shirt buttons.

She grinned, glancing down at Tollan's arousal, then winked

at him, though he suspected that she misinterpreted its source. She leaned in and whispered in his ear, "It needs to be wet."

Confused and dazed, Tollan stared as she spit on his cock— once, then twice, and then a third time. "Sorry, Your Grace," she whispered daintily before she settled her wig perfectly straight atop her head.

He turned and saw Wince rubbing spit onto his own cock, his face red, and his back shaking with laughter. Perhaps if Tollan weren't a virgin, he'd have seen the humor in the situation, but all he felt was an agonizing combination of dishonor and disgust. Especially because he'd grown hard at the sight of his naked best friend.

He heard Gemma flop onto the bed, behind him and then squeal as if she'd been poked by a needle. Just as Wince threw open the door, naked to the world, she pressed her mouth to Tollan's ear, and he felt the warmth of her body slide against his skin. "Whatever you do, don't let anyone see your back. The mark will give you away," she hissed, as the opening door revealed a large bald man with pointed teeth who searched the room with a hard gaze.

Tollan realized he had completely forgotten about the mage mark on his back. And just as suddenly, it began to tingle and burn.

"I'm terribly sorry, sir," the man raised an eyebrow in Tollan's direction. "We've had word of a young street boy breaking into rooms and stealing purses while our guests were otherwise . . . occupied. Would you mind if we check your room? You'll be well compensated for the interruption." The man was watching

Gemma even as he was speaking to Tollan.

"Let them in," she whispered, relaxing against him.

"Of course, of course," Tollan croaked, realizing too late that he'd forgotten to affect his accent. "My lady doesn't mind the interruption." The burning and pulsing on his back was growing worse, and his mind felt clouded, heavy and unresponsive.

The giant of a man brushed past Wince without a glance and was followed by a smaller man with cold, assessing eyes and messy brown hair. The large man made a pretense of searching behind curtains and in the wardrobe, but the smaller man moved straight toward Tollan, nearly knocking him over.

"What is it?" Gemma asked, her voice dripping with worry. "What's happened?"

"Gem," the man whispered, pushing Tollan aside. "Don't go home. You know where to go. And don't let this walking erection go to Above, either. Things are bad. Get out of here now. The back way." He dropped a pack on the floor in front of her, then pulled her to him. "I'll be there when I can," he said, eyes bright. "Please be careful."

Before Tollan knew it, the men had left the room and Gemma was unloading clothes from the pack they'd dropped. As she slid into a pair of nondescript breeches, he noticed Wince pulling on clothes, too. She threw a bundle of clothes at Tollan, and though he tried, he couldn't catch any of them. His heart thudded in his chest.

Gemma ripped off her wig and shoved it and her gown into the pack along with the book, the pencils and her leg sheaths. Then she wiggled into an oversize shirt and deftly buttoned it up before reaching into the pack and drawing out a knife belt, which she wrapped low on her hips and fastened snugly. He watched in awe as she did something similar on each of her wrists. She glanced up at him then and nodded at his wilted manhood. "Get dressed, Your Grace," she whispered.

He shook his head, then turned to see Wince pulling on a second boot. His friend nodded at the clothes in Tollan's hands. "Hurry," he mouthed.

His back burned as if someone had spilled acid on it, and he couldn't make sense of what was happening around him. Sound came and went like the tide.

"Prick," Gemma said, shoving Tollan's discarded eye patch into the pack as she glared at him. "We've got to go. You'll have to dress on the way." In two graceful strides, she crossed the room to the wardrobe. Standing on tiptoe, she ran her fingers along the top, and Tollan heard a click. He saw her lips moving, but all he heard was the pounding of his blood in his veins.

Wince shoved a pair of breeches into Tollan's hands, "Hurry, Toll. Goddess, what's wrong with you?" Stars flared in his field of vision and the thumping of his heart changed its pace.

Somehow, he found himself shoved into the strange pair of pants. A shirt was thrown over his shoulders as he pulled on one boot, then the other. The edges of his vision grew dark as he slumped onto the bed. His back burned like the fires of the Void.

Gemma eyed him warily and then ran her fingers behind the wardrobe, pushing it open with a grunt. "Pick him up and carry him, Wince. I don't know what the prick is wrong with him, but we've got to run. Now."

Tollan was tossed over Wince's shoulder and carried, head down, into a dark hallway. Gemma pulled the wardrobe shut behind her, then whispered, "Sixty-seven paces, then turn left."

Tollan tried to keep count, but he lost his numbers somewhere after the twenty-eighth pace. "Wince?" he said groggily.

Wince stopped walking, and Tollan felt his head rest against his friend's ass cheek. "Forty-four. What?" Wince asked, his voice ragged.

"Who were those guys back there?" Tollan's tongue was thick in his mouth.

"Weren't you paying attention when Gemma told us? They're nobodies, really. Just Fin the Fish and Devery Nightsbane. You know . . . the prickling master of assassins," Wince spit out.

"Oh," Tollan said, as brightly colored spots appeared before his eyes. "They seemed . . . nice."

Suddenly Gemma's breath was on his face. "That's because Fin is my friend and Devery is my lover. Now can you shut up? Come on, Tollan. We've got to get out of here, or we die."

"Why will we die? What's happening?" Tollan asked, weakly beating his hands against Wince's back. He blinked away tears and saw, in his mind's eye, an image of his brother holding a bloodstained sword. His sword. "Help me, Aegos," he moaned. "Have mercy on me." Darkness and stars and the tide overtook him and he slipped beneath the waves.

Gemma fumbled in the pack Devery had given her until she found a bundle of candles in the bottom. With practiced fingers, she pulled her flint from her pouch and snapped a spark into life. Darkness gave way to dancing shadows.

They walked in silence for several minutes before Wince said, "Devery Nightsbane is really your . . . lover?"

"Why do you say it like that? *Lover.* You have a lover! Why shouldn't I?"

"How do you know about her?"

"I'm just observant. That's why Melnora chose me." She choked back tears and kicked at a loose stone. "But you didn't answer my question. What makes it so goddess-damned shocking that I take a man to my bed?"

He grimaced. "Because if a man marries a woman and then discovers she isn't a virgin, she can be thrown into jail or kept in the stocks. Only whores would risk it. But you're not a whore. You're the most respected woman in Under."

"Your laws are barbaric," she said. "You goddessless bastards don't even know that being a whore is a prickling privilege. Aegos kisses those who share themselves, and blesses them even before the queen and king. The whores I know are some of the most generous and compassionate . . ." she growled in frustration as he shook his head in disbelief. "Pretty much everyone I know has a lover. If you love each other, you stay together. Only folks in Above get married. Wedlock is just another way to claim ownership over someone. In Under, we own ourselves." She exhaled. "Look, your lot have balls to meet girls and get married, and we . . ."

Wince chuckled softly.

"What? What could possibly be funny about that?"

"Did you just say that we have balls?" His chuckle turned into outright laughter.

"You're a twelve-year-old, Wincel Quintella."

He nodded, almost proudly.

"That makes it easier, though. Doesn't it?" Gemma looked at him with distaste. "Laughing over your cocks and balls instead of trying to really understand." She spat at the ground as her temper threatened to get the best of her. "That's what I mean, Wince. That's exactly what you do in Above. Make every prickling thing about what's hiding in your breeches, instead of what is happening right in front of your face."

His grin faltered. "Sorry," he whispered.

"Look . . . in Above, you can bury your head in the sand. You judge us because we're whores and thieves and murderers, and you get to keep your hands clean. We scratch your belly and you scratch ours. But your goddess-chosen king is just as much of a twisted prick as the rest of us. And that's worked out just fine, except . . ."

Wince was looking at her now as if he were meeting her for the first time. "Except what?"

"Except," she went on, "maybe we were too busy scratching each other's bellies to notice that a snake had slithered into the cottage."

CHAPTER SIX

THE TUNNELS

They had stumbled through eleven different tunnels and were approximately 1,839 paces from the Six-Mast, near Canticle Center, when it struck her like an iron pipe to the gut.

"Stop," Gemma said, dropping her pack. "I know what's wrong with him." Wince gingerly put Tollan down, and the king murmured something as if in slumber.

"What is it?" Wince said breathlessly.

"Hold this." She pressed the flickering candle into Wince's hand. His face was a study in angles, his eyes sunken and haunted.

"All right," she said. "I remembered something." She thrust her chin in the direction of the sleeping king. "But I need to get his shirt off of him to be sure."

Wince nodded and undid the misaligned buttons on Tollan's shirt. The King of Above's skin burned with fever. His pulse fluttered and his breath was coming in painful gasps. His arm and leg muscles twitched uncontrollably. Gemma slid one quaking arm and then the other out of their sleeves, and rolled the dead weight of the king over onto his stomach.

Holding the candle near the raw, freshly drawn mage mark, she looked at the strange symbol—part brand, part tattoo—and knew immediately she was right. She drew a sharp breath. "Did you ever see King Abram's mage mark?"

Wince's mouth turned downward in consternation when he saw the mark on Tollan's back. "My father is the weapons master. The king would come and spar on occasion, and he usually removed his shirt. I never saw his so inflamed, though. Is that what's wrong with him?"

"I think so," she said, fumbling in her pack once more. She pulled out the blank book and pencil they had used to pass notes earlier and drew a mark on a blank page. "This is what I was taught to look for on the back of the King of Above."

"Yes," Wince nodded. "That's the mark."

She shook her head, brushing her finger along Tollan's red, irritated skin. "Not exactly. Look," she said, pointing to one of the curves. There was a difference to one of the flourishes and a slightly different curve to the bisecting line.

Wince groaned low in his throat and pushed himself backward, as if distancing himself would somehow help. "But this has to be the true mark. Doesn't it? I mean how . . ."

She looked up, meeting his gaze. "I was forced to draw this mark a hundred times a day for four straight months when I was fifteen. It has always been one of the Daghan family's greatest concerns, that someone would try to impersonate the king, and this was their way of ensuring that it didn't happen. You can always identify the true king by his mage mark. If I'd have made this mistake in my drawing, Melnora would have had me scrubbing chamber pots for a month. Which means . . ."

"No mage woman could have drawn that mark by accident. Prick me! They did this to him? Are you sure?"

"I'm not sure of anything, but it makes a lot of sense. Who in all of Yigris is powerful enough to take out both the King of Above and the Queen of Under simultaneously? Yesterday, I'd have said no one. But seeing this . . . the King of Above keeps four mage women as servants to the crown—insurance that the Vagans would never start another war. They are the only people who have done mage work in Yigris since the end of the Mage War." She met Wince's gaze. "Do you know how the king's mage mark is supposed to work? Do you know what it does?"

"It marks him as Aegos's chosen ruler."

"Well, sure, but Melnora taught me that the mage mark is triggered when it's looked upon. It's supposed to infuse its bearer with confidence in himself, in his divine right to lead the people of Yigris. As if their view of and belief in the mark actually makes a stronger, better-equipped king. That's why Abram would take his shirt off to spar—it made him more self-assured."

"What does this have to do with Toll?"

"He was fine until I looked at the mark."

"Are you saying what I think you're saying?"

"I think a mage woman took the opportunity of Abram's death to try to kill Tollan, too." She rolled her neck, staring upward at the tunnel's ceiling for a moment. "Is it a crime of opportunity or something else? Why would they want to attack Tollan?" She remembered the strange, emotionless mage woman who had hovered behind Tollan when they'd first met. A sliver of fear stabbed at her spine.

"Really, Aegos? It's my first prickling day as queen."

They were silent for a long moment as she pondered what to do.

"If what you say is true about the mage mark, can we just—I don't know—can we break it?" Wince said.

"The mark?"

"Yeah. Can we just make it so that it won't work?" His gaze was on the raw brand on the king's back.

Gemma stared at it, too, looking at the way the blackened skin almost seemed to pulse. She could feel the mage work. "It's carved and burned into his skin, Wince. I don't know. Maybe cutting a piece of it out might do it, but it's going to hurt a lot, and might not work."

Wince stared at Tollan for a few moments as Gemma grew antsy. They shouldn't be standing still, and she was nearing the point when she would have to get them moving again when he said, "Look, Gemma. I'm a little out of my depth, at the moment, but I can't just sit here and let those scorpions dig their claws into my king any deeper." He looked away from her, then mumbled below his breath, "Twisted prick or not."

She nodded. "All right." She reached for her dagger, but he stopped her.

"Does it have to be a blade?" he asked. "Do you have a needle? Maybe we could just drag a needle through the outline, mar the edges a bit..."

It was Gemma's turn to burst into laughter. "Oh, sure . . . let me just dig through my sewing basket, here . . ." She withdrew a stiletto blade, a garrote and a vial of near-toxic sleeping powder from her waist pouch. "Hmm." She grinned broadly. "I'm afraid I left all my good embroidery at home." She shoved the tools of her trade back into her pouch. "There's not much I know how to do that isn't at the back end of a weapon. But I'd be happy to do the cutting, if you'd rather not."

He shook his head. Gemma was impressed that he hadn't balked at her little display.

"If it's going to cause him pain, then let it be me." He drew a dagger from his waist and tested the blade along his thumb. "Thank you, though."

When his eyes met hers, she ignored his tears. She'd let him have his silly Above masculinity.

She put her knees atop Tollan's shoulders in an awkward position, the king's head cupped between her thighs. But by putting her weight on his shoulders she could keep his upper body mostly immobile, despite the muscle tremors that continued to rack his frame.

Wince sat astride Tollan's ass, holding his lower half still. "How deep, do you think?" he asked.

"I don't know. A quarter of an inch, maybe? Not so deep that you cut through muscle but all the way through the mark."

He nodded, holding his blade over the center of Tollan's back. "I'm going to cut through the middle of this line, here," he said, gesturing with the tip of his blade, "and then maybe cut through the outside circle, just in case."

She nodded, trying to reassure him.

His breath gushed out of him, and then, not wasting any more time, he sliced through the center of the mark.

Tollan's skin separated and Gemma felt the tingling that accompanied mage work, but instead of blood seeping from the broken skin, light erupted.

The last thing Gemma remembered was the floor shaking beneath her.

There was pain, somewhere distant. There was warmth and light and something was tugging at his mind, but Tollan clung to the darkness, to the freedom of dreams that kept him afloat.

Waves tipped the ship gently as a light breeze tugged at Tollan's hair. He closed his eyes to the bright sun reflecting off the Hadriak Sea. He was alone in the place that made him happiest—on the deck of a ship. Free from the politics and pressures of home. Free to think thoughts that back home were forbidden and shameful. He stood straighter here on the boat, relieved of the usual weight on his shoulders.

Footsteps approached, and he opened his eyes. The captain was older than he remembered—wisps of silver touched her temples and made the black of her hair stand out all the more. She wore a cheaply carved talisman on a leather thong near her heart.

"Mother," he whispered.

"Get to work on those lines, sailor," she groused as she moved past him, checking knots and shouting orders to the men and women who bustled about the ship.

The salt air turned to ash in his lungs. She'd forgotten her own son. He meant nothing to Isbit Daghan, former Queen of Above and wife of Abram, his father.

The weight of stone and water pressed upon him, and he clawed for the surface. Dream turned to memory.

The seas began to heave. A man was in the water clinging to a piece of flotsam. He wore a carved wooden talisman at his neck, like the one Isbit wore. Deep in the corners of his mind, Tollan felt the overwhelming urge to let him drown.

There was pain. A fire in his chest. The blackness pulled him back under.

Time passed and the sailor woke. Tollan steeled himself to the pounding in his chest. He was nearly a man, and he was brave enough to speak to the sailor who watched Tollan's mother with a gaze that made Tollan's belly twist. He stood tall and announced in a quavering voice, "I am Tollan." He took a step forward and held out his hand in formal greeting. "Crown Prince of Yigris and heir to the throne. Son of Abram Daghan and Isbit, his wife." His chest swelled at his official-sounding introduction. He almost wished his father could have seen him.

The sailor's eyes darted back toward Tollan's mother who slept in a chair, unwilling to leave the nearly drowned sailor's side, then back to Tollan. "Are you really?" he asked. He sniffed, ran a hand over his forehead and through his greasy hair, then stuck out his hand to accept Tollan's. "It's good to meet you, Prince Tollan. I'm Jamis. Captain of the now defunct Siren's Call *and the luckiest man in the Four Winds."*

Tollan nodded. "I'm sorry about your ship."

Again, the sailor's gaze flicked to Tollan's mother, then back again.

"Well, Your Highness. That makes one of us."

Then the waves tossed and turned again, time passed and Tollan stood before his father's desk. His hands grew clammy with fear as he clutched the letter that his mother had written. Her goodbye echoing in his ears so loudly that he couldn't understand why the king didn't look up.

"You're back, then?" King Abram grumbled, his gaze never rising from the papers before him.

"Mother sent this." Tollan pushed the envelope across the desk and fled.

Tollan could still hear the crystal shattering within his father's rooms. He was falling. He could no longer be sure if he even had a body. Memories and dreams tangled him, the lines snapped at him, dragging him under. He gasped for air and found nothing but salt and storm.

He was back on the Hadriak. The sky was black as pitch, and the ship began to come apart on the wind. Bits of wood and crimson sail, hemp rope and tar, flaked off into the air around him. The once grand sloop disappeared, and in its place was the throne room of the Yigrisian Palace.

Tollan sat on the throne, his hands and feet manacled to it with gold chains. Beside him sat his brother, also bound. Iven looked back at him with their mother's eyes.

CHAPTER SEVEN

UNDER

Tollan opened his eyes. The ground trembled beneath him, and for an instant he prayed for death. He didn't know where he was. The flame of a candle fluttered nearby, casting eerie shadows. He rolled over and saw a large chunk of stone crash to the ground just a few feet away. The roots of some sort of plant pushed their way into the tunnel and continued to grow, winding along the ceiling and then down the wall like a vine. In the distance, Tollan could hear more stones falling. "Aegos!" he shouted, leaping to his feet.

He remembered. He was in Under—wearing pants and boots that were not his own. He picked up the candle and searched his surroundings for something familiar. "Aw, prick," he snapped and dove toward the prone figure of Wince, who was sprawled on the floor nearby, a knife clutched in his hand.

"Wince, wake up!" he shouted, slapping his friend's face and shaking him. "Come on, mate."

The cavern continued to tremble and shake, and a fist-size piece of stone fell from the ceiling and smashed to bits a foot from Wince's head. Tendrils of thorny branches unfurled all around them.

"Come on, Wince, you mother-prickling half-wit!" He slapped his friend as hard as he could and prayed to Aegos.

Wince's eyes flew open. "What? Oh, shit. Shit!" He scrambled to his feet. "Toll? Oh, goddess. Tollan, is that you?"

Tollan grabbed hold of Wince's face. "It's me. What's wrong with you?"

"I can't see, Toll, I-" Another tremor shook the cavern and Wince screamed. "What is happening? What is that sound?"

"I don't know," he said, grabbing his friend by the arm, "but we've got to get out of here."

"Right. All right." Wince took a step and stumbled over a small pile of stones. "I'm . . . all right," he said, trying to regain his footing. "Where's Gemma? Gemma?" he called out.

Tollan finally spotted her twenty feet away, crumpled awkwardly against the wall.

"Gemma," Tollan said, bending down to help her up. Her eyes were glassy and her pupils were very large. A stream of blood ran down her forehead. "We've got to get out of here. The tunnel's coming down."

He held his hand out to her, but she waved him off and in an instant she was on her feet. "I'm all right," she said, though she wavered a little. She thrust her chin toward Wince. "What's wrong with him?"

"He can't see," Tollan said, taking Wince's arm. "I don't know what happened."

"I do," she said, running fingers along her scalp. She grimaced as they came away crimson. "Ugh. Head injuries bleed like a virgin." She wiped her fingers on her breeches. "Wince, close your eyes, press the heels of your palms against your lids and count to ten. It'll help."

Wince followed her instructions.

"And for goddess' sake," she said, reaching for her satchel, "take a deep breath. We're going to be all right." She groaned as she bent to pick up her pack but waved Tollan off when he tried to help her.

She took Tollan by the shoulders, turned him around and looked at his back. "Huh. Worked better than I thought it would. Nice work, Wince. You can put your shirt back on, Your Grace." She patted Tollan's shoulder and said, "We've got to get out of these tunnels before they come down around our ears." By the time Wince removed his hands from his eyes, she was grinning.

"What's going on, Gemma?" Tollan asked, though he followed her advice and picked up the shirt that lay discarded on the tunnel floor.

"How's that?" She asked, taking Wince by the hand.

Irritation flared within Tollan at the way that Gemma ignored his question.

"Maybe a little better," Wince said. "I can see some shapes, now."

Another tremor shook the tunnel, and small bits of rubble peppered the floor around them.

"Good—it was just a flashbang. Things will be fuzzy for a while, but no permanent damage. We don't have time to waste, though. Follow me."

Gemma took the candle from Tollan, and he followed the bobbing, flickering flame. Wince held tightly to Tollan's elbow. The tunnel was dusty, and occasionally, a plant root twisted and writhed through the tunnel ceiling or wall, lending a greater sense of urgency to their already fast pace. Tollan trembled as he walked, sure that the earth was going to crumble in on them and his final moments would be choked with stone and blood.

"Where are we . . ." Tollan croaked. He cleared his throat and tried again. "Where are we going, Gemma? And what are those plants?"

She stopped and stared at him in exasperation. "We're going to Canticle Center," she said. Somehow, her breath was not uneven despite the rapid pace they'd set. "And I have no idea what those plants are or where they're coming from, but this whole tunnel reeks of magic. Do you have any other questions that are more important than getting out of here before there's a cave-in?"

CHAPTER EIGHT

CANTICLE CENTER

Before long, Tollan found himself being led into a hallway that ended abruptly. Gemma stopped and ran her fingertips along the wall then turned and said, "We're here," gesturing to the blank wall behind her. "Try to keep your heads down. The first part is a bit of a gauntlet. When we find Brother Elam, it'll get better. We'll talk inside," she said, and she pressed her hand against Tollan's arm for an instant. She blew out the candle.

He tried to watch what she did in the dim light, but her hands slid rapidly into hidden cracks and crevices, and before he knew it, a wide section of the wall was sliding aside. She waved them in after her, and they stepped into a small, poorly lit storage room.

Gemma pressed her body against Tollan's and his back pushed to Wince's front as she flipped the invisible switch that slid the stone panel closed behind them. "Hello there," she whispered breathily.

He wished in that moment he could say something witty—something smart and funny and a little crude. Something that Wince would say. Instead, he stared at her, tongue-tied, trying to ignore his unease. A lifetime as royalty apparently gave one very little to go on in the jesting-when-bodies-are-pressed-together department. Instead, he averted his gaze and blushed.

He tried to make sense of what had happened in the Under, but the last thing he remembered before waking up in the tunnel was Gemma very inelegantly spitting on his . . .

"Prick me," he mumbled.

"Come on." She laughed as she flung open the pantry door and strode up a set of stairs into Canticle Center as if she owned the place.

They wove in and out of corridors, passing statues of Aegos in all her forms. The goddess never slept, but it seemed that her temple did. Tollan had never been in this section of the church, but given the serene décor and the silent nature of the rooms they passed, he assumed they were in an area of the temple known as the Head.

Just like Yigris, the goddess Aegos had an Above and an Under. Aegos wore two faces—the mindful, peaceful mother, cerebral and beneficent; and the vital, sanguine lover and warrior, carnal and fierce. The Head was where the prayer keepers meditated, prayed and sought the goddess's wisdom and light. The main, public, temple was called the Heart—where the people of Yigris came to seek the enlightenment of Aegos, as well as the blessings of the prayer keepers. There was also a hospit within the Heart, and a school for the children of the craftsmen and shopkeepers of Merchant Row and Brighthold.

Soon, Tollan began to recognize areas of the Heart. Though the royal family had a private temple within the palace, some public ceremonies required their attendance at Canticle Center. His memory conjured images of the singing, dancing and stories that had inspired faith in him as a lad, the air heavy with incense, and his father's boredom. He was struck by a memory of his mother swaying to the sensual music—her face alight with a joy he rarely saw. A powerful sense of familiarity surged within him. This was the place where he belonged, he controlled. This was the place where things were as they should be, a part of his history, not a part of his city that he'd never even entered before.

They passed through the large ceremonial hall, silent and empty of inhabitants, and moved down a corridor that branched off into private worship rooms. Gemma led them down the hallway through empty schoolrooms and past the stretch of pallets and cots filled with sleeping patrons of the hospit, where the sick and injured of Yigris came for healing. They passed below an archway painted bright red, then took a long set of stairs down into a distinctly separate section of the temple that consisted of dozens of small offices.

People bustled around as if it were broad daylight. Men and women sat at long nondescript tables laden with coins of all denominations, counting and tallying.

"Gentlemen," Gemma said, grinning over her shoulder, "welcome to the Slit."

Gemma watched with glee as Tollan's eyes grew round in his face. She knew she shouldn't enjoy tormenting the young monarch quite so much, but the extent of his innocence was something that she had never in her eighteen years encountered. She thought he was probably only a year younger than she, but she'd bet a week's honeycakes that he was still a virgin. And so it was with no small amount of pleasure that she led Tollan and Wince into the depths of the church, where the prayer keepers not only maintained the largest bank in all of Yigris and trained an elite military unit—the Ain—but they also maintained an exclusive society of the most exotic sex worker priests in the Four Winds, the Dalinn.

Wince drew in a breath beside her. "Praise Aegos."

Tollan squared his shoulders and held his neck straight. He sighed. "Lead the way, Gemma."

Chuckling and shaking her head at the strange, dogmatic behavior of the Above, she strode down the hallway. A graying prayer keeper approached them. "Is there some assistance I can offer you?" he asked, gaze turned down and hands clasped before him, covered by the wide sleeves of his brown robes.

Gemma leaned in close to the man's ear and whispered, "I am Gemma Antos, the Queen of Under, and I come as head of the Guild." The prayer keeper's eyes darted to her face, then away again. Then she raised her voice. "I need Brother Elam," she said.

"Of course, Regency. I live to serve."

They followed the gray-haired prayer keeper into the depths

of the Slit. If Tollan was nervous now, she could hardly wait to see how he would respond to Elam—a member of the legendary Dalinn. If their behavior tonight had told her anything about Wince and the king, she'd bet they'd laid awake plenty of nights fantasizing about the pleasures of the fabled Slit.

The hallways grew narrower and more dimly lit as they moved deeper into the secret areas of Canticle Center, and a haze of incense and the distant strums of a harp filled the air. Day or night, the Slit bustled with activity—economic, sensual or visceral. Some business qualified as all three.

They were led to an alcove hung with brightly colored silk curtains. The floor was polished wood and several brightly colored pillows dotted the space. A low table, bare save a large bottle filled with black sand, was the only furniture. "Please wait here," the prayer keeper said, bowing deeply to her. "I'll alert Brother Elam that you seek an audience."

She chose a rose-colored pillow made of velvet and sat down, stretching her legs out in front of her. Tollan seemed rather reluctant to sit but eventually chose a blue silk cushion. The breeches that Devery and Fin had brought for him were a bit snug, and as he sat, Gemma admired the muscles in his calves that pulled the thin material taught. The King of Above may be naive, but he was not weak.

Wince sat down beside her on a yellow pillow. He rubbed at his eyes and then grinned caddishly.

"Calm yourself, there, lightning," she chided, though she could not keep a smile from her own face. "We're here on business—not pleasure."

"So it's true, then?" Tollan asked. "The church trains women in the art of—"

"Not just women," Gemma interrupted. "Men, too. The priests of the Dalinn are the best at what they do, but that's not why we're here."

"Why are we here?" Wince asked, leaning back and stretching his own legs out.

"Privacy, and a place where I can think and talk to someone I trust. The tunnels are unstable, Aegos knows what's happening with those plants up above, and Devery said that neither of us should go anywhere near our homes. We need information and we need someplace we can talk without fear of someone overhearing, until we figure out who's a friend and who's not." She heard footsteps coming and quickly tucked her feet beneath her, putting herself in a regal, meditative position. Wince and Tollan nervously followed her lead.

Elam entered the alcove, his expression serene. "Thank you, Lamwin," he said, nodding to the gray-haired prayer keeper.

"Follow me, please." Elam offered a hand to Gemma, then smiled at Tollan and Wince. "Good sirs."

Gemma stood, her skin burning with nervous energy, and took his hand. It had been far too long since she'd been to church.

They made their way down a narrow passage, dark save the red-covered sconces that lit the hall in a warm wash of color. At the end of the hallway, Elam produced a key from a chain around his neck and unlocked a stone door. He opened it with a small grunt of effort, ushered the three of them inside and then turned and relocked the door.

He had barely finished with the door when Gemma threw her arms around his neck and kissed his cheek. The serene demeanor of prayer keeper vanished, and the boy she'd known as little more than a street rat suddenly appeared. "Goddess, Gem," he said, reaching up to brush at the bloody streak on her forehead, "Are you all right? What do you need? How can I help?"

"Gentleman, this is Brother Elam of the Dalinn. Elam, may I introduce Tollan Daghan, King of Yigris Above, and his associate, Wincel Quintella."

"Prickling Void, Gemma. It's even worse than streetword has it, then?" Elam asked, his brow furrowing behind his spectacles.

She nodded, chewing her lip. "We need a place to lay low for a few hours. Can we . . ."

"You don't even need to ask . . . Regency."

She saw then, that he knew about Melnora. "What news have you had?" she asked, wishing she'd made time to come visit him before she'd needed to cash in a favor.

"I was at the assembly," he said, squeezing her hand gently. "Since then, we've had word of a fire at the Six-Mast. A few of those displaced from the docks have made their way to the temple. They're saying that giant bramble bushes have grown up around Dockside. Some urchins came in saying that Guildhouse is surrounded by fire and thorns. People are saying that the Guild has disbanded—that there is no head—they're saying that the Queen of Under is dead."

"Prick that," Tollan growled behind her. "Gemma, you've got to—"

"Elam, give us as much time as you can," she said, talking

over the King of Above. She didn't have time for his naivety. "But don't risk yourself or the rest of the Center. Keep your ears open for me. I'd like to think that the church will be safe no matter what, but I don't know who is behind this yet, and we cannot be dealing with anyone from Above just now." He nodded, dark eyes shadowed.

"And don't tell anyone we're here. Unless . . ." she paused, unsure if she was tearing open old scars. "Unless Devery comes, or Fin."

Elam, always stoic, nodded. "Of course, Gemma." If she hadn't known him as well as she did—if she hadn't grown up with him, stolen, fought and bled with him—she'd never have known that he was still in love with Devery. But she knew, and that knowledge clawed at her heart.

Wince watched the blood drain from Tollan's face as Elam left and Gemma locked the door behind the sex priest.

"Gemma," Tollan said, "can you explain to me why everyone in the most highly guarded place in Yigris is willing to do your bidding? Ten minutes ago, I didn't even know this place existed, but you seem to be old friends with everyone here. I want to know what's going on here!"

Wince hadn't thought to wonder this, but as soon as Tollan asked, he realized it was true. He turned to Gemma. "He's got a point," he said.

She sighed, sliding into one of the two chairs that sat across from an enormous, lavishly draped bed. The rug in hues of red and gold on the polished floor was probably from Ladia, where the best textiles were made.

"All right," she said, the toe of her left boot kicking aimlessly in the air. "You have to understand that this is top-level information." She grinned, eyebrows bobbing. "And yes, the irony of saying that to you, Tollan, does not escape me."

Tollan nodded, still stick-straight and tense. It had been a long while since Wince had seen Tollan this anxious. Of course, it had been a long time since Wince had seen Tollan in the same room as his father, and that had pretty much always made Tollan look that way.

Gemma went on. "A hundred and some-odd years ago, just before the Mage War was first called off, Jenn Daghan and his sister, Olyn, signed the secret pact that created Above and Under, making him king and her queen."

Tollan sighed, and Wince knew that his friend already knew all of this, but Gemma ignored him and went on. "Yigris had traded away nearly all of its land and mines just to get the Vagans to leave. Above was strapped for gold and Jenn saw Olyn and her Under as his ticket back to prosperity. Olyn, however, saw the pact as her ticket to freedom. She'd gone from feeling like a pretty backdrop who didn't even have the right to choose who she married in House Daghan, to the leader of a powerful criminal underworld nearly overnight. She was smart and brutal, and while Jenn believed that he'd found a way to control both the nobles and the thieves, Olyn had other plans."

Ever since Wince had snuck a copy of the secret pact away

from Tollan's tutor, they had talked about the pact and what it meant for Above, but Wince had never really thought about the leaders of Under. The idea that Olyn had thought she'd gotten the better of the deal was foreign and strange to him, and he turned his gaze to Tollan, wondering how the king would take that information.

Gemma went on: "It didn't take long for Olyn to realize that the church would be a problem. The pact was perfect in the way that it divided power and kept both the legitimate and the criminal elements loyal to what was left of House Daghan, but that would do little good if the church stood against them. There is only one thing people fear more than their king, and that is the goddess.

"But Olyn also knew that the greater part of the priests and prayer keepers were lecherous, money-starved miscreants. So she figured why not bring them into her fold? She infiltrated the Slit, learned of their underground dealings and used it for her own benefit."

Wince looked around at the splendor of the Dalinn's room. The sex priests were obviously taken very good care of, and the few glimpses around the Slit had told him that the Holy Aegosian Church had far more wealth than he had ever imagined.

"Olyn took the seedier leanings of the church and bent them to her will. Nobody outside the church—and I mean nobody living except for you, me, Wince and a couple of top members of the Guild—knows that the Yigrisian temple of the Holy Aegosian Church became a branch of the Shadow Guild four years after the pact was signed. They have their own leadership, their own bylaws and they handle all of their own conflicts internally, but they answer to the Queen of Under." Gemma finished with a sigh as she met Tollan's steely gaze.

Tollan bristled. "And why exactly would they answer to the Under rather than the Above?"

Gemma smiled. "Because Olyn had them by the balls, and because she was way too smart to tell her brother. Once the pact was signed, the income made by the Guild by paramours, assassination-for-hire and bloodwork was taxed by the king and overseen by the king. That was all part of the benefit of signing the pact in the first place. If the church refused Olyn, she vowed that she would report their less-than-sacred activities to her brother, thus putting them under *his* control. If they agreed to Olyn's compromise, then at least they maintained the illusion of autonomy, and they were protected anonymously under the parasol of the Guild."

Tollan's nostrils flared, but he said nothing. Wince knew his friend well enough to know that a slow, simmering rage was boiling beneath his surface. Wince could see the telltale twitch in Tollan's right eyelid and the twist of his mouth in distaste. He should diffuse the situation, but he was in so much shock over what Gemma was telling them that he let the moment pass.

Gemma continued. "Olyn was the true intellect behind the pact, and she manipulated her brother into wording it so she maintained control of the Under. She knew the pact wouldn't stand a chance of succeeding if the church maintained its self-government, and her newly found freedom would disappear as well. She made it work—and for five generations, it has. I know that's a lot to take in, but..."

Tollan moved toward Gemma. He shook with rage, and for an instant Wince thought the King of Above might strike the Queen of Under. She put her hand on the hilt of her dagger. They were of equal height, but for a moment, she seemed dwarfed by him.

"A lot to take in?" Tollan growled. "All of Yigris thinks I've killed my father and perhaps Melnora, too. I've been in two whorehouses today—one of which is a prickling church. I've been dragged through Under, which appears to be collapsing, while Above is supposedly consumed by burning bushes. And now I find out the king doesn't wield much power anyway. Even the church is controlled by the Under!" He balled his fists at his sides.

Wince's heart pounded in his chest. Tollan was right, but a fight with the Queen of Under seemed like a good way to meet a blade.

Tollan seemed to come to the same conclusion, because his shoulders sagged. "I'm sorry," he said softly. "That was ungentlemanly of me."

"You're damned right it was," Gemma replied, smiling brightly. "It's about time you started thinking like a rogue. It's the only prickling way you're going to survive this!"

After Gemma and Wince explained their discovery of the tainted mage mark on his back and their conclusions about a potential mage uprising, Wince could see the panic growing behind Tollan's eyes. Pacing, Gemma continued. "How could this happen? What made the mage women suddenly choose to act against you? Was it just your father's death? Did they see this as their opportunity to start trouble? They've been alone in the castle for so long . . ."

A deep, painful sigh pushed its way out of Tollan. "But they aren't alone, anymore. My brother married a Vagan princess, Elsha, a few months ago. I was gone when it happened," Tollan said, his voice little more than a whisper.

And suddenly, it was Wince's turn to panic. He didn't want to hear this story, didn't want to relive what couldn't be relived. Heart pounding, he said, "No, it's not your . . ."

But Tollan pushed forward, his shoulders slumped and his eyes glassy with unshed tears. "Wince and I grew up with a friend—a noble girl named Uri. A while back, Uri got into some trouble with a common-born boy who worked in the stables. She had this mare she doted on, and she spent a lot of time there. This stableboy took care of her horse—the one thing she loved most in all the world—so she loved him for it. And one thing led to another. She got pregnant."

Wince could barely believe what he was hearing. Was it possible that Tollan really didn't know the whole truth?

Tollan turned his back to them, his words heavy with guilt. "Uri came to me, hysterical. We were really good friends—and she was sobbing that her parents would disown her, that she'd lose everything. I thought I was helping. I told her to tell her parents that the baby was mine."

"Oh," Gemma said as if she'd been gut punched. She couldn't know exactly what had happened—but she was a smart girl. Wince was sure she could imagine.

Tollan squared his shoulders and turned to face her. "My father was livid—as angry as I've ever seen him. He said that under no circumstances could I acknowledge the child; that Uri and her family would be sent away so that no one would notice the resemblance. He said that I ought to have known how to keep the useless girl from getting with child if I wanted to climb on top of her, and that he wouldn't let House Daghan be saddled with my indiscretions. Then he sent me to sea on his private merchant vessel to give me time to calm down, as he put it."

Wince felt bile rise in his throat. The weight of his own grief was as vast as the Hadriak. He didn't want to hear about Tollan's pain. He didn't want to feel responsible for that, too.

"After that," Tollan went on, despite Wince's silent pleas for him to stop. "I couldn't tell him the truth—it would have ruined Uri even more than the lie." He met Gemma's gaze. "I was at sea for four months, but three days after I set sail, Uri hanged herself in the stables. I was a prickling coward and my friend died because of me. Her family thinks I abandoned her, but I..." He trailed off.

Wince gagged on a sob, his throat squeezed tight by the tears he had refused to shed for her—for them.

Tollan crumpled onto the bed, as if his spine had all but gone out of him. "While I was away, my brother was...he got married. She was a foreign visitor—a princess. A Vagan princess. It seems my brother and Princess Elsha fell madly, deeply in love within just weeks of her arrival and refused to be separated. She's been living in the palace, ever since."

"Are you suggesting she's a mage woman? Do you think he's somehow magically compelled to be with her?" She shook her head and spat as if dispelling a foul taste. "If it's mage work, then there isn't a damned thing you could have done," Gemma said soberly. She moved toward Tollan—almost as if she meant to comfort him—but she stopped short, her mouth twisted downward. "And if you hadn't been sent away, then you'd probably be the one married to the Vagan princess."

Tollan stared at her. As much as Wince could see he wanted to deny it, Tollan knew she spoke the truth. If he hadn't been away, he'd have succumbed to his father's will, or to Elsha's. Wince barely heard Tollan as he said, "When I returned, six weeks ago, she and Iven had already married. Uri was in the ground. Everything was different, except . . . except my father. He was the same."

Wince couldn't listen anymore. He couldn't let the conversation continue to dwell in the depths of the pit he only allowed himself to fall into when he was alone and drunk. "We need to know more," he blurted. "We don't know shit about magery or about the Vagans. Both halves of Yigris strut around pleased as prick that they've got a secret pact. We closed what was left of our borders for a hundred years, pretending we could banish anyone who wields the kind of power that the mages do, and then"—he rubbed his hands together—"we forgot about the whole damned mess."

"How did the king's mage women seem?" Gemma asked Tollan. "Have you noticed any increase in hostilities?"

Tollan chuckled bitterly. "You've not actually met a mage woman, have you?"

She shook her head. "I mean, I saw the one who was with you . . ."

"The mage women haven't spoken since the war, since they were signed over as part of the truce. They are silent, emotionless servants to the crown."

"Signed over? I thought they chose to stay." Her eyes grew hard. "Do you think they see themselves as servants to the crown, Tollan?" she asked. "Because they sound like slaves to me. You noblemen do love to keep your women prisoner, don't you?"

Tollan opened his mouth then closed it again.

"So what do we do?" Wince asked, thankful to the goddess that the conversation had swerved far away from his grief. "Can we talk to them? Can we set them free?"

"Prick that," Tollan growled.

Gemma's gaze cut hard and fast at Tollan as she snapped, "Goddess-damn you, with your prickling *morality* and your noses turned so far up to the sky that you trip over your own feet. Aegos! Wince's smallclothes were so twisted about who I let stick what where, in *my* body, that he could barely speak, but keeping people locked up against their will, using them and . . ." Gemma spat on the floor again. "And you bastards have the balls to call us evil."

Wince felt color rise to his cheeks. She didn't have to be quite so descriptive.

"The mage women might have murdered my father," Tollan grunted.

"They might have murdered Melnora, too," she barked, and Wince saw, without a doubt, just how dangerous Gemma could be. "I imagine that you'd also be ready to kill someone if you'd been chattel for a century." Her hand rested on the hilt of her knife. "What the Void am I supposed to do about . . ."

A small bell tied to a velvet rope that ran across the ceiling and down the wall rang softly and all three of them jumped.

"Aegos," Wince said. He drew his sword and turned to Gemma. "What was that?"

"I don't know," she said, pulling the key from beneath her shirt and heading for the door.

Wince stood next to the door as Gemma opened it. The prayer keeper, Brother Elam, stood in the hallway, his face pale and his shirt blood spattered. His glasses were askew, and it looked like he'd been crying. "Gemma, hurry," he said as soon as he saw her.

Gemma followed him at a dead run, leaving Wince and Tollan to hurry behind.

By the time Wince and Tollan caught up with Gemma, she was in the hospit on her knees beside a low cot. A large man, bald with smooth skin was spread out, his feet hanging off the end.

Tollan wore an expression of bewilderment, so Wince whispered to him, "Aw, Aegos. Fin the Fish."

Understanding settled on his friend's features.

"Oh, no . . . no . . . no." Gemma moaned, clutching at Fin's hand. There was blood everywhere, as if he'd been gutted like his namesake, and when he tried to speak he coughed more onto her face.

"Shhh," she said, squeezing his hand and leaning into him. She kissed his cheek and whispered into his ear, but he kept struggling, fighting to talk.

"It's going to be all right," she said, smoothing hair that wasn't there and caressing his cheek. "The priests will fix you up, and you'll be good as new." Her tears fell on his face, and he opened his mouth to form words but no sound came.

"Fin, I don't know what you're trying to say." She sobbed.

He coughed once and thick, dark blood bubbled from between his lips. He hacked out a single word.

"Dev."

She stopped moving for a heartbeat, then stood up. "I have to go. Fin, if he needs me, I have to go. Is he hurt? Is he . . . dead?" There was a tremor in her voice.

Fin shook his head—or at least Wince thought he did—it was difficult to tell because at the same moment a shudder ran through the Balklander and his breathing stilled.

Gemma's knife was in her hand. "I'm going to gut whoever did this, Elam," she snarled. "I'm going to cut them from carotid to cock, I prickling swear it."

Elam squeezed her shoulder, leaving a bloody handprint on her shirt, then looked at Fin. The prayer keeper's eyes brimmed with tears. He snapped his fingers twice, and though Wince didn't understand it, something about that made Gemma stand straighter.

Gemma took a moment longer to turn back toward the gurney where Fin's body rested. Though the Balklander had been bigger than any man she knew, he'd had a kind heart and a gentle tongue. Even when he'd punished her as a girl, he'd always hugged her after. In many ways Gemma believed that she had grown to be the woman she was because of Fin the Fish's guiding hand—a hand that now swung lifeless off the edge of the cot, fingers covered in blood.

Elam sagged to the floor and sobbed raggedly. "I wasn't ready to say goodbye," he choked, and Gemma reached down to wrap him in her arms.

The other prayer keepers gave them a wide berth. Though the church was officially a branch of the Guild, it was rare for one of their ranks to have come from Under. Most of those within the walls of Canticle Center had been sent there by their merchant fathers and stayed, having found the voice of the goddess a willing mistress. Elam was an oddity, so it was no surprise that no one else in the Heart cared about the man Fin had been. Elam swallowed a choking sob and wiped his face on his tunic, staining the silk with his tears.

A young woman wearing the light-brown robes of a prayer keeper in training approached them, eyes wide with fear. "Brother Elam. Regency," she said, bowing respectfully. "There may be a fire. Father Mahpir has ordered the immediate evacuation of Canticle Center."

Other novice prayer keepers rushed into the hospit from the

Slit, carrying out patients and gathering supplies. Elam looked down at Fin's body, but Gemma turned her back to it. It was said that the kings of old used to be burned on great funeral pyres and sent to the goddess with all of their wealth, and if ever she had known a king of men, it was Fin. Elam leaned down, closed the Balklander's empty eyes and kissed his forehead. "May Aegos welcome you with open arms and legs, my friend. Give Melnora my love, and send us any luck you can spare. I have a feeling we're going to need it."

Then he looked up and said to Gemma, "Go on, go find him. I'm right behind you." She kissed his forehead and turned to leave, motioning for Tollan and Wince to follow.

Outside, Canticle Square was in chaos. Brambles had erupted from the ground around the Head, and when they burst into sudden flame, they lit up the night. Gemma could hear a child screaming in the distance. A man driving a cart barely slowed down to pass them, and Gemma let her dagger fly. It pinned him neatly in the back of the neck and he slumped over onto the seat. She was dimly aware in the back of her mind that she should feel guilty for killing him, but in the forefront all she saw was Devery, bloodied and alone.

"Come on," she barked, running to catch the slowing horse. She yanked her dagger from the cart driver's neck and pulled him down to the ground before claiming his seat.

Tollan stared, disconcerted, as he climbed onto the cart with her. Wince didn't meet her gaze.

She opened her mouth then snapped it closed again. She didn't need to make excuses. She was the Queen of Under.

She steered them toward Guildhouse, her throat tight. The clip of the horse's feet on the cobblestones reminded her of the two finger snaps that Elam had sent her off with. As she pushed the horse to go faster, she remembered the years she'd spent with Devery and Elam, honing their craft, in their apartment together on Thieves Row. Their jobs got bigger and more difficult as time went by, but it wasn't until they pulled off the assassination of a Farcastian baron when Gemma was nearly sixteen, that Devery had finally opened up.

As the three of them sat around their tiny table passing a bottle of congratulatory wine between them, the excitement that appeared in Devery's eyes lit the room. "Nobody's ever going to find that prickling shitbag! It was a brilliant plan, Gemma." He handed the bottle to her, grinning.

"I didn't know you could smile," she said, taking another swallow. "I asked Fin about it once, and he said the muscles that pull your lips up had been severed in a tragic accident involving a goat, a printing press and a harvesting scythe." Her own mouth turned upward in a devilish smile as she continued. "But he told me not to bring it up. Said you were a little touchy about your affinity for goats."

Elam erupted with laughter, but Devery just looked at her—eyes glinting. Something within her—probably the wine—made her match his gaze. Until that moment, she'd been too afraid of him, too unnerved by him to ever even try to make him warm to her. She glanced away demurely. "I'm sorry for the loss of your goat, though. What was her name? Sugartits?"

Warm, hearty laughter tumbled out of him. She was sure he was mocking her until she saw his face. It was as if the Devery she had known for three years had vanished in the blink of an eye and was suddenly replaced by someone who didn't hate her. Who maybe even liked her a little bit.

The sound of his laughter tumbled through her mind as she raced through the empty Above. They were one street over from Guildhouse, and Gemma was positive that the geyser of flame she saw just beyond the closest row of buildings was the aboveground portion of her home. But she did not slow down. She snapped the reins against the horse's ass, urging it onward.

She was prickling done with slowing down.

There was a point earlier in the day, before Tollan's whole life had gotten away from him, when he'd thought that he should be wary of Gemma. But wary didn't even begin to describe his feelings now. The rage that boiled off her as they careened through the city was terrible to behold. She had gone cold, and there was violence in her that he had underestimated.

Wince had gone stiff. He was clearly weighing the risks versus the benefits of staying with Gemma. "We need to get out of here," Wince hissed in his ear.

Tollan agreed. Gemma's vengeance fantasy was not theirs, and he needed to get back to Iven to see if he was being controlled by magery, or if he did truly want Tollan dead. If Elsha was compelling Iven, and there was any way to free his brother from her talons, he had to do whatever he could. Iven was just a kid.

They took a corner too fast, and the horse faltered. "Prick!" Gemma shouted, whipping at the horse with the reins.

"Gemma, it—"

She interrupted Tollan with a glare so icy that he shrank from her. Her lip curled. "Get out," she snarled.

He looked at Wince, who shrugged.

"Gemma, we need to talk," Tollan said. "I know you're worried about your . . . Devery, but I need to find out what's going on with my brother. I can't just leave him if he's caught in a mage woman's trap. They could control all of Yigris if we leave them there. Let's just take a minute and think this through. If we could break into the palace through the Golden Door, maybe we could find out the truth . . . " He hated the clumsiness of his tongue. He wished he had some of his father's authority behind his words.

She hopped down from the cart and drew a knife. When she met his gaze, there was a glimmer of madness in her eyes. "Right now, I don't give two shits about Yigris. You want to head back to the palace, that's your funeral." She looked at the blade of her knife, glinting in the streetlight. "But I'm going to find Devery." Her hand drifted over her midsection as she added, "It would take a whole army of mage women to stop me." She offered Wince the reins. "If I were you, I wouldn't be heading into their den without some friends at my back, but maybe you're better swordsmen than I think."

"My brother . . ." Tollan said and shook his head. "I can't leave him if our suspicions about the mage women are correct. If I'm wrong, I . . . "

She nodded. "I understand. Sure. Family is important. I'm going to go find what's left of mine." She turned and walked away, but a few steps later, she called over her shoulder, "If you're right, and this is Vaga, House Daghan is to blame. If I lose Devery . . ." She didn't bother to finish the threat. Tollan knew exactly what she meant.

Wince gathered the reins, then snapped them to urge the wounded horse gently onward. "Well, that could have gone better," he muttered.

Tollan couldn't argue with that. He may have just made an enemy of one of his only allies. They plodded through the city streets. No one paid them any heed. The shops and homes were shuttered tight. There were no people about. Fires raged, but the streets had an eerie silence to them. Tollan picked at the gum paste that still clung to his chin. He settled into a sullen silence and ignored Wince's prying gaze. "This whole city feels like a mummer's show," he said. Tollan's eyes continued to search the horizon. Nothing else was burning. Not even the buildings adjacent to the fire. How was that possible? It was a windy night. The flames should be dancing from rooftop to rooftop. Prick, half the city should be engulfed by now.

"I know. It's hard to believe it's real."

"No, I mean . . . it . . . this . . ."—he held his arms wide—"feels staged. Remember the stories of the Mage War? Hundreds of mage women swarmed through the streets, the Yigrisian army decimated. Remember the riots and the refugees and the mass chaos?"

Wince nodded.

"Why are people not fleeing? Where is the chaos? Back by Canticle Center there was a little, but here . . . almost nothing." He turned in a circle and pointed to a column of smoke.

"It's a farce," Tollan said. "The flames aren't spreading. The only thing that could explain it is mage work, but . . ."

Wince met his eyes, and his hand drifted to the hilt of his cutlass. "Bloody Aegos," he groaned. "The mage women don't leave the palace. And I find it awfully hard to believe that Iven's princess has been down here in the shit and mud."

"It has to mean that there are other mages here within the city. Someone must have marked the Guild buildings to make them, and them alone, burn."

"But, why?" Wince fidgeted with his sword. "Sure, the Guild may have lost Melnora, but the king holds insurance on all the buildings, right? It's in the pact. They could rebuild without much trouble, and the Guild members aren't going anywhere."

"I don't know, Wince. But we need to get moving."

"Back to Gemma? She may be walking into a trap." Wince picked up the reins.

"No. We are going to the palace. Gemma's a grown woman, and she made her choice. Iven might not have had a choice. I have to figure out a way to help him." His voice trembled as he said, "I need to go home to the palace."

CHAPTER NINE

GUILDHOUSE

As Gemma neared Guildhouse's courtyard, she saw a hundred or more children standing outside the gate watching the flames rage. Several dozen Guild members, men and women she recognized but didn't know by name, stood about, hats removed in respect. A whisper ran through the crowd as she approached. All around her, faces were streaked with tears and Gemma's throat tightened with her own, left unshed. The looks on the faces of her people tugged at her, demanding her attention and forcing her to stand straighter and remember her position.

A little girl came racing toward her, and Gemma gasped with the swell of gratitude she felt when she recognized Katya's white-streaked hair.

"Hey, mite," she said, picking the girl up and swinging her into a hug. "I'm glad to see you're safe."

Katya looked at her in confusion. "Gemma, I thought you were asleep in Guildhouse. I . . . you should be asleep."

"I was on an errand, Katy. I'm safe. Everything is going to be all right." She squeezed the little girl tightly and looked into her sea-glass eyes. "I have to find someone. You stay safe. Listen to Lian, and keep the urchins in line."

An odd look, serious and conflicted, crossed Katya's face. She nodded. "Yes, Regency." Gemma ruffled her hair and watched the girl scramble away then push through the crowd until she spotted the slight, stoic figure of Lian.

Gemma approached quietly, raking the crowd for signs of Devery. As she neared the maid, Lian looked up, eyes wide with fear. "Oh, thank the goddess, Gemma," she sobbed, catching Gemma in an embrace. "We didn't know where you were. Melnora's gone."

It was no more than she'd expected, but the words and the faces of the people she cared about took the razor coldness out of her. She felt the ice in her veins melt as she hugged Lian. "Have you seen Devery?" she managed to ask.

Lian released her. "He left with Master Fin a couple of hours ago. Not long before this all started. They said they were going to meet you somewhere safe."

Gemma wanted to kick herself. She'd forgotten in her mad dash to escape the collapsing tunnel and the aftermath of Fin's death that Devery had told her to meet him at the safe house. "I hate to ask it, but . . . were you able to get Melnora's body out of the house, before . . ." Her gaze drifted to the fire.

Lian nodded. "The men argued with me, but I demanded that they get the mistress out or I'd leave them inside."

Gemma grinned. Lian would have absolutely let them cook to a crisp while she watched if they'd refused to do her bidding. Gemma cupped the maid's face in her palm and kissed her on the cheek. "You're brilliant, Lian. I need to see her immediately."

Melnora was laid out on a stone bench, a sheet covering her. Gemma knelt on the grass beside her. "We need to search her skin. I'm looking for a mark—any sort of odd character."

The maid blanched but nodded, and the two of them set to checking over their mistress's body. It didn't take long to find what she was looking for. A mark—part brand, part tattoo—rested on the inside of her left forearm just below the elbow. Much smaller than Tollan's mage mark, but it still left no doubt in her mind. Gemma placed her hand on the mark. She couldn't help but notice that Melnora's limp hand now rested nearly on the corresponding area of Gemma's arm.

The air was thick in her lungs. The clasping of arms was the final step in signing a business arrangement. "Do you have any idea what Melnora did today, Lian? Who she met with? What business did she attend to?"

Lian shook her head. "I'm not sure. I went to the apothecary, and when I came back, Fin said she'd been called away. She arrived home a little after luncheon and said she had a headache and needed to lie down. I went to check on her an hour later, and she was . . ." A fresh wave of tears rolled down Lian's cheeks. "I don't know who did this, but I . . ." She hiccupped.

"I know," Gemma said. "I'm going to find out who's responsible." She didn't have the heart to tell Lian about Fin.

She covered Melnora, tucking in the edges of the sheet. "I have to go. Look after the children for me. Take them to Canticle Center, if need be, but beware the tunnels. The brambles have made them unsafe. I'll be back when I can."

"Yes, Regency. I'll see them safe. But, Gemma . . . the palace. It's happening there, too . . ."

"We're not going to worry about what's going on up the hill, Li. We take care of our own, and that's all we do just now." A flame of guilt flared within her as she thought of Tollan, but she pushed it aside and kissed Lian on the cheek once more, then turned and ran.

The streets surrounding Guildhouse, beyond the courtyard, were oddly deserted. The crackle and hiss of flame was the only sound. Gemma stopped, staring at the column of flame and smoke that was her former home. While a warm breeze ruffled her hair, no flames moved beyond Guildhouse. For all she knew, the people in the buildings nearby were still asleep in their beds. Truth be told, the only people she'd seen out and about were the people who'd been taking their night's rest within the walls of Guildhouse proper. The hair on the back of her neck rose in alarm. There was mage work to blame.

Without warning, a palm was over her mouth and a body pressed against hers. She flung an elbow hard, but it was caught by a strong and dexterous hand.

"Shhh, Gem," Devery whispered in her ear. "It's just me. I didn't want you to scream."

She turned around, scanning his body for injury. His fitted jacket and tunic were spattered with blood, but he looked whole. She threw her arms around him, hot tears flooding her eyes.

"I thought you were dead. Aegos, when I saw Fin, I . . ." She couldn't stop the sob that ripped its way out of her chest.

"You saw Fin?" he asked, pushing her out to arm's length. His blue eyes went hard and cold. "Is he . . . is he all right?" There was a thread of fear in his words.

She shook her head, fresh tears filling her eyes. "Dead," she whispered. "But he sent me for you. His last thoughts were of you. What happened?"

He pulled her close to him then. Years of keeping their relationship a secret dissolved in an instant as she leaned against his chest. He didn't answer her, only sobbed against her as she cried against him.

"Dev," she finally said, "there's magery at work here. I saw the mark on Melnora. I've seen Tollan's mark—a blasphemy of what it should have been. The fire is wrong, and I . . ."

His face did an odd sort of crumpling. "Where is Tollan?"

"Headed back to the palace, I think. We had a bit of a disagreement about tactics. He was none too thrilled with mine."

Devery smiled, his eyes lit eerily by the flames. "That doesn't make any sense. Did you tell him about the mage work? Why would he head to the only place we know for sure that there are mage women, if he even suspected they were responsible?"

She shook her head. "Of course I told him, but Tollan's got some noble idea that he needs to rescue his brother. Honestly, he's not our problem. He and Wince are big boys. They know what they're walking into. Let them spring the trap. It keeps the mage women out of our hair. I had to find you, and no whining King of Above was going to talk me out of it."

Devery reached out, cupping her chin in his palm. "It's your call, Gem. If you're done with them, then prick the Above. Tollan Daghan's a half-wit not to listen to you, but I'm fine. We're fine." He ran his thumb along her jaw, sending little bolts of lightning through her skin.

She was struck, looking into his eyes, by the overwhelming urge to take him by the hand and run as far from Yigris and the shambles of the Guild as they could get. She knew the secret bank codes in Ladia and Balkland. They could live extravagantly for the rest of their lives, without a care in the world. They could take a ship to Far Coast and beyond and never look back. Everything she loved, except Devery and the secret she carried, was already gone.

He must have seen it in her face. He snapped his fingers three times. Their old code from when they were little more than children. One snap meant "run," two meant "I've got your backside" and three meant "have patience."

Tied up in that memory was Elam—the third in their triad. She couldn't leave Elam any more than she could leave Devery. "Prick me," she growled.

He caressed her cheek as he swooped in for a quick kiss. "I tried, darling. But you were too busy. And now, in the middle of a goddess-damned revolution, it doesn't quite seem the time."

She kissed him again. "I should have listened to you, then," she said, languidly pressing herself against him. "You couldn't have warned me that the Void was about to break loose?"

Tears wet his eyes as he leaned in, this time kissing her deeply. "I love you, Gemma, and we've got all the time in the world," he whispered. Then he added, "Lead the way, my queen. I always did enjoy watching you run away from me." He patted her ass gently and that was all the prodding she needed.

CHAPTER TEN

THE STREETS

Gemma and Devery threaded their way through vacant streets. They almost always traveled through the city via the now compromised tunnels and walking beneath the stars with him made her smile. In the emptiness, Devery reached out and took her hand.

Gemma was queen now. If she wished to take an assassin as her lover, there was no one to forbid it. The very thought sent a thrill through her.

She had never planned on disobeying Melnora. It should have been simple for them to follow this one rule. And it had been simple for a long time.

Once, Gemma had even understood Melnora's reasons. The ruler of Under must be accessible to all, and if Gemma was romantically involved with a trained murderer, she would not be approached by those who feared her displeasure. In fact, any who approached her might come to fear for their lives.

There had been plenty of logical reasons against it, but logic had nothing to do with love.

And for all of Melnora's protestations, the very bylaws that addressed the training of the future Queen of Under had complicated the situation. The bylaws made it clear that no team was to stay together for more than a period of one year, except in the case of the heir apparent—who was to be placed with a team that would serve as conscience and backbone to the future ruler of Under. In their world built on lies, Melnora had handed Gemma two people she could trust no matter what. If she hadn't known her better, Gemma would've almost thought that Melnora had forbidden the relationship just to make them want it more.

She squeezed Devery's hand, feeling the pulse in her thumb throb against his own. She was distracted in the very best way. She wanted to put her hands in his hair, to scream out to the world that she loved him. She wanted to forget all the other shit she was going to have to remember soon enough.

Desire swelled within her and Gemma stopped walking.

"What is it?" he asked.

She released his grasp on her hand and began to unbutton her shirt.

They had been lovers long enough that Gemma no longer experienced the flutter of wings in her belly at every brush of his hand. But this new public touching set her skin aflame. Despite her exhaustion, despite her grief, she felt the stirrings of heat.

They were half a mile from the edge of Yigris—in the heart of Brighthold Above—surrounded by the stately manors and lush keeps of the wealthy. From here they could barely see the fires that were decimating all the prominent offices of the Guild, though the palace lit the night with eerie shadows in the distance. There was not a soul to be seen.

She slipped out of her oversize bloodstained shirt and started to unlace her breeches. Then she crooked her finger, beckoning him closer.

"Gem, I . . ." he began, but she pounced on him, ravaging his lips with her own as her fingers began to work on his shirt buttons.

"Is this all right with you?" she asked. She leaned away and offered him the chance to stop her. She would have expected nothing less from him.

He smiled shyly. "You just surprised me, is all. Of course it's all right. Goddess, you are beautiful." He admired her as she basked in the lantern light. "What if someone sees?"

She looked around at the silent sleeping city. Here, she could almost believe they were the only two people in the world. She imagined a life where she and Devery could be together, could talk or touch or kiss whenever they wanted to. Just the two of them, disentangled from all the concerns of Yigris and the Shadow Guild. And then a thought tickled at the back of her mind, and she grinned. It wouldn't be just the two of them for much longer.

"There's no one to see. Maybe the mages have killed everyone. Maybe they've put them all to sleep for a hundred years. Maybe you and I've been swept away to the land of the dead and we await judgment from the goddess. I don't care anymore. I want to lie down on this grass," she pointed at the manicured garden in front of the adjacent manor. "I want to make love until the sun comes up. I don't want to think about my duty or what is happening over there." She waved toward Shadowtown. "I just want you."

She slipped out of her boots and stepped the rest of the way out of her breeches, then unbuckled her knife belt and pouch. She ran a hand through her hair. Then she walked to the grass, and lay down on her side, propping her head on her hand.

"I love you, Gemma," Devery whispered as he moved toward her. His shirt blew open in the breeze, exposing the line of soft, dark hairs that ran down his belly.

She patted the ground in front of her, biting her lip. "I love you," she whispered, as he sank onto the grass, flat on his back, his hands behind his head and his legs spread out.

She laughed at his pose. "Too many clothes," she murmured.

Together they unburdened him of his wardrobe. His pale skin glowed in the lantern light. Each time his fingers brushed against her, she squirmed at the overwhelming sensuality of unrestricted caresses. Despite her grief and the losses she felt so keenly, she felt vividly alive.

They explored one another as if they'd never touched before. She pulled at his hair, dug fingertips into his back. The gardenia blooms nearby scented the air. Their laughter and groans of pleasure sounded like murmured prayers.

His mouth pressed against hers then suckled at her breasts and later, between her legs. She bucked against him, her thighs wrapped tightly around his shoulders as he lapped at her. Her fingers tore at the pristine grass as moans of ecstasy escaped her mouth until a sun exploded deep within her. She shuddered beneath him, and when he looked up at her, his eyes were hungry and dark.

CHAPTER ELEVEN

SHADOWTOWN

Tollan and Wince were lost.

One would think that a king would know his own city—but there were sections of Yigris that a king wouldn't be caught dead in. Or rather, if he were to be caught there, he'd probably end up dead.

"Any idea which way?" Wince asked as he stopped the cart at a narrow intersection. The street lanterns here were more widely spaced than any area that Tollan was familiar with—and there were empty, forbidding zones between the puddles of dull light that they provided. The streets remained deserted—even the public houses and inns were locked up tight.

Tollan shook his head, then realized the street was too dark for Wince to see him. "None whatsoever," he groaned, listening to the silence.

They passed slowly through a pool of light, and Tollan saw a glint of gold running across Wince's knuckles. Wince only ever played with the ancient Vagan coin when he was truly nervous. He called it Uri's Blessing, and he believed that the gold piece she'd given him as a girl still held some of the luck that she had wished on him.

"I think we're going to have to retrace our steps," Wince said. "I don't see any other way to get back to some semblance of civilization." The heavy, uneven clopping of the horse's hooves on the cobblestone street was the only sound they heard until the sudden crystalline ping of a coin hitting the street.

"Oh, balls!" Wince stammered. He pulled the horse to a stop. "Prickling Void!"

Tollan heard Wince fumble in his pouch for a long moment, then he lit the nub of candle they'd salvaged from their race through the tunnels with Gemma.

"I have to find it," he said. "It's the only part of her I'm ever going to get to keep." The panic and pain in Wince's voice shook something loose within Tollan, something that he should have seen long ago. The coin, which Wince had always associated with Uri, had become his only connection to her, and the grief in his words wasn't a friend's grief. It was so much more.

"Of course," Tollan replied. And it was suddenly as if he'd never really looked at Wince before. There was a distant wound there that would not heal—an injury he didn't want to examine too closely. *How could I have been so blind?*

They scoured the street in search of the lucky coin to no avail. Wince had gone stonily silent, and Tollan tried desperately to ignore the tracks of wetness he saw running down Wince's face. This wasn't about a coin. This was about a girl who would never be coming back.

Goddess, what a mess I make of everything.

When they'd exhausted their search of the street, they started to look through the scrubby grass that surrounded the homes that lined it. Tollan continued to run his hand along the ground. More than once he encountered a thorny weed that left his hand stinging and itching, but the hunch of Wince's shoulders and the trembling of his chin kept Tollan searching.

There was an alley between two buildings that was mostly bare of vegetation. As they moved into the narrow passage, Tollan prayed silently to Aegos for a small miracle. The path was full of refuse and the overwhelming smell of human waste.

Tollan was nearly overcome by the odor, but Wince seized a long piece of wood and began sweeping aside garbage in search of his talisman with a seemingly single-minded focus. Sighing, Tollan bent to look along the edge of the bedraggled wooden house, brushing aside the sparse foliage in search of the glitter of gold.

If he had not been bent over, nearly crawling on his hands and knees, he never would have found the coin. And if he hadn't been on his knees in the alley looking for the coin, he'd never have seen the mage mark, burned into the rough shingle of the house. His breath was a trembling thing as he pointed it out to Wince.

"Thank Aegos," Wince said, knees in the muck as he snatched up the coin. His damp eyes clung to it for a moment, and a small sound escaped his throat before he remembered himself.

He shoved the coin into his pocket. "And thank you, Toll."

Tollan nodded, afraid his voice might betray his guilt over Uri and his sudden realization that Wince could have been the true father of her child. If that were the case, he had failed both of his best friends. Desperate to change his train of thought, he gestured to the mage mark. "What the prick do you make of that?"

Wince's fingers traced the charred edges of the symbol.

Tollan had also touched it and could feel the mage work tingling. The mark was working, though what it was made to do he couldn't imagine. In all of his life in the palace, Tollan could almost count the number of marks he'd ever seen. To find one on a random dilapidated home in the middle of Shadowtown made no sense to him.

Wince stood. "Toll, I don't think you should go home."

Tollan watched as Wince shoved all of his emotions into his pocket along with the coin. His expression went blank, his voice no longer trembled. It was as if he had put on a mask to cover over his pain. "All of this feels . . ."—he ran his filthy hand over his face—"wrong isn't a strong enough word. Maybe we should find a place to stay close to the ground for a few days, see how things play out? Maybe find a ship to take you to Far Coast? If something happened to you I'd probably hate myself for a month or two." He winked.

What Wince said made logical sense, but his brother was at the palace in the clutches of a Vagan princess and four mage women. "I can't abandon Iven," he replied and sighed. Even as he said the words, he pictured his mother. She'd had no problem abandoning any of them. "But I think you're right. Even if I could somehow make it into the palace without being killed by mage women, the guards won't follow my commands. They think I killed my father. They'd probably just hang me." Tollan had grown up a prince in a place ruled by men. Acknowledging that he'd lost access to that privilege was more difficult than he would have thought.

He sat still, thinking, whispering a quiet prayer to Aegos. When they had fled the Canticle Center, a priest had stood atop the base of a large stone statue preaching about Aegos's loving, protective arms and the safety she provided for all who were faithful, but Tollan had his doubts. He didn't believe that this night was being watched by Aegos the Merciful. This night reeked of blood and violence—the realm of Aegos the Victorious. The goddess, like most women, wore many faces, and tonight she prepared Yigris for war.

The Ain had been there, assembled in ranks, their red-and-gold armor glittering in the light of the flames. Tollan could picture the steel glinting in the hands of each of the two hundred men and women who made up the exclusive fighting force. It had been so long before Tollan was born that the Ain had last been sent out to defend Yigris that the soldiers had fallen into legend, but Tollan had seen them with his own eyes, just before he'd gone chasing after Gemma. Perhaps they were the answer to his problem. Perhaps they could get him into the palace and closer to his brother.

Just as quickly as the idea came to him, he remembered that the Ain's loyalty lay with Gemma Antos and the Under. He would need her, if he were to gain access to the Ain, and getting her to listen to him might take a kind of diplomacy that he'd never been taught.

It had been a long time since he'd wished for his mother's return from the sea, but now he fervently longed to see the mast of the *Heart's Desire* rising above Dockside. If there was anyone who would know how to deal with this situation, it would be Queen Isbit.

As Tollan was dreaming of the miraculous return of his swashbuckling mother, Wince approached the building to the west, which nearly butted up against the marked one. Tollan heard him hiss, "Prick's sake."

Tollan approached. There, not three paces farther, was another mage mark. The same mark.

"Come on," Wince growled.

It didn't take them long to conclude that every building in the area bore the same mark. "Goddess!" Tollan hated the self-pity he heard in his own voice. "Are we looking at a whole army of mages?"

Wince took his elbow and guided him back toward the cart. "I won't be party to you going back to the palace. Whatever we'd be walking into, it's more than we're prepared for. If you won't leave Yigris, then we need to find a place to hide."

Tollan yanked his arm away from Wince. "Like the Void I'll leave Yigris." He couldn't believe that Wince had suggested it. "But I see your point. We need to find Gemma. We're going to go find her, and we're going to get on our knees and beg because she's the only one who can help us now."

The horse went down onto the cracked and broken cobblestone street with a throaty scream an instant after Tollan heard the snap of its leg. Wince leaped from the seat of the cart as the animal writhed in agony. Tollan climbed down from the cart and drew his sword, heart pounding in his chest.

"Aw, prick," Wince groaned. "He stepped in a hole." He glanced up at Tollan, then drew his own sword and swung at the horse's thick neck. A geyser of blood blew back in his face, and he wiped it off on his sleeve. The horse twitched and kicked, then went still.

Tollan scanned the street. How could the people inside have slept through that clamor?

Wince put his back to Tollan's, both of them circling, eyes alert for danger that did not come. "It's prickling eerie," Wince whispered after a moment, then sheathed his sword. "It's got to be the marks, but I..."

"Shhh..." Tollan warned, his ears picking up the sound of approaching footsteps.

Wince dragged his bloody cutlass back out of its sheath. A hundred yards ahead, a figure turned in their direction. He could make out a frown on the man's face in the lamplight.

"Odd night for a walk, Your Grace," the man said, bowing formally.

Tollan felt his breath rush out of him in relief as he saw the familiar spectacles and close-cropped hair of Brother Elam.

"Where's Gemma?" the prayer keeper asked.

"Run off with her lover," Wince replied, taking a step

toward the priest. "We didn't much feel like accompanying her as she went about murdering folks." Elam gave Wince a sideways glance and Wince continued, "She wouldn't wait to find Devery and we thought that the fate of the city and Prince Iven were more important."

"Though, in the long run, that may have been our mistake," Tollan said.

Brother Elam chuckled, "With Gemma, you can never be sure, but getting between her and Devery is never a good idea. You're going the wrong way if you're heading home, though. If you want, I can lead you as far as Brighthold."

Tollan and Wince shared a glance. At this point, they were going to stumble into a sewer pit and drown in Shadowtown's shit if they weren't careful. They might as well take what assistance they could get.

"What are you doing here?" Tollan asked.

"The temple's surrounded by burning brambles," Elam said, eyes downcast. "And so is your lovely palace. The Guild is falling, and . . . my place is with Gemma and . . ." He trailed off.

For a moment, Tollan couldn't breathe. *The palace is burning?*

Wince grunted. "We appear to have come to a similar conclusion. We were actually hoping we could find Gemma and take advantage of her hospitality."

Elam eyed them, his smile growing broader. "So, you gentleman are pissing yourselves, then, eh?"

Wince laughed. "I believe that is a fairly accurate description of our current state, yes."

"Well, then," Elam said, turning his back on them and pointing into the distance, "You are in luck. I happen to know exactly where Gemma will go once she's found Devery."

Something in his tone brought to mind the ancient pain that Tollan had so recently heard in Wince's words—"I have to find it."

But then the prayer keeper smiled over his shoulder at them. "So what do you make of what's going on in Yigris, tonight?"

As they walked, Wince told Elam about the mage marks on the buildings and the mark on Tollan's back. They stopped at a corner house, located the mark, and showed Elam what they meant.

He stared at the mark, brow furrowed in concentration. Then he turned to Tollan. "Your Grace," he said, "I'm afraid that you are well and truly pricked. If I were you, I might consider a fast ship to Far Coast and a new name."

"That's what I said!" Wince laughed, but no one joined him.

"Can you take me to Gemma?" Tollan asked. Wince didn't like the tone of his voice. Something about it brought Tollan's father to mind.

The prayer keeper nodded. "I believe so, Your Grace."

Tollan stood straighter, and despite his stained rags, he thrust a measure of confidence into his words that surprised Wince. "And she, as Queen of Under, can command the Ain? Is that correct?"

Elam inhaled sharply through his nostrils. He nodded slowly. "She can, yes, but . . ."

"There is no 'but'," Tollan snapped. "She has to do what's best for Yigris! What if I commanded her?"

Jovial laughter erupted from the slender prayer keeper. "You don't know Gemma very well, Your Grace, if you think that line of reasoning is going to work. Your Yigris is a different Yigris than hers, and you're going to have to make her see the benefit of ordering her people to help you. You're going to have to approach this with some humility, if you don't mind me saying so, Your Grace. Commanding her might be a good way to get your throat slit, but that's probably not the outcome you're looking for."

Wince watched all the steel go out of his friend's spine as Tollan said, "Do you think she would—is she really capable of that?"

It was difficult for Wince to watch his best friend, the prickling king, shrivel under the gaze of a trumped-up whore, no matter how genial Brother Elam seemed to be.

"Oh, she's capable," Elam said, patting Tollan on the arm. "But I'm more worried about Devery. He's got to be on edge, with Fin and Melnora, and—" he gestured back toward the fires. "He is not a man that I recommend trifling with. He has a good heart, and he's saved my life on more than one occasion, but he's a killer, and a prickling good one at that."

Wince said wistfully, "Maybe he's already dead, and we won't have to worry about it."

In one instant Brother Elam had his arm pressed against

Tollan's back, and in the next, his knife was pressed to Wince's throat.

"I will thank you kindly not to speak such things about my friends, again, Master Quintella," he hissed into Wince's ear. "There are few things that we in the Guild take as seriously as death threats. And by that, I mean in all seriousness . . . if you say such a thing to me again, I will slit you from ear to ear."

Their eyes met for an instant, and Wince glanced away. His heart pounded an uneven beat in his chest.

The three of them stood in silence until Elam sighed. "We've got a long walk, gentlemen. Might as well make the best of it." He let go of Wince and began to whistle, the sound echoing and eerie in a night that seemed to never end.

An hour later, Tollan was wavering on his feet.

Wince watched him, mouth pursed and eyes dark. Finally, when Tollan stumbled and nearly collapsed, Wince said, "We're going to have to stop so the king can rest."

Elam assessed Tollan for a moment before he said, "You have two choices then. You either sleep on someone's grass, or we're going to do a little thieving."

Tollan glanced at his surroundings. They'd moved into a more prosperous area of Yigris—he assumed that they were on the edge of Brighthold—and the homes here were spaced out, with large lawns surrounding them. Street lamps lit the way, and the paving stones were smooth and well packed. He eyed the small manor in front of them, and his body yearned for a warm bed, a soft pillow. He shook his head. He would not break into one of his city's homes. He was better than that.

He thrust his chin at a small grassy patch beside the house. "We sleep there," he said.

Wince shuffled forward, head hung low. Elam moved toward the knoll with lithe muscles. The thought of the prayer keeper's body—nimble and warm—sleeping beside him, made Tollan's breath catch in his throat. He could not deny the surge of energy that raced through him when the man had touched his arm. And though Tollan knew these thoughts would bring him nothing but pain, he moved forward like a man sleepwalking. To be nearer to that beautiful man, he would gladly sleep in a gutter.

Elam began to hum softly as they settled on the lawn. "It's a lovely night for it, Your Grace," he said, and Tollan had the distinct impression that the man was mocking him.

CHAPTER TWELVE

THE SAFE HOUSE

It didn't take long to walk the last distance to the safe house. They stood at the very edge of Brighthold in front of a small manor, windows ablaze with light. Devery squeezed her hand as they made their way up the front walk, and Gemma found that she was nervous, though she had no real reason to be.

He knocked on the door. Before he'd finished his third rap the door flew open, revealing a tall, stately woman with brown hair, pulled back severely. She had full lips and shrewd blue eyes.

Gemma drew in a deep breath, reminding herself that she was the Queen of Under. Brinna had no reason to . . .

"Hello, Mother," Devery said, his voice vacant of all warmth.

Brinna's gaze snapped to her son, and she seemed to remember herself. "Come in, come in," she said, her words betraying, only slightly, the odd accent she bore. She waved them inside and closed the door behind them.

Glancing around the entryway, Gemma noticed a chair that seemed out of place. A steaming cup of tea sat on the floor beside it. "You were expecting us," she said.

"I saw the flames. I was worried, and I suspected my son might need solace." She glanced at Devery. "I did not realize he'd be bringing company."

"Mother, we're tired. Save your judgment for morning." There was a dangerous edge to his voice.

Brinna's nostrils flared, but she stayed silent.

"Excellent," Devery said. "We'll be using the guest room, then."

Gemma followed him through the entryway and into the hall. She glanced back over her shoulder. Gemma was grateful that Brinna was only throwing glances. If they'd been blades, she knew her blood would be staining the woman's Ladian carpets.

Devery led her upstairs to a bedroom that was lushly furnished, then locked the door behind them. When he turned to meet her gaze, his expression was somber. "I'm sorry, Gemma. I don't know why I keep expecting her to change."

"It's all right." She pulled him to her by the front of his shirt. His arms slid around her waist. "You're worth it."

He grinned at her, crookedly, and she laughed as he slid into a chair. She sat down on the edge of the bed. "We can stay here until the smoke clears," he said, his expression growing more serious. "The inhabitants are pretty awful, but..."

"We need to get a plan in place. I'm thinking that if we end up having to assault the palace, we'll have to go through the Golden Door. I think the rest of the entrances are blocked by brambles and fire. We can put the Ain in the tunnels, in case somebody manages to sneak past us, and I guess we'll have to count on anyone else who's able to surround the palace Above. Maybe Lian can take charge there." She had no idea how many of the Ain or the Guild members had survived the night's massacre, but it was at least the skeleton of a plan.

"Or we could just stay here and pretend that the world isn't ending." Devery kissed her, his hands wandering down her body.

"Dev," she interrupted him. "I can't just sit here while Yigris goes to shit. In the morning, I'll have to gather together what's left of the Guild. We'll need to start assessing how many mage women are in the palace—it looks like there's at least four, if Iven's princess is one, too."

Devery looked up at her in surprise. "Princess?" he asked, and something in his eyes scared her, but an instant later, he was standing beside her. "Of course, you're right. But can we worry about all of that tomorrow?"

She nodded and leaned into him as he kissed her long and slow. Soon, they were removing each other's clothing once again until they were completely bare.

She drew him toward the enormous canopied bed.

"Prick the goddess," he murmured as they slid between the smooth, cool sheets. "I don't want to go to the After when I die. I just want to be here with you."

He shuttered the lantern, and the room fell dark. She could feel the beating of his heart. His breath was warm on her neck, and his hand rested on the round of her belly. Tears stung at the back of her eyes. She grinned, stupid-happy in the dark.

I'll tell him in the morning when I can see his face.

PART TWO

THERE'S THE RUB

CHAPTER THIRTEEN

THE SAFE HOUSE

Sun filtered through the window, eliciting a groan from Gemma as she pulled the pillow up over her face. "Blessed goddess, can't you just keep the sun asleep for another day or two?" Her skin slid across satiny sheets as she snuggled deeper into the warm spot that lay beside her, almost as if another person was . . .

Her eyes flew open and she tossed off the covers, taking in a room she barely recognized. The night—and day—before came flooding back to her. Despite the warmth and the Devery-shaped divot in the bed beside her, she was alone in Brinna's guest room. She slid from the bed and dressed.

As she neared the top of the staircase, she couldn't help but hear whispered voices. She knew she should turn around, but something pulled her forward. As she reached the top of the stairs, she hid herself behind a pillar. She listened, confused, as she heard Devery and his mother arguing in whispered tones.

In Vagan.

Her mouth went dry as she fought to understand, but she had only learned a scrap of the language—just enough to recognize it for what it was. She swallowed hard, heart pounding in her chest.

Devery was fluent in all the languages of the Four Winds. It was one of the Guild's requirements before an assassin could be named master, so his ability wasn't astonishing. But his use of the language at a time like this was nothing short of bewildering. And Gemma could see no reason at all why his mother—a wealthy immigrant from Far Coast—should ever use the Vagan language. Unless . . .

Her heart was pounding so loudly that she could barely hear their whispering, when a sudden knock on the front door interrupted thoughts she could not believe she was having.

The door downstairs opened and Brinna said warmly, "There you are. You had us worried."

A young girl's voice answered, "I'm sorry, Grandmother."

Gemma heard the door close, then Brinna said, "Come here, darling. Give me a kiss."

Small footsteps darted across the wooden floor, and after a moment, Gemma heard Brinna say, "I've a surprise for you. Look who's here."

More movement, and then the girl squealed. "Papa!"

Gemma's eyes began to well, her throat tighten. She couldn't breathe, and her trembling hands fluttered upward to cover her mouth. Below, she heard Devery's voice, bright and clear, though low.

"Shhh. We've a guest sleeping upstairs. Come here, my girl. I'm glad that you're safe. You've done so well."

There was a tremor of emotion in his tone that Gemma had thought belonged only to her. Love. Devery loved this child. This was not an act.

"You're filthy," he chuckled softly. "Go on up to your room, and I'll send the maid up with some water for a bath. But do be quiet, love. We don't want to wake our guest."

Unable to make sense of what she'd just heard, Gemma turned and slipped back into the guest room, her shredded heart pumping adrenaline through her veins. She paced the room in a fog of regret, and sat down on the now cold bed, the hilt of her blade clutched in a steady hand that managed not to betray her terror.

Several long moments passed as Gemma sat on the edge of the bed, waiting for Devery's return. Her knife lay across her lap, its blade bared. She was cold and empty. Nearly everything she had ever believed in was a lie.

When he came into the room, his movements meant to be quiet and not awaken her, she met his gaze with as much ferocity as she could. "Close the door," she said, and when he stared at her in surprise, she threw her dagger at the wall where it stuck with a thud. "Close the goddess-damned door."

When he did, she growled at him, her words more animal than human. "What did you do, Devery? How could you?" She pulled another dagger from the sheath on her ankle.

Devery's shoulders slumped as he met her gaze, then looked away. He looked everywhere but at her as he began to pace the small room, his feet making no sound despite what appeared to her to be plodding, weary steps.

Gemma's hand twitched on the hilt of her dagger. Her blood was pumping through her veins with such fierceness that she could hear it pounding in her ears. She allowed the rhythm to fuel her rage as she stared at him.

"I need to explain something to you, and I'd appreciate it if you wouldn't stab me, but . . ." He looked at her once more, a wealth of emotion in his eyes. "I understand if you must." He spread his arms wide. "I am without a weapon, and I offer myself to the queen for judgment."

A lump formed in her throat. She nodded. Tears stung her eyes, and she found her hand gripping the hilt of the knife in her lap until her knuckles turned white.

Devery opened his mouth to speak, then snapped it closed. He walked the length of the room, then back again, before kneeling in front of her. His face was a white mask, his eyes vulnerable and panicked. "I've practiced these words a thousand times. " His voice trembled, but Gemma refused to let him see that it pained her.

He continued slowly, the words pulled from him with great effort.

"I planned and prepared and the words...they're inadequate. Nothing I say will ever change what I've done."

Her mind raced. Was he responsible for the king and Melnora? Did he set the fires? Why? Her heart ached as the most painful question bubbled to the surface. "Did you kill Fin?"

His eyes went wide, and he nodded as tears slid down his cheeks. He shook with sobs as he said, "I didn't want to, Gem. I... It wasn't supposed to happen that way. He was supposed to be asleep, just like everyone else. Like you were supposed to be. I planned and worked my ass raw making sure this whole thing would be as bloodless as possible. I—"

She found her gaze pinned to the throbbing of his pulse in his throat. If she reached out with her blade, she could end this, right now. She'd never have to hear what else he had to say. Her voice was low despite her urge to scream. "Not entirely bloodless. There was Melnora."

He sighed. His hands cupped the back of her legs as he said, "No. Not entirely."

"Keep your prickling hands off of me, you bastard," she growled. "You killed Fin! He loved you, and you killed him!" Vomit stung the back of her throat and she gasped for air, but there was none in the room. Every inch was filled with betrayal and rage and agony, and there was no room left for anything else.

He leaned away from her, his eyes streaming tears. "I had no choice, Gemma. I was protecting..." He trailed off, his eyes flickering in panic. "Gemma, I love you. I would never hurt you. Everything I've done has been to protect you!" He shook with emotion and Gemma couldn't tell whether it was fear or anger or something else.

"You've already hurt me! You may as well have sliced me open the way you cut Fin!" she screamed, slapping at him and pushing the hilt of her knife into his hand. "Go ahead and kill me like you killed Fin. Get it over with. It couldn't possibly hurt worse than this."

"Gemma," he sighed. "If I wanted you to die, you'd be dead already."

He said it without threat or malice. Just a statement of fact. All the fight drained out of his eyes as he met her gaze.

Her heart turned to stone. She flung the dagger that he refused across the room, and it stuck in the wall beside the first. He might have lost the will to fight, but she was just getting started.

"Tell me about your daughter, you lying shit! Is she the one who was worth killing Fin for?"

He stared at the dagger still quivering in the wall. The rage that rolled off her filled the room with black energy. Death lived in rooms like that. Death and words that couldn't be taken back. He didn't touch her again. "How did you—" he croaked.

"I overheard you and Brinna arguing. In Vagan. I heard the girl arrive, and I . . ." She choked on a sob.

There was an ache in his eyes, a depth of emotion that was too much for her to look at. It wasn't fair that he could dampen all the rage within her with just one expression, but she had loved him too long not to see the devastation within him. A wisp of pity snaked its way through the barely caged violence within her, and she hated him for it, even as she allowed it to grow.

"Will you let me explain? I want to tell you everything. And then I swear by the goddess, if you think I should die, I will bare my throat for your blade."

She forced herself to look into his blue eyes, which suddenly seemed like an unknown sea, when she had so often swum in their familiar depths before. She nearly gagged as she thought of Melnora—ashen eyes staring blankly at the sky. And Fin—gutted from neck to navel.

Her mind cleared. She had trained for this all her life. She was good at what she did—good enough to be queen—and she wasn't going to sit here and heave yesterday's luncheon all over his lap. Prick that.

She stared into his eyes and was filled with regret. She couldn't tell him about the baby now. That future was lost to her. Her words sounded like a death rattle. "I don't even know who you are."

"Yes, you do," Devery said, leaning toward her once more. "But there were things I could not share with you. I'm so sorry, Gem. May I?" he asked, reaching for Gemma's hand. "I want to show you something." He moved slowly. Gemma had produced another blade that was bare in her hand, and she could almost see his blood coating its edge. It wouldn't take much to push her to violence. "Put your hand here." Yesterday, that would have turned into a lewd jest, but today, she doubted that Devery would ever hear her laugh again.

She nodded, though she kept her right hand firmly on the

handle of the knife in her lap. She placed her fingertips on his scalp.

He moved closer, his gaze never leaving hers. "I was born in Vaga sixty-eight years ago."

She couldn't help her shock. She had expected nearly anything but what he said.

"Here," he said, bending his neck and guiding her fingers along his scalp. "Do you feel this one?"

Her lip trembled, and her eyes filled with tears. The tips of her fingers brushed through his tangled hair, and the moment she felt the raised scar on his scalp, she knew what she was feeling. It had been easy to assume that they were the scars of his trade, but she began to weep as he said, "That is the mage mark for long life. It was placed upon me when I was twelve, and it has slowed down my years to a crawl." She hated that he had unnerved her. She hated that that wisp of pity was growing within her, even though she couldn't explain why.

He reached out and brushed away a tear that ran down her face as he moved her hand to another scar. "This is the mage mark for speed," he said, then moved to another, "and this is the mark of the light-footed." He moved her hand half a dozen more times, naming scars for strength, stamina, intelligence, dexterity, calm and cunning, while tears continued to stain Gemma's face.

"Who did this to you?" she choked, though she was sure she already knew the answer. A new, darker hatred was growing within her as she thought of the woman downstairs.

He licked his lips, then looked down at the floor and said,

"My mother. What do you know of mage work?"

She shook her head, then wiped her face on her sleeve. "Almost nothing, really."

He met her gaze and said, "Of the female population of Vaga, only one in ten thousand women is a mage, and there has never been a man who can do the work. It is a mystery as old as the goddess herself, but only a few very honored women are capable of being trained. The marks are the written word of Aegos herself, and very few are gifted with the ability to imbue their marks with the goddess's power. Those who are gifted are celebrated and respected throughout Vaga—they are our priestesses and our queens. The more mage work that a woman does, the longer her life span. Those who are most gifted have been known to live for five hundred years, but if a woman stops working magic or if she does very little, she begins to age more quickly."

Gemma opened her mouth, then closed it again as she thought of the king's mage women, who were kept like chattel and only allowed to do mage work at the king's bidding.

"You see it, now, don't you? The Kings of Above have slowly been killing them." He sighed, and though she wanted to look away, the desperation in his eyes held her gaze. "My mother is the youngest daughter and sister of the mage women kept in the palace. The other three are Brinna's elder sisters; Jaree, Manil, and Valone. My mother was very young when the Mage War broke out, and Hannai, her mother, would not let her come to Yigris to fight.

"Hannai was a lesser Queen of Vaga, third in command, but

she had gained a great deal of support during the war against Yigris. The greater queen felt threatened by her popularity, so at the signing of the peace accords, she signed away the lives of Hannai and her daughters in exchange for a greater share of Yigris's gold mines. She caught two fish with one hook by crippling Yigris economically and ridding herself of her closest competition."

Gemma chuckled bitterly. "And people think that we're criminals."

He watched her in silence for a moment. "Brinna was only thirteen when the greater queen signed away her family, and the greater queen thought she could be controlled. My mother played her part, but in her heart she vowed she would do whatever she needed to get her family back. First, she poisoned the greater queen's tea. Then, my mother spent a lifetime training herself, honing her skills and learning even the most obscure mage marks. She became one of the greatest mage women in Vaga. She took a lover, and when I was born, she took another—until a daughter was born."

Gemma remembered the strange look on Devery's face the night before, when she had mentioned Iven's wife. Another piece of the puzzle slipped into place. "Princess Elsha," Gemma's voice was thick.

Devery nodded. "My mother has spent her entire life trying to rescue her family, and this is the reason that I was born. For most of my life, I had no reason not to go along with her demands, and then suddenly, I had every reason in the world to.

When Brinna realized how much I cared for you and Elam, she gained a hold over me. I would do anything to keep the two of you safe, even if I had to murder everyone in this city."

She stared at him for a long moment. "Why didn't you tell me?" she asked. "I'd have helped you free them all."

Tears filled his eyes, and he couldn't look at her. "It isn't enough anymore for my mother that the mages be freed, Gem. House Daghan has to fall. And . . . I knew you'd never turn against Melnora. I didn't have a choice." As the tears streaked down his face he said, "You don't understand my family."

"I thought we were your family." She hated the weakness in her voice. She hated the way she'd let him hurt her. "And your daughter? I heard her voice. She can't be more than eight or nine. How could you lie to me like that?"

He closed his eyes, and when he reopened them, they were wet. "I didn't . . ." He sighed, running his hand across the top of his head. "I didn't know about her. Not at first, and then . . . by the time I found out the truth, it was too late to introduce you to Katya as my daughter."

A sound somewhere between a sob and a laugh escaped her lips. Katya had been hers. She had worked hard to earn her trust, to get close to her. Now he was taking away the child whose hair she'd braided, whose wounds she'd stitched, the strange, somber child whom she had seen so much of herself in . . . the little girl whom Gemma saw as her heir. Gemma's heart twisted within her. She should have seen the truth. It was her job to see the truth.

She flopped back onto the bed, tears flowing unhindered.

"How many other children do you have running around that I don't know about?"

"It isn't like that," he said. He was still kneeling in the center of the room, but there was more heat in his words. "I wish I could have told you, all those years ago, but ... I was half a man for such a long time. My wife had died, and I thought the child she carried had died with her. I'd come to Yigris to run away from it all and avenge my family, to become the killer I'd been born to be. I closed off my heart for so long that I didn't even know how to tell the truth anymore. I hated myself, I hated what I'd become, I hated this city and its people and its prickling king, and all of this would have been as simple as breathing if I hadn't fallen in love with you. Because everything got complicated then. And at the same time, everything got much, much simpler."

The truth had blown a hole in her chest, but rage filled it back up. "How do I know you're telling the truth? How do I know this isn't just another lie to make me ... to get me to ..." She couldn't even imagine what else he could want from her. He'd already taken everything. She wanted to hurt him worse than he'd hurt her, but she couldn't think clearly. She couldn't see past the storm swelling within her. She knew there were questions she should be asking him. About his wife and child, and other things, but she just couldn't do it.

He pulled the collar of his shirt down, baring his throat, and tipped his head to the side. "I submit to your judgement."

Something in his voice—utter resignation—made her believe. Brinna had used him, had created him and toyed with him, had broken him until he fit the mold she wanted him to fill. The fact that anyone could do that to their own child filled Gemma with black rage. She covered her belly protectively. The fact that anyone could do that to Devery twisted her in knots. She wanted to hate him, for Fin and Melnora and everything, but she found that she couldn't. She sighed and patted the bed beside her.

He sat down. The smell of him overwhelmed her and tears fell anew. She leaned into his chest and sobbed until her eyes ran dry, knowing now, for the first time, that her time with him might be less than infinite.

Time passed without either of them speaking. A soft knock on the door jarred her from her daze. Devery stood, moved across the room, and opened the door. "I asked the cook to put together some breakfast for you," he said softly, returning with the tray that the maid had brought. "It's been too long since you've eaten." He set the tray on the bed in front of her and waited. When she made no move to eat, he touched her hand hesitantly. His fingers drew a pattern across her knuckles. It had the distinctive shape of a mage mark.

"What was that?" she asked, yanking her hand away.

"I don't possess any magery, Gemma. I . . . it was the Vagan word for love. I love you, Gem. Please, at least a bite of bread and some tea."

If he'd only told her about the mage women, she'd have sneaked him into the palace herself. No one in Under held with keeping someone against their will. Sure—if you crossed someone in Under, they'd gut you like a fish—but they'd never hold you prisoner. Slavery, torture and rape were weapons of the Above. Why hadn't he known her well enough to know that he could trust her?

Full of only grief and emptiness, she picked up a slice of bread oozing with melted butter. She took one bite and put it back on the plate. She coughed, choking it down.

He picked up the cup of tea and pushed it gently into her hands.

She sipped at it, and as soon as she swallowed it, she felt her throat begin to close. She couldn't get any air as she cried out, dropping the cup to the floor. Her hands flailed at her throat as she sputtered.

"Gemma!" Devery screamed, taking hold of her hands. "What's happening? Goddess, what's wrong?"

She let out a wail before slumping, boneless, to the bed.

He fumbled at the collar of her robe, feeling for a pulse. As the edges of her world went black, panic filled his voice as he bellowed, "Mother!"

Prick, she thought as the room was swallowed by the abyss. *I should have seen that coming.*

CHAPTER FOURTEEN

BRIGHTHOLD

Tollan opened his eyes to find himself staring at a bug's eye view of a carpet of grass and Wince's boots. "Goddess, am I dead?" he groaned, rolling onto his back. Every inch of him hurt as if he'd been tossed around ship's quarters during a hurricane.

"He's gone," Wince said, voice tight.

Tollan pushed himself up, then regretted it immediately. "Who?"

"Brother Silken-Pants," Wince growled. "We're absolutely pricked, and I don't mind saying I wasn't thrilled that our only ally was a whore from Under, but at least we had someone." He gestured wildly around them. "Do you even know where the prick we are?"

He tossed Uri's coin in the air and caught it, the way Tollan had seen him do a thousand times before.

From the back of the house, a voice called, "You're just across Thieves' Row in Brighthold, and, frankly, Master Quintella,

I prefer to be called Brother Tight-Pants or simply Silky. No need for formality among friends."

Elam came around the corner, his arms laden with loaves of bread, a wheel of cheese and two bottles of wine. His pockets bulged with what Tollan presumed was some sort of round fruit. "Breakfast is served, gentlemen," he said, tossing a loaf to Tollan and grinning broadly at Wince.

Tollan tore the loaf in half and passed the other piece to Wince, then stifled his own laughter by tearing off a large bite, and chewing ecstatically.

"Robbing houses, then?" Wince asked, staring down at the bread in his hands.

"I understand that you have some misgivings, but, really, there is no one who's going to mind. I suspect that until we figure out what is going on with those mage marks, nearly every citizen in Yigris is going to stay sleeping like a babe in arms." Elam pulled the cork on a bottle of wine and raised the bottle toward the sky. "To the goddess," he said brazenly, "May she protect us from the rough prickery ahead."

Wince choked on his laughter, and Tollan exhaled, relieved. He needed the Wince who told ribald jokes and remembered how to laugh. He didn't think he could handle the world if Wincel Quintella stayed serious forever.

"What do you mean about the mage marks?" Tollan asked as he caught an apple that Elam tossed in his direction.

Elam took a bite of his own apple, chewed it properly, then swallowed before answering. "I went in that house last night. There's a whole household in there—two maids, a nursemaid, a man and his fat-but-lusty wife, and a spit of a kid—and no matter what I did, I couldn't wake a soul."

"Are they . . . dead?" The apple turned to ash in Tollan's mouth.

Elam shook his head. "Snoring away, perfectly peaceful. They just can't be awakened."

Wince snatched the bottle of wine from him, and tipped it toward the sky. "Aegos. The whole prickling city is asleep?"

Elam stood, motioning for them to gather the rest of their breakfast. "I suspect so, but let's go have a glance, eh?"

Tollan's body ached from sleeping on the ground, and by the time Elam stopped an hour later and said, "We're close to the safe house," he was grateful for the reprieve. "I want to have a look before we go up to the door and make sure that we weren't followed and that no one is watching the place. I don't want to expose Gemma or you, Your Grace."

Tollan nodded, and he and Wince stayed in the shadows of a tall manor house.

"Do you think Gemma will call the Ain?" Wince asked once Elam had disappeared.

Tollan thought for a moment. "Can't say. I'd like to think she would, but I don't think the girl who was bouncing on the bed and spitting on my cock is the same girl who killed that man at Canticle Center. I think it all depends on what's happened since we left her and what she's found." He didn't want to think about what would happen if things had gone badly. Gemma Antos was the barrel he was clinging to in this storm, and if she and her Ain couldn't help him float, he'd most likely go under.

Elam came from behind them. "I don't know," he said softly, his brow furrowed as he removed his spectacles and pinched the bridge of his nose. "Something is ... odd."

Tollan arched an eyebrow at him.

"We haven't seen a living soul anywhere, right?"

Tollan and Wince nodded.

He went on. "As I was watching the safe house, a little girl approached and knocked on the door. Devery's mother, Lady Brinna, opened it—I saw her, and hers is not a face I'm likely to forget. She let the girl in, and—"

Wince shrugged. "This is a Guild safe house, right? So anyone in the Guild could have made their way here. Perhaps the kid is one of your street rats."

"That's what's odd. I recognized the girl, too. She's one of the urchins. But this isn't a safe house that's known to the Guild. This is a secret place. Only Gemma, Devery and I know it exists." Elam's amber eyes held real fear. "But stranger still, why isn't Lady Brinna asleep?"

Tollan looked at Wince. "What do we do?"

"We can't go in there," Elam said, turning his gaze upward. "Not until we have a better idea of what's happening. Something here isn't right, and I think we should stay put until we figure out what it is." He grinned at Tollan. " Come, Your Grace. I'm going to teach you the first rule of bloodwork."

A shudder ran down Tollan's spine. "And what's that?"

"Get to know your victims as well as you know yourself."

Quicker than Tollan would have thought possible, Elam picked the lock on the back door of a tall manor house, and the three of them scuttled inside. He balked at the idea of breaking into someone's home, but Elam laid a gentle hand on his lower back and guided him in. Wince began to search the first floor for any danger.

Elam brushed past Tollan. "Let's get the lay of the place," he said, but Tollan was still focusing on the warmth that remained where the prayer keeper's hand had been. All his life, he'd pushed that part of himself aside. He was to be king, and the king must have a queen, because the king must have an heir. Desire had nothing to do with it. He shook his head.

Elam was moving through the kitchen. He bent over a trapdoor in the floor. He pulled up the handle and quickly disappeared. An instant later, his head reappeared. "Root cellar," he said, grinning. "We can stay down here tonight. We'll be able to have light without anyone seeing."

"Do you think we'll be here long?" Tollan asked. In the back of his mind, he saw his brother. He couldn't bring himself to believe that Iven was participating in the mage women's plans willingly. If the mage women hadn't killed him, the fire may have. That thought made him tremble with impotent rage, but Tollan refused to give up hope. If they had no proof that Gemma was even at the safe house, and if they were going to have the Ain assist them, they had to find Gemma. And without the Ain...

"I'm a prickling idiot," Tollan groaned, leaning against the wall in resignation.

"How's that?" Elam asked, as he climbed back up and closed the trapdoor.

Tollan sighed. There were a million reasons, but in this case, he had one thing in mind. "I'm not the king. Not really. I don't have the mark anymore, and everyone thinks I'm responsible for my father's death. No one at the castle will listen to me, and I've got no assets to help rescue my brother, if there's even anything left to rescue. I've been trying to do the right thing, but it's useless. It's all pricked."

Elam shrugged. "I learned a long time ago that the lines between right and wrong aren't worth paying attention to. Those of you from Above think you're in the right, that your hands are clean. But those of us from Under—the ones lining your pockets—we know that there's no magic wall that divides us. We're all just doing what we can to get by. We hope that at the end of the day, when we lay down, at least our hands don't look too dirty."

Tollan stared down at his own hands. After his night spent on the lawn, his search in the alley for Wince's coin, his escape through the tunnels—there was a map of filth laid out on his hands. He chuckled ruefully. "At least there's no blood."

Elam's gaze softened. "Some days, that's the best you can hope for."

Sobered, Tollan nodded. "Can I ask you a favor?"

"Of course, Your Grace."

"I've just told you that I'm not really the king. So, will you call me Tollan?"

"As you wish," he said softly.

Tollan turned to see what was keeping Wince, but he felt the Dalinn's eyes following him long after he'd left the room.

Hours passed. Sitting off to the side of the wide north-facing window, they took turns watching the safe house. They raided the larder and played a game of cards. Elam won handily, and Tollan turned out his pockets. "I guess I'll have to owe you," Tollan said.

"I look forward to cashing that in," Elam replied.

Tollan turned away, unsure what Elam meant—or what he wanted him to mean. An embarrassed silence settled over the room until Wince whispered, "Someone's leaving!"

Elam crawled across the floor, rising up just enough to peer over the sill. Too curious to wait, Tollan followed suit. A man was standing in the front garden of the safe house, arms crossed in a stance that spoke of frustration or anger. He began to pace the walk—running his hand through his hair and occasionally stopping to stare off into the distance.

"What's got you so irked, Devery?" Elam whispered, never taking his eyes off the man.

"That's Devery Nightsbane?" Tollan asked.

Elam nodded, his mouth turned downward. "Yes, and he is anxious about something."

"How do you know?" Wince whispered, his back still pressed to the wall beside the window.

"I just know. How do you know where the sun rises?"

"Some things you just know," Tollan answered.

"Exactly," Elam said. "And the last person anyone wants to meet is an anxious Devery Nightsbane."

In the dark of the root cellar, Tollan could barely breathe. If he did, he drew in the scent of Elam—who lay so near to him, Tollan could feel the man's breath on the back of his neck. The scent of the prayer keeper had driven him to the point of distraction, and he could not push aside his desire to touch him, here in the dark where it was safe. He would have never dared, in the light of day, in the world Above.

Fighting the urge to flee, Tollan found he had only two options—to give up entirely, or to be brave. His decision made, he rolled over, his hand coming to rest very near Elam's. His fingers were close enough that he could feel warmth radiating off Elam.

He heard Wince tossing once more and realized that Elam's breathing was no longer even. He was awake. Long, empty moments in the dark spread out between them until Tollan's finger brushed gently against Elam's hand. Tollan held his breath, waiting for the inevitable rejection.

Elam stretched out, curling his fingers around Tollan's trembling hand. Tollan gasped at his touch but said nothing, afraid to break the perfect sweetness of the moment. And soon, fingers intertwined with Tollan's, Elam's breathing steadied and the prayer keeper drifted off to sleep.

Sometime later Tollan awoke. Elam's breathing still had the ring of slumber, and he heard Wince's quiet snores. His hand, still clinging to Elam's, was warm despite the chill of the cellar.

His heart hurt from too much grief, his shoulders ached from the stone floor on which they slept and his head throbbed from lack of sleep. He felt weary beyond his years. He longed for some sense of normalcy, a thread of familiarity in the unknown waters he found himself in. He longed to feel safe and at home. He knew he should let go of Elam's hand, but he didn't. It was the only safety he could find.

On the evening of their second day in Brighthold, Tollan and Wince were sitting in the sweltering attic of the manor house, their gazes fixed on the newly discovered view of Dockside. They had exhausted their desire for cards and dice games and had fallen into a watchful stupor.

A handful of people scuttled along the shore, their movements as fleeting and mysterious as that of an anthill. There was no telling whether the people there were friend or enemy, the distance was too great, but Tollan was infatuated with them as they went about their business.

Suddenly, beside him, Wince gasped. "Look," he said, pointing away from the shore and into the depths of the Hadriak. Tollan's gaze followed where he indicated and his heart began to pound. There were ships coming, a whole fleet of ships. As he watched Tollan counted at least ten. Then, across the horizon, he saw the crimson sails of his mother's ship. "Oh, Aegos," he said, his mouth dry. "The pirates have come home."

As he raced down the attic's ladder and through the rooms of the manor's top floor, Tollan pondered the arrival of the pirate fleet, and more personally important, his mother. Just days before, he had wished fervently for her return, but now all he felt was a nervous panic.

Without stopping to think, Tollan burst into the library, trembling with pent up energy.

"Ships!" he hissed, flailing his arm to point in the general vicinity of Dockside. "Ten, at least!" His hand struck a tall vase, which tumbled off its pedestal, hit the floor and shattered with enough noise to wake the dead.

"Oh, prick," Elam moaned, turning back to the library window. He looked out the window with a pained expression before a hint of relief crossed his face. He held his hand up before the window and snapped his fingers twice in the same odd way he'd done to Gemma at the hospit.

Tollan cleared his throat, drawing Elam's attention back to the library. "I'm sorry," he said, bending to pick up a piece of the shattered vase. "Did someone see you?" His voice trembled slightly.

Elam moved toward where he knelt. "Devery was out there,"

he said, bending to help Tollan pick up the pieces. "For good or ill, we're not alone any longer." His hand brushed Tollan's, and their eyes met for a long moment as each of them leaned over the shards. "You were saying, about the ships?" Elam leaned closer, a soft, reckless smile on his lips. Tollan, eyes wide and heart pounding unevenly, leaned in, too. Tollan took a shaky breath. Their lips met. A thrill of excitement raced through Tollan as his lips parted slightly at the probe of Elam's tongue.

"What are we going to do about those prickling boats?" Wince blurted, bursting into the room.

Tollan bent to examine the piece of vase in his hands, while Elam scooted quickly away. Neither one made eye contact with Wince, who stood in the doorway, mouth open and eyes wide.

"What in the Void happened to that vase?" Wince stammered. "I, um, I'll go look for a broom in the kitchen."

"Sorry, uh, ships!" Tollan said, before he, too, fled the library. His face was flush with desire and embarrassment. He felt both like he could fly, and also like he was drowning. Afraid to look back, he ran to find someplace to hide from Wince.

Suddenly, everything in the world made sense to Wince and yet nothing did. He trusted Tollan like a brother. Void, sometimes he trusted Tollan more than he trusted himself. He knew Tollan Daghan as well as he knew anyone. Or so he'd thought up until the instant he had walked into that library.

He stood with a broom in his hands, overwhelmed by the

sense of shame that he felt. He slid down to the floor and put the broom beside him. He pulled Uri's coin from his pocket and stared at the sharp-nosed woman whose face graced one side. "I cocked everything up, Uri," he whispered, his voice cracking. "I never asked him . . . I just . . . I just assumed that he . . ." Wince glanced over his shoulder, making sure that no one was within earshot. "I loved you from the minute I laid eyes on you. And like the big, dumb ass that I am, I assumed that he did, too. Especially after . . ."

He couldn't bear to speak of Tollan's offer, and her death. It rattled his chest to think of the enormous sacrifice that he now saw Tollan's offer had been. He couldn't bear to think of the all-too-brief love affair he and Uri had. He couldn't dwell on the baby—because no amount of wishing and hoping and sobbing would change that she was gone and that she'd chosen death over him.

He rolled the coin across his knuckles and wiped away his tears. As much as it hurt, he didn't blame her. He only wished he'd been enough to keep her here. "Thanks, Uri," he whispered as he slipped the gold piece back into his pocket. "I'll make sure to do better by him than I did by you."

CHAPTER FIFTEEN

DOCKSIDE

Tollan was surprised at how swiftly things had moved, once Elam made contact with Devery. The same evening that the ships arrived, Devery had signaled Elam, and with their help—and a few well-placed burning bottles of whiskey—the master assassin had managed to escape the clutches of his mother with Gemma's unconscious body.

Days passed in a whirlwind, and Tollan grew quite adept at the art of avoidance. He'd been avoiding putting himself in any situation that would give Wince the opportunity to mention the scene in the Brighthold library. He'd been avoiding his mother, though, goddess knew, that was getting more difficult by the hour since she'd sailed in with the pirate fleet. And he'd been avoiding facing what was going on in his head like the plague.

He and Wince had taken up residence in Dockside, one street from the waterfront in a tumbledown inn called the Sea Dragon's Tail. The straggling Guild members now filled its rooms to overflowing.

A petite woman with graying hair named Lian had taken charge, and Tollan was glad to take orders from someone. In the days since they'd come to Dockside, Elam had shown up several times, speaking in hushed tones with Lian and with a ridiculous-looking man named Riquin, whose beard was trimmed into the shape of a bird. Apparently, he was the captain of all the pirates in Yigris. Tollan had seen Elam passing messages to thieves and whores and murderers, had seen him laugh with street rats and share a meal with a pair of filthy sailors while they threw a set of bone dice. Twice, Elam had found Tollan alone and had taken the opportunity to kiss his cheek. He told Tollan that Gemma was still unconscious, and that he'd let them all know as soon as she woke up. Tollan could still feel the soft pressure of the last kiss—warm, tickling with new beard growth—and it sent shivers down his spine.

On the fourth night, he stumbled out of his room to take his turn on guard duty. Lian demanded that the streets be guarded at all times to ensure the mage women didn't try to finish what they'd started with the Guild. As he tumbled down the steps, he found himself staring at Wince. "Hey, Toll," his friend said cordially. "Fancy meeting you here. Looks like we're on watch together."

Wince chucked him on the shoulder. There seemed to be no avoiding the questions now. They sat on the front stoop of a pub called the Kraken's Grave. Wince stopped grinning and glanced around to make sure they were alone. "You're a hard man to find these days," he said, his attention fixed on the blade of the sword he held across his lap.

"I'm sorry," Tollan said. "There's been a lot to do."

Wince nodded. A long, painful silence followed, until he finally said, "Can I ask you something, Toll?"

Tollan sighed and dropped his head into his hands. "I don't suppose I could pay you not to?"

Wince chuckled, though the laugh sounded forced.

"Why didn't you tell me?"

There was an emotion in his tone that Tollan had not expected. Not anger. Not disgust. Something else—pity perhaps or maybe something closer to empathy. Without meaning to, Tollan met his gaze. "Would it have changed things?" he asked. "I was the heir to Abram's throne. What I wanted was of no consequence."

One side of Wince's mouth turned up, and he laughed. "Well, I might not have flashed my cock about so much when we were kids. I was always pissing in front of you or swimming in my skin. I mean, that sort of temptation could have been distracting, I'm sure."

"Aegos, Wince. Just because I'm attracted to men doesn't mean that I was driven mad by the sight of your childish, flaccid cock. You're not my type."

"Yeah?" Wince said, his smile growing wider. "Well, you're not really my type, either." He held his neck straight and his nose in the air, feigning indignation.

"Wince," Tollan said, his own voice low. "Why didn't you tell me about Uri?"

Wince looked at him, his blue eyes like slate. "You said it yourself, Toll. We're born who we're going to be, and no amount of wishing was going to make me an acceptable match for her. Before we . . . before the stable, I thought that I'd spend my whole life pining for her, and I wasn't wrong. I just pine differently now."

"I'm sorry, Wince, I—"

"You offered her what I couldn't, Tollan. It isn't your fault that your father was a prickling shit, and it wasn't your fault that she felt there was nowhere else to turn. I just wish that I'd have been brave enough to tell her how I felt. I wish I'd given her the chance to choose a life with me and the baby. Honestly, I wish I'd thought more like the people in Under."

Tollan nodded in silence. There was nothing more to say. A few moments later, he looked up at Wince. "Did you arrange for us to be on guard together?"

Wince grinned, torchlight dancing in his eyes. "These bloody thieves. I had to pay Lian a silver for the privilege."

Tollan and Wince sat the next hour of their watch in silence as the sun crested over the horizon. Tollan had to fight against tears of gratitude for Wince's friendship.

Then, the clang of steel on steel broke the morning calm. They stood, swords at the ready. Tollan pounded on the door to alert those inside. They took the steps two at a time and rounded the street corner just in time to hear his mother, Isbit, snarl, "I don't care who you work for, you runny little shit. You come onto my boat without permission to board and I'll end you."

"Prick," Tollan said under his breath.

The man on the ground was bleeding from his face and shoulder.

"I'm glad we got that cleared up," she said. "Be gone before I decide that I'm not in the mood for mercy." Then she looked up and saw Tollan.

Wince bowed slightly, but Tollan stood his ground. "Hello, Mother," he said, meeting her gaze as she cleaned the sailor's blood from her blade.

"Hello, Tollan," she said. "Wincel." She nodded. "Come. I'll have breakfast prepared." She didn't wait to see if they followed. She sheathed her long, curved blade and walked, swaying gently as if she were still at sea, toward the waterfront. Her black-and-silver hair hung past her waist in a mass of braids. It was held back from her face by a pale-yellow turban. She wore loose-fitting breeches and a long coat that came down over her hips. She was barefoot and had several hoops dangling from her ears. The collar of her shirt was open, exposing sun-freckled flesh and a jagged scar along her collarbone, which was accentuated by the leather cord that held a wooden talisman.

Tollan sighed. "What, no bells, Mother? I thought all pirates wore bells in their hair."

She stopped walking. "Only idiots wear bells, son. You never know when you'll need to sneak up on someone, and when you do, there's rarely time for a haircut." She arched an eyebrow at him.

Seeing the set of her shoulders and the tilt of her head, he was stunned to find that he couldn't hate her. A piece of him understood why she had run away.

"I was sorry to hear about Jamis's death," he said. For most of his life, he couldn't help but hate the pirate lover who had stolen his mother away from him on the *Heart's Desire*, but the view he had from a burning, mage-ensorcelled Yigris had softened his opinion of her and of the pirate, Jamis Heliata.

She smiled, then turned and began to walk once more. "There isn't a day that goes by that I don't miss him. But there hasn't been a day that I haven't missed you and your brother, too."

Guilt twisted his insides. Elam had assured him that they were maneuvering all the pieces of their plan into place to save Iven, but Tollan still felt helpless. The Ain would not help until Gemma awoke or died, and Tollan did not even want to think about the chaos that would ensue if she did not recover.

Pushing futile thoughts aside, he followed his mother into the waiting dinghy, manned by two greasy-haired sailors who bobbed reverently when they saw her. They were rowed toward the *Heart's Desire*, the ship that so many of his nightmares had ridden on. As they approached, he saw what a beauty she was— gleaming wood and scarlet sails, her single mast tall and straight. His mother's eyes were full of pride.

Aboard the ship, Wince made his excuses. "I'll leave you to it," he said, standing firmly outside the door to Isbit's cabin. "I'll just stand watch."

Tollan smirked. "Very brave of you, Master Quintella."

Wince shrugged. "You want me to fight brigands or bastards, I can do that, but your mother . . ." He trailed off. "That is a set of skills I lack."

Tollan entered the room alone. His mother was seated at a small table. She was pouring wine from a skin into wooden cups. He sat down in the chair opposite her and took a sip. "I expected golden goblets and the finest Balkland vintage," he said.

"You've come from Above, Tollan. The tales of pirate riches are, I'm afraid, sorely exaggerated. Our funds are most often procured by selling necessities we've stolen to the Shadow Guild, which supplies them to the Under. My greatest spoils are medicines, grain and cured meats."

He grunted. "So you're a humanitarian, then?"

She laughed, clear and honest. "Not exactly. We sail because there is no place else we want to be, and we make a living by stealing from those who can afford to lose some. I know who is willing to pay for what I've taken, and I know when to move on to safer waters. But I don't do anything for free, and I've almost never done anything without the assurance of payment."

"Almost?" he said, taking another sip of wine.

Isbit sighed, lounging back in her chair. "Almost." Then she leaned toward him, her eyes flinty. "Tell me—where do you stand in this conflict, son? Are you still king? Do you support the Under? Where do your allegiances lie?"

Tollan swallowed hard. "I . . . I am not really the king. The mage women marked me, but it was a corrupt mark. It would have killed me if Wince and Gemma hadn't destroyed it." He couldn't look at her face. "I . . . I don't think I ever even wanted to be king."

She chuckled, hard and bitter. "I cannot say I blame you. It always seemed like a shitty job for someone like you."

"Why?" he asked, afraid of her answer. Afraid of her.

"I only wondered if you would be willing to help me gather my bounty. On the night Gemma Antos proclaimed herself Queen of Under, Riquin Hawkbeard fled Guildhall with the intent of a mutiny. As soon as he heard that the King of Above had died and Melnora was on her deathbed, he decided to use the unrest to his advantage. He sent out a hundred birds, calling in every available ship with promises of glory and the favor of the future King of Under."

Tollan's eyes grew wide.

"I have no love for the system in Yigris," she said. "It leaves good people without basic resources, and it keeps the pompous elite blissfully ignorant in their glittering manors. It made me a prisoner in my own home, a pawn whose only purpose was to breed, like one of Abram's prize mares. The women of Above are treated like . . ." She trailed off. They both knew what the lives of the women in Above were like.

"I'm not going to lie. I've become an ambitious, brutal woman. I saw in this the possibility that I might be able to take back what should have been mine. I was risking my ship, my crew and myself on a chance—but I thought it was a chance worth taking."

Tollan watched her. Her glittering gaze stayed firmly fixed on his face. "Do you plan to overthrow Gemma, then? Help Riquin, or take her seat for yourself?" he asked.

She shook her head, a wicked smile on her lips. "No, son," she said calmly. "I have no interest in Under. I intend to remake my place as the Queen of Above."

CHAPTER SIXTEEN

THIEVES' ROW

Dreams returned slowly to Gemma, as if she had swum up for air from the depths of the Hadriak for days before catching the first glimpse of the sun's rays.

They were laughing. Elam had just told a funny story, and she was doubled over with laughter. He slipped out of his shirt and hung it over the back of a chair in their room. He had his own room down the hall, but he never slept in it. They'd taken to keeping their weapons there, spread out on the bed like it was a shop in Merchant Row.

She undressed and pulled on a shift, not bothering to turn away from him. She had never trusted anyone like that.

Then Devery pressed himself against her, and she felt his desire through the thin shift . . . but wait, that was wrong. She wouldn't make love with Devery for several more years, long after the night when Elam had been asked to slap his patron's ass with a dead fish.

She blinked, confused, the memories all jumbled together . . .

She was a little girl. Her mother lay huddled on her cot, wheezing. They didn't have money for medicine. Her mother's skin was the color of mud after the rain. One side of her face drooped.

She shook her head as tears sprang to her eyes. That wasn't her mother—it was Melnora. A trail of spittle leaked down from the queen's mouth, and Gemma wiped it away.

But it wasn't saliva . . . it was blood on Fin's chin as he coughed blood and tried to speak. Devery leaned over him, eyes wide and black, slitting Fin open.

Gemma screamed, and Devery looked at her. He was crying, but when he held his hands out to her, they were covered in blood.

She fell back, away from him, but there was nothing but air to hold on to. She tumbled and fell toward the earth, which rushed to meet her as she screamed.

And then it wasn't her screaming, it was a baby. She placed it on her breast, put her nipple in its mouth, and the child fell silent. Then a garrote crossed her body from breast to womb . . . and the baby was Katya, with a white streak of hair. Gemma dropped her, but the girl turned into Devery, and she pulled him back to her. He held the wire in his hands. He put it around Gemma's neck and drank from her breast until he was sated. The wire pulled tighter and tighter until Gemma was all but gone.

She awoke screaming in a darkened room that she did not recognize. A flame flared nearby. Devery stood over her holding a candle, his pale face haggard. Tears welled in his eyes as he whispered, "Thank the goddess."

She tried to get away from him, but she couldn't move and there was nowhere to go. She was tangled in bedsheets, damp with sweat, trembling. Pain forced the air from her lungs. She doubled over and screamed again.

"Gemma," Devery said, his hand hovering above her but not touching her. "What's wrong? What's the matter?" He was crying, tears streaming down his face.

By the time she'd caught her breath, he was lighting the lantern by her bedside. His face crumpled as his gaze fell on the bed. She looked down at the white coverlet. It was twisted and tangled and soaked in blood.

Her heart shattered. Too many fractures in such a short span of time had made it weak. She hadn't been certain that she was with child, but she had hoped. She didn't have the strength to stop herself from whispering, "Our baby . . ."

His hands were balled into fists as his face crumpled with grief. "I'm going to gut my mother for this, so help me goddess."

It had been years since she'd seen that sort of rage sweep over him. Not since Elam had been taken by that bastard Ragram had Devery been so angry. A sob of fear and heartbreak escaped her lips, and he wrapped her in his arms and cradled her against his chest.

Devery was staring at the blood-soaked sheets. He echoed the words that Gemma had said. "Our baby? Our baby? Oh, Aegos," he moaned, pressing his lips against her forehead. "Gemma, I'm so sorry. I don't know how to make this better. I can't make this better. This is all my fault."

"What happened?" Gemma groaned, as another pain raked through her. Her arms pressed against her belly.

The air stuttered in and out of Devery. "My mother . . .

poisoned you," he said. "It was not enough to kill, but enough to make you sleep for a long while, and also, apparently, enough to . . ." He trailed off and swallowed hard. "We've come to violence over it." He held up his hand, which she now noticed was heavily bandaged.

He chuckled. "I gave her as good as I got. She can toss burning mage marks at me, but so far as I know, there's no mark that will grow back an ear."

Gemma bit her lip and turned away from him. She could feel another pain building within her, but it was less than the pain of grief that threatened to swallow her whole. It was all too much.

"Where are we?" she croaked, when the wave of pain had passed.

Devery held a cup of water out to her. She eyed it for an instant, then drank. He noticed her hesitation. His voice trembled as he said, "Our old apartment on Thieves' Row. It wasn't my idea. I wanted to get you closer to Shadowtown, but—"

A soft knock on the door interrupted him. "Come in," Devery said hoarsely. The door creaked open to reveal Elam dressed in rough woolen breeches and a loose-fitting linen shirt. It had been years since Gemma had seen him in such simple garb. It made him look younger.

"Hey," he said, slipping through the door. He purposefully overlooked the blood on the blankets and focused instead on her face. "How are you feeling?"

She drew in a shuddering breath, and when she exhaled, it came out as a broken sob.

"Oh, doll. Come here." He sat down beside her and ran

fingers through her hair. "You're a mess," he said, chuckling softly. For an instant, his gaze fluttered to Devery, who watched her with raw emotion.

"Dev, you haven't slept in days. Bring me a tub of hot water, and I'll help Gemma get cleaned up while you rest for a while."

Devery started to shake his head in protest, but Gemma stopped him. "Please," she breathed. "I can't think with you here."

A few minutes later, Devery came back with a tub of steaming water, a sponge and a stained towel. "Best I could find," he said, setting the tub down beside the bed. He reached out to Gemma, fingers hovering above her hand before clenching his fist and turning to the door. "Will you be all right?" He looked back.

A sudden wave of emotion ran through her. She nodded because words wouldn't form. It wasn't true, of course. Nothing would ever be all right again.

"I'm so sorry, Gemma," Devery said. He ran a hand over his face and took a deep breath.

"I know," she choked. "I . . . I love you." She wondered if she was the only one who could hear what was unspoken. The slump of his shoulders as he turned to leave told her that she was not.

When he was gone, Elam bent close to her. "That was a kindness you did for him."

Hot tears stung her eyes. "Being a kindness doesn't necessarily make it a lie," she said, as she swung one leg over the edge of the bed.

"No," Elam said, as he began to untie the robe she still wore, "but it doesn't necessarily make it the truth, either."

"I'm beginning to think that there are only versions of the truth and degrees to a lie," she said, as he pressed the wet sponge to her forehead. Rivulets of water streamed down her face. He started to gently scrub her hair.

"You know, I usually get paid twenty gold to give a bath, Regency."

She laughed, in spite of everything. "I seem to have left my purse at home. Can I get a line of credit?"

He chortled. "Whoring on credit is very, very bad business." He grinned and lathered her up with soap. "Tip back," he said, as he poured a cup of steaming water over her head and down her back. "I'm not sure that I can give the lady credit," he went on, scrubbing sweat and grime from her arms, breasts and belly, "but I know a sad-eyed gentleman who would pay anything to see you smile."

She sighed. "What am I going to do?"

"That's not my place to say, but I believe that Devery is telling you as much of the truth as you'll ever hope to see. That man loves you, and he's made himself sick with worry. He's been making plans while you slept—he's trying to undo as much as he can." He moved around to her back, scrubbing away the residue of the past few days.

The soap he was using smelled like lavender. Gemma breathed it in. Some things could never be undone. "How long did I sleep?" she asked, turning away from the question of Devery, as Elam began to work his way lower, sponging away the remains of her too-brief pregnancy.

"Six days," he said, as he rinsed out the bloody sponge and

continued to gently bathe her. He had the touch of a caregiver—efficient, but gentle. "We moved you on the night of the third."

She shook her head, confused. "Brinna just let us go?"

He laughed low in his throat. "Not exactly. When Devery realized I was watching the safe house, he put a plan into action. He left me a message on your window asking me to cause a distraction and then meet him in the tunnels. Apparently, when he commissioned his mother's manor, he created a quick escape route that he never bothered to tell her about, but in the chaos we caused, he wasn't able to get his daughter out. He had to leave her there. He's confused and angry and worried and desperate."

"He's not the only one."

Elam rinsed the sponge, again. "I know," he said. "And for what it's worth, so does he."

Gemma didn't want to hear what Devery knew. "We should just leave, Elam. The Guild is destroyed. Melnora and Fin are gone. They burned everything."

"They didn't." He wiped away a tear that was running down her cheek. "Devery and I had a long, not entirely cordial conversation, while you slept, and he told me everything." Elam met her gaze, then continued. "It's all an illusion. Apparently, Devery's daughter is the most talented mage woman, well, mage girl, in a millennium. She and Devery worked together—against Brinna and Elsha and without their knowledge—to save the Guild. Elsha's marks were meant to trap us. Nearly everyone in Above was tucked into their homes for the night, so the sleeping mage marks that Elsha made held all of Brighthold, Merchant Row and Whitebeach at bay. But those of us down the hill—

Shadowtown and Dockside—never truly sleep. The brambles were supposed to keep the Under trapped."

He continued, as he scrubbed her arms and legs, "Katya realized that her aunt could easily slaughter the whole Guild, if she decided she wanted to. And Katya didn't trust her not to want to, so she created the flames to drive us out of the Guild buildings before the brambles trapped us. Her mage marks created the fire, but the flames consumed nothing. They were meant to help Under, not destroy it. She gave you as much of an army as she could, even though they had both still hoped you wouldn't need it."

"I don't understand."

"Devery had a deal with his mother. After they destroyed House Daghan, she would flee back to Vaga with the captive mage women. Elsha would take the throne of Yigris and their revenge would be complete. But you aren't a Daghan and as a final payment for his help, you were not to be touched. You and Dev would be allowed to rebuild Under, remaking the pact in a new image." Elam met her gaze, his eyes full of grief. "He really did mean to leave the Guild intact—entirely intact—save Melnora. Fin's death was an accident. Fin caught Katya drawing the mark at Canticle Center. When he realized what she was doing, he deduced in error that she had killed Melnora. Fin was going to kill his daughter, Gemma. You know Devery couldn't just . . . " His voice trailed off and she let it. Of course he couldn't let that happen, but it didn't make the truth hurt any less.

She waited several long minutes as Elam continued to scrub her clean. "Then what happened? Why did his plan go so wrong?"

"You were too clever," he said, and squeezed the water from his cloth back into the tub. "You helped Tollan escape Elsha's grasp at the palace, and then you figured out the mage mark on his back before it could kill him."

"Shit. What happened to Tollan?"

Elam blushed inexplicably as he handed her a towel. He brought her a pair of clean breeches and a shirt and helped her wad rags into her smallclothes to absorb the bleeding. "He's at Dockside," Elam finally said. "There have been some developments."

When Elam finished fussing over Gemma, he went to go fix her something to eat.

It had been more than half an hour since the last pain had ravaged her, and she could tell that the bleeding had slowed. It was strange how something so monumental could pass by so quickly. Gemma settled herself into the bed and vowed that she wasn't going to let grief pull her under. She had wanted a child to solidify an heir before it was ever an issue. She knew of the trials Melnora had gone through to find her own replacement, and Gemma didn't want that added burden. She wanted Devery's child because she wanted to share a piece of herself with him that no one else could ever have, but perhaps everything about their affair had been unrealistic.

She watched as Elam pulled the door closed behind him, then she counted to one hundred. She slipped out from beneath the covers, padded across the floor and opened the door slowly. Glancing down the hall, she saw she was in the room that had once been Elam's. She tiptoed down the hall and slipped past the entrance to the kitchen. She peered into Devery's room. Four people she didn't recognize were stretched out on the bed. She remembered what Elam had said and realized that these were probably the rightful inhabitants of the apartment, sound asleep because of the mage marks.

She continued until she reached the door of her old room. She turned the handle and slipped silently inside.

Devery lay atop the covers fully dressed. His eyes were open. He was staring at the rafters, his hands behind his head.

She didn't wait for an invitation. She lay down beside him. Without speaking, he wound his arm around her and pulled her close. She felt as if there should be some unease but there wasn't. She listened to the familiar sound of his heart beating—and his stomach growling.

"When was the last time you ate?" she asked. Strange how her first instinct continued to be his well-being, even when she knew she couldn't trust him.

He shrugged. "It didn't seem very important at the time."

"It sounds like it might be important now."

He rolled onto his side and cupped her face with his hand. "It is so far down the list of important that I can't even see it." He stared at her, then asked, "Are we going to make it through this?"

She bit her lip. "Well, if I have to go to war with mage women, there isn't anyone I'd rather have beside me than Devery Nightsbane, so we have that going for us."

"That's not what I meant," he said as he ran his thumb down her jawline.

She stopped pretending that she didn't know what he meant. "I don't know," she whispered hoarsely. "I hope so."

He pressed his lips to her forehead. "That is all I can hope for," he said, voice thick.

"You have to be honest with me, Dev. No more lies, not ever."

He sighed. "We're of Under, Gemma. We lie the way that others breathe."

"Not to each other," she whispered. "Not ever again. That is the payment I demand for Fin's life. If you ever lie to me again, then I am gone. And it starts right now. Tell me about Katya's mother."

He sat up. "Do I have the right to say no?"

"Of course," she said, pulling herself to sitting and leaning against the wall beside him. "But I'll always wonder why if you do."

Gemma watched as Devery paced the room. His eyes had a bruised look about them, his skin was pale and his cheeks gaunt. Gemma found it hard not to comfort him. All of her instincts were off when it came to him.

Finally, he said, "It was a long time ago. When Rucheal was alive, you were still living on Lord Ghantos's estate." He stopped, pausing to stare out the window. "I was nobleborn and the son of a mage woman. Tradition meant that I should have long since offered myself up to several wives as a proper breeding husband, but I ... I was never very good with people. My mother had little time for me, especially once Elsha was born. I knew from the time I was a young boy that I was to be the instrument of my mother's wrath, and I always felt that tools of violent revenge make terrible husbands."

Gemma's heart ached for him and she had to force herself to sit on her hands. She would not go to him.

He smiled weakly at his own joke. "Rucheal was a tavern maid. She was uneducated, half my age and kind. I spent more time than I should have at the tavern, and we became friends. Then we shared a bed. Then she became pregnant."

The word struck Gemma harder than she'd expected. She clutched her hands to her belly and bit her tongue to keep from sobbing.

Devery stopped and looked for a moment as if he would reach out to her, but then his expression changed to guilt as he refused to meet her gaze.

"When I found out I was going to be a father, something inside of me broke open. I wanted to give my child a family—the kind I'd never had. So, I married Rucheal. It wasn't love. It was, at most, kinship and familiarity. But it was enough. I was . . . happy.

"I went to the Balklands to pick up some documents my mother was having forged, and while I was there, Rucheal went into labor and died. My mother told me that the child died, too. In a fit of impotent rage, I came to Yigris to become an assassin of Under."

Gemma exhaled. "But Katya didn't . . ."

He shook his head, laughing bitterly. "No, she didn't. My mother felt she would be nothing more than a distraction.

Convinced that the daughter of a bar wench could never carry the gift of the goddess, she had handed my newborn daughter over to one of her maids to raise. But the maid brought her back to my mother, terrified, when Katya began to do mage work before her first birthday.

"Of course, my mother thought this was a sign from the goddess herself. No child in recorded history had begun mage work so young. So she took her back to the Vagan Palace and raised her as her own. Five years later, my mother brought Katya to Yigris and assumed all would be forgiven. But it was too late. I was in too deep, and I'd already . . ." His voice shook with emotion. "I'd already fallen in love with you. The only thing I could do was find a way to protect you and Katy and hope that someday you'd understand."

A knock sounded at the door, and Elam entered carrying a tray laden with food. He smiled when he saw them, then said, "I thought you promised to stay in bed."

"I am in bed," she said.

"Yes, well . . ." he chuckled, putting the tray down. "I'm not sure that anything going on in here could be considered restful." He arched an eyebrow at her, then pointed at the tray. "Eat. Both of you. We have some royal company, and I think you might need your strength for this." He turned to go, then glanced over his shoulder at them. "Take your time," he said, grinning. "I'll stall him . . . somehow."

Tollan could barely breathe as he sat, facing Elam, their hands clasped together across the small table. Every nerve in his fingers sang at the other man's touch, and he found that he could feel the whirls and grooves of Elam's fingerprints upon his skin. It could have been moments or hours that they sat like that, a soft, sensual tension building between them as they snuck glances at one another. Tollan couldn't help but remember the feel of Elam's lips against his own, a feeling that he had dwelled on nearly every waking moment since they'd first kissed.

Dragged out of his reverie, Tollan stood up when Gemma and Devery entered the kitchen, yanking his hand from Elam's in a gesture that felt like tearing off a piece of himself.

Gemma grinned when she saw Tollan, then glanced across the table at Elam.

"Well," she said, sitting down in the vacant chair, "that explains quite a lot."

Tollan opened his mouth, but Elam erupted in laughter. "Welcome back, Gemma," he said. "We've missed your smart-assery."

Tollan doubted he would ever have the sort of careless banter that the three of them tossed around. Even Wince couldn't read his mind that way.

"How are you, Your Grace?" Gemma asked, sitting herself gingerly in the chair.

"I'm not the king, Gemma. Never was, and to be honest, I never plan to be. I've come here on behalf of my mother, Isbit Daghan, captain of the *Heart's Desire*."

"And what can I do for Captain Isbit? It's been a long time since the lady graced our gentle shores."

"Well," he said, "my mother wishes to help you quell a pirate uprising and get rid of the Vagans, and in return, she asks for the throne."

Gemma barked out a laugh. "Oh, is that all?"

Tollan recoiled, but Gemma leaned forward. "Tell me about this uprising."

When Tollan had finished telling them what he knew, Gemma stood up, her eyes flashing. "Bloody Riquin Hawkbeard," she snarled, slamming her hand onto the table. "Goddess damn him and his obsession with his eerie prickling facial hair!" She stood up, then wavered on her feet.

In an instant, Devery was across the room, and Elam was out of his chair, both of them reaching to support her. She threw her hands in the air. "I'm all right, damn it!"

Elam slunk back, but Devery stood his ground. A look passed between them, and Tollan felt as if they were holding an entire conversation, though neither spoke. Finally, Devery shrugged in resignation and returned to his post against the wall.

"Now then," she said, beginning to pace the kitchen slowly. "Where were we? Ah, yes. I'm going to gut that little bird-loving bastard and tie him onto his own mast."

Elam burst into laughter. "Prick!" Gemma grinned. "I'm the goddess-damned Queen of Under until I choose not to be, or until someone kills me."

"That isn't going to happen," Devery said.

"Prickling right it isn't," Gemma snapped. "What is he thinking?"

"Apparently, he just couldn't resist the siren's song of a city in chaos. He sent a hundred messenger gulls out to recall the entire fleet on the very night you proclaimed yourself. Told Isbit that when he heard the King Above was dead, too, he knew it was a chance for change. He said it was time that the pirates ran things for a while."

Elam picked up where Tollan left off. "Isbit thinks he'll move soon, since the last of the fleet has just arrived. He's holed up at the Belly Up, so it's hard to say exactly when he'll get bored there and decide to come for you, but he knows you've been ill, so he's sure to use that to his advantage. We've managed to keep the truth of the mage women quiet to keep panic to a minimum. We spread some well-placed rumors about Farcastian assassins and strange devices that might be attributed to the makers of Far Coast. Under knows something unnatural is going on, but up to this point, we've kept the details secret."

"And how exactly did he find out she's been ill?" Devery's eyes were ice.

"I'm not sure," Tollan said. Though now that he thought about it, it *was* possible that he'd been speaking to Lian about Gemma's health where some of the urchins could hear. But he'd keep that information to himself.

"It doesn't matter. He already knows." Gemma looked at Elam and said, "I need you to find Lian and get me a restorative. If she doesn't have any, she'll know where to find the herbs. I'm going to need quite a bit."

Elam stood. Devery took hold of his arm. "Don't tell Lian who it's for," he said, sharing a glance with the other man. "You know how she can be about . . ." He gestured to Gemma.

Elam laughed. "Are you kidding? I'm going to tell her it's for me! I've been running this city ragged for days." He grinned, then looked at Gemma. "I'll be back soon. Don't do anything stupid without me."

"Wouldn't dream of it," she said, matching his smile.

As he walked past, Elam brushed Tollan's arm with his fingertips and a thousand shivers ran up and down Tollan's spine. When he looked back up, Gemma was grinning at him.

When Elam was gone, she turned back to Tollan. "Now," she said, as if she'd been waiting the whole time for Elam to leave, "how much assistance can I expect from Lady Isbit?"

Tollan shrugged. "I hardly know my mother anymore. But I can say that she has her mind set on Above, and I'm not sure she gives two shits about whether Under survives or not."

Gemma paced the room, nodding and rolling her neck as if she were arguing with herself. Then she stopped, ran a hand through her spiky hair, and said, "Okay. We take Riquin when he doesn't expect it, make a very public scene to deter any further unrest and then make a move on the palace. Efficient, smooth and if it pleases the goddess . . . not too bloody."

Devery nodded, his gaze hard as iron. "But just bloody enough."

CHAPTER SEVENTEEN

THE BELLY UP

The street outside the Belly Up was clear, thanks to a well-placed whisper here and a coin in the pocket of an urchin there. Gemma watched from the shadowed alley as Elam strolled up to the door of the tavern. A handful of drunken sailors lounged on the front stoop, mugs half-filled and eyes half-lidded.

As he climbed the steps, Elam said, "I'm looking for Becka Bright-Eyes. Is she inside?"

One sailor smirked, his eyes bloodshot. "You'll have to wait in line, there, prayer keep. Becka's got quite a queue."

Something in the man's tone turned Gemma's stomach.

"Well, she'll have to take a break at some point," Elam said, and pushed the door open.

As the door swung closed behind him, Gemma could hear the sounds of dishes breaking and men swearing. Things inside the tavern were getting out of hand, or perhaps they had already been out of hand for a while.

Every hair on the back of Gemma's neck was standing on end before the screaming started.

Gemma signaled to Devery, who flowed out of the shadows like a wraith. She followed behind him and the sailors on the steps fell away like water. As they burst through the door, they almost crashed into Elam. Three sailors blocked his path.

"That's none of your concern, Brother," the toothless man in the middle grunted. "Just sit back down and have a drink."

Dev was swinging even before he reached the men. They cried out and fumbled for their weapons. Elam picked up a mug and threw it at a sailor's head. Chaos broke out around them as Elam brandished his dagger in the direction of a Balklander, then pivoted and smashed his truncheon atop another man's hand.

"What the bleeding prick?" Gemma shouted. "Where's Riguin?"

"Go, Gem," Devery grunted. "Through the doors. Riquin must be in there."

Elam's opponent disappeared in a spray of blood and Devery stood grinning where the Balklander had just been. "Just like old times, eh?" Dev said, as he put his back to Elam's and they spun around. They were now in the middle of a circle of red-faced drunken pirates, who were armed to the extreme and screaming for blood.

And Devery was laughing.

Gemma sent up a silent prayer for their safety and flung herself through the swinging kitchen doors. Her heart was pounding but nothing prepared her for what she saw in the Belly Up's kitchen. A woman was stretched out across the butcher block naked and unconscious, her back a mass of raised welts and cuts. A man was chained to the bread oven, his flesh sizzling while Riquin pricked him from behind. The man's screams had obviously been enough to cover the sounds of the fighting outside, because Riquin turned to her in surprise.

"Aegos, Hawkbeard," she said. "I've seen tits that didn't sag that low on a dead milk cow."

He reached for his sword, which rested beside the unconscious woman, and Gemma let a dagger fly. It stabbed his hand and pinned it to the butcher block. To Riquin's credit, he didn't cry out—even when he pulled the blade from his hand and dropped it to the floor. "I heard you were dead," he said.

"Funny, but I'd heard *you* were dead," she replied. "I'm afraid that only one of us is correct." Her gaze flicked to the man who was still painfully close to the oven, but he shook his head.

"Gut him, my queen," he croaked.

Riquin laughed. "This prettied-up street rat is nobody's queen. She was born a rat, and she's going to die like one, too."

"Perhaps next time you decide to rape someone in my Under, you should keep your pants around your ankles, Hawkbeard. It really is quite pitiful to have to kill you in this state." She glanced down, raising a disdainful eyebrow in the direction of his cock. "Of course, I don't see next time being much of a concern."

He lunged toward her, and she dodged to the side, swiping her blade down at his shoulder. She felt resistance as her blade bit into muscle.

Riquin grabbed at his wounded arm. "I'm going to enjoy cutting you, bitch." He drove toward her, drunk and old and slow as prick.

She dropped low and brought her blade across his hamstring. His leg gave out beneath him, his sword skidded away from him, and she put her foot across the blade.

He spat at her. "You've no right! You're just a . . ."

She picked up his sword and held it to his cock. The words died on his tongue.

"Crawl, you sadistic shit."

It was a law of nature, so far as Gemma could tell, that if you threatened a man's cock, he would do what he was told. And it appeared that Riquin Hawkbeard was no exception. He left a trail of blood across the kitchen floor, but each time Gemma nudged him with the tip of his sword, he moved. His whimpering was pathetic and beautiful to her ears.

At the door, Gemma looked back at the man who was still chained to the ovens. "Help will be here soon."

He nodded, snot and tears streaming down his ash-stained face, as he said, "It's already here."

When she kicked Riquin through the door, the tavern floor was strewn with groaning, bleeding men. Elam was breathing hard as Devery wiped his blade off on an unconscious man's sleeve. "Hey, beautiful," Devery said, grinning broadly.

She winked at him, then gestured at Riquin. "I don't suppose you'd lend me a hand, Dev. Master Hawkbeard has an appointment."

Devery bowed, the smile never leaving his face. "Regency, I would like nothing more in all the world."

The whimper that Riquin let escape, added to the puddle of piss he left on the floor, was almost satisfaction enough. Almost.

Gemma scanned the room, making sure that all the threats were eliminated, then patted Elam on the back. "You all right?" she asked.

He nodded, still panting. "Yeah, just—a little out of practice."

"I've got to get out there and deal with—" She waved vaguely in the direction that Devery had gone. "But there are two people in there who need help." She thrust her head toward the kitchen. "It's ugly, Elam. If you'd rather, I'll send Lian in."

Elam shook his head, though his color went a bit gray. "I'll see to them," he said softly.

She leaned forward and kissed him on the cheek. "I love you," she said. "I don't tell my people that enough."

Riquin Hawkbeard was strung up, arms and legs spread wide, between two dock posts. His infantile bird-shaped beard trembled as did his flaccid manhood. Blood was caked down his left leg and across his right shoulder, but somehow, the man held his head straight.

Tollan watched as Gemma approached him from the Belly Up. She looked out over the crowd, which had grown to fill the street. She didn't raise her voice, but as she started to speak, a hush fell over the group. Tollan scanned the unfamiliar faces for Elam, as a small coil of fear unraveled in his stomach. He had to force himself to listen to Gemma.

"It's been a dark few days in Yigris, friends, and I must apologize for my absence. But I'm so proud of the way my people—my family—came together to protect our own." She glanced over her shoulder at the pirate, then said, "But sometimes, even the healthiest of houses can be struck by a plague, a cancer or the clap . . ."

A few people in the audience chuckled.

"One week ago, when I ascended to the throne of Under, I stood before Guildhall and offered myself to anyone who chose to challenge me. Many of you were in that hall, and you saw that no opponents came forward." She turned and spat in Riquin's face. "Riquin Hawkbeard was in Guildhall that night. But too craven to challenge me there, he ran like a whipped dog to gather his followers."

A low grumble rolled over the crowd.

Gemma held her hand up for silence. "The slate is wiped clean for all those but the ringleader." She paused, and Tollan wondered how he would forgive those around him if they had betrayed him and mutinied against him. He was surprised to see that Gemma was more forgiving than he would be.

"But, unfortunately, mutiny and revolt are not his worst crimes." Gemma gestured at the Belly Up. "Within our own walls, Riquin Hawkbeard raped, tortured and imprisoned two of our own."

A hiss drew out of the crowd. In Above, mutiny and treason

were punishable by death, but rape and torture were often overlooked. Tollan didn't know if he would ever understand Under, but he realized that he felt safer here than he ever had in the palace, surrounded by guards and his father.

"We have little in Under," Gemma said. "We have each other, our pride, our sharp blades and sharper tongues. And we have a code. When we kill, we kill quickly. We do not bask in another's pain, and we do not cause it unnecessarily. That is the monstrous horseshit that festers in Above. We are liars and thieves and whores and killers, but we are not evil!" Her eyes flashed in the torchlight.

The crown erupted in cheers. Tollan found himself cheering, too.

Gemma raised her hand to quiet them. "I have a bit of a conundrum, my friends. A part of me wants to make Riquin's screams last, but the goddess tells us to be merciful. So, while I could gut him—spill his innards here on the docks for the gulls to feast on—I don't want our seabirds poisoned with his bile. I could strap him to an iron weight and drop him below the waves, but then I risk polluting the entire Hadriak."

A few cheers were raised and quickly quashed, as she went on.

"What I really itch to do is hand over some blades to our brother and sister in there and let them cut him until he isn't capable of raping anyone ever again."

The paramours shouted with a single voice.

"But we are of Under, and we are better than that."

Next to Tollan, Isbit stepped forward. "Excuse me, Regency," she said. "I believe I have a solution."

Gemma nodded for Isbit to continue.

"You all know my story. I was not born in Under. I became one of you because I fell in love with Jamis. But now that he's gone, now that Abram is gone, my place is in the palace. I've decided to pass on the *Heart's Desire* to my son, if he'll have it." She looked at Tollan, and he found himself nodding. He was stunned by her offer, but he realized immediately how right it felt. The only place he'd every truly been happy was at sea. He was nodding and smiling before he'd even collected his thoughts.

His mother smiled back, flashing a golden tooth that hadn't been there when he was a boy. Then she turned back to Gemma. "I believe I have a solution to your"—she waved her hand at Riquin, disgust clear—"little rapist problem. I am of Above, and you're right. We are evil, sadistic pricks. I have no problem doing what should be done to this animal."

Gemma nodded. "It is done then. Let us leave this monster to her work."

The crowds cleared out. Tollan felt sick as he watched his mother take the knife from Gemma, but then he spotted Elam by the tavern stairs. Tollan ran to him, covering his ears. But the screaming had already begun.

Gemma's legs trembled as the crowd followed her instructions, and she made her way back inside the Belly Up.

"What I did out there," she said, resting her head in her hands upon the sticky table, "was wrong." She could still hear

Riquin's screams, and her stomach twisted.

Devery reached out to put a hand on her arm but then didn't, his hand hanging in midair and then settling again on the table. Elam clicked his tongue as if he were going to say something, but then he stopped himself, too. Tollan and Wince stared off blankly, as if at any moment, they would ask how they had gotten here.

She told herself it had been necessary, that unless she wanted a civil war, she had to excise Riquin's poison, but his screams only pierced that argument full of holes. "Goddess above," she growled. "That woman is merciless."

Tollan chuckled, and Gemma turned her attention to him. "I'm sorry," she said, meeting his gaze. "She's your mother..."

He shook his head. "No apology needed. My entire life I loathed my father and thought my mother was a being of mercy and warmth. But it strikes me tonight that at least I can say I actually knew my father. That woman"—he gestured toward the door—"is a complete stranger to me."

Wince looked as if he wanted to comfort his friend but didn't know how. So it was Elam who reached out and took Tollan's hand. His thumb caressed the former king's hand gently, and Gemma caught herself staring at the bare honesty of the moment. It was unlike Elam to be so open. A gurgling scream found its way in through the closed door.

"Maybe that's the last," Devery said, just as another, higher-pitched keen began anew.

"Prick this," Gemma said, pushing away from the table and getting to her feet. "It's over." She stormed out into the night.

CHAPTER EIGHTEEN

DOCKSIDE

When Gemma reached Isbit, she couldn't believe that Riquin was still alive. "Enough!" she growled, snatching the knife from Isbit's hand.

The Queen of Above turned her gaze upon her and said, "Come to finish the deed?"

Gemma was surprised to see that Isbit's eyes were wet with tears.

Gemma placed the blade to what was left of Riquin's throat. "I can't say you deserved this, you prick, but neither did Jost and Becka." He stared at her with blank eyes, and she drew the blade across his throat.

"Is this not what you wanted?" Isbit asked softly.

Gemma felt ill. Her legs and arms trembled. She turned and slid down to sit on the dock, putting the pulp and bone that had once been Riquin Hawkbeard behind her.

Isbit sat down beside her.

"How can you . . ." Gemma wasn't sure how to ask the woman how she could live with herself.

Isbit sighed and wiped her bloodied hands on her breeches. She was silent for a long moment before she said, "For much of my life, I was someone's property. Have you ever known that feeling? To know that you have no value?"

Gemma shook her head, which was beginning to throb.

Isbit went on. "No, I suppose you haven't. I look at you, and I see what I might have been. If you walk through the halls of the noble houses, you would never think that a woman might choose a low birth. It makes no sense. But I can tell you from experience that I would have done so in a heartbeat had I known what it was like in Under."

She sighed. "In Above, daughters are sold to the highest bidder. Their own choices and desires mean nothing. I had no say in whether or not I married the king. My friends had no choices. We were first our father's property, and then our husband's. If we did not please our husband, we could be beaten lawfully. If we did not satisfy our husband, he could take as many mistresses as he liked. If we dared to question our husband, we could be declared a whore, humiliated, used and broken until we learned our place. Every girl's mother warned her. We were raised on horror stories. Every girl grew up knowing how to lay still and take it."

Bile rose in Gemma's throat.

After a moment, Isbit continued. "When Jamis washed up on Whitebeach, he was terribly ill and injured, yet he spoke to me kindly. It wasn't respect for my station or fear that he would break some silly rule. It was actual kindness. I ran headlong into him, and in our years together, he never once treated me as his possession. In Above, that is rarer than you can imagine.

"Had I known that the world could be other than it was, I'd have left before my father signed the nuptial agreement with Abram. I'd have come to Melnora and offered myself as a maid or a thief or a whore. I'd have done so willingly and with a smile on my face.

"Because, as I discovered much too late, I was always a whore. I let Abram prick me and get me with child because I was paid to do so with plush carpets and silver platters, with a torn slit and bruises and a hatred of myself that was only eclipsed by my loathing of him."

Gemma couldn't help but be moved by Isbit's story, and she reached out and silently took the other woman's bloodstained hand. After several long moments, the queen went on.

"Life Above doesn't have to be rotten. But if anyone is going to change it, it must be me. I'm the only one who knows how different things can be. And if that means cutting every prickling rapist and sadist I come across, I will gladly do so, until the women of Above walk with their heads held as high as the women of Under. Until every person in Yigris is free."

Gemma smiled, ignoring the cramp that was building in her belly. "It's funny you should bring that up, Your Grace," she said. "Because I need to talk to you about some mage women up on the hill."

In Gemma's mind, two things were clear. First, the mage

women in the palace must be released and allowed to go home to Vaga. Second, Brinna could not continue her vendetta against the Daghan family. Isbit's son (or sons, if by some miracle Iven still lived) must be given his freedom. And Gemma hoped, for Devery's sake, that his family would somehow be convinced to see reason, but she feared that Brinna's taste for vengeance had poisoned her and Elsha both beyond the point of return.

Isbit stared at the sky, her fingers tracing the wooden talisman she wore on a leather cord around her neck. "I always hated the way the mages were kept," she finally said. "I wasn't allowed much contact with them. I was told they were too dangerous, and I was too weak to control them." She sighed. "You must think that I'm a milquetoast half-wit."

Gemma laughed. "I think a lot of things about you, Your Grace, but milquetoast is not among them."

"Well, my dear, I'm afraid you're wrong. I was as weak as a person can be for much of my life. I saw how those women were treated but never said a word. In my mind, I thought there was nothing that could be done, and in my heart, I thought I was as much a prisoner as they were. Brinna saw what I could not—that there is always something that can be done. But I can't let her have my sons. I have done them enough wrong already."

"Can I ask you a question, Your Grace?" Gemma said.

"Only if you call me Isbit," the queen said. "You and I are going to have a lot of work to do together once this is over. It'd be best if we were friends."

Gemma couldn't help but glance over her shoulder at Riquin's mangled corpse. "Friends, huh?" she chuckled softly.

But Isbit just nodded.

Finally, Gemma continued. "Why didn't you take your sons with you when you went?" She couldn't help but think of the baby she'd lost, and she couldn't imagine giving up a child willingly.

Isbit's hard eyes went soft. "Jamis wanted me to. He said that we could raise the boys together, on the boat. But . . ." Her voice cracked, and she looked away from Gemma. "What I did to Abram—I left him a cuckold. Your King of Above was scared pissless of any confrontation, any unpleasantness, save against those who shared his blood or his bed. Tollan and I always took the brunt of his impotence, and I will never forgive myself for leaving him and Iven there. But the fact of the matter was that if I had taken the boys, it would have meant war. Abram would have wasted every one of Yigris's resources to retrieve his heirs and put an end to me and Jamis.

"I was just selfish enough to run, but I wasn't selfish enough to destroy my city." She cleared her throat, then continued. "I know you must think me an abomination. What sort of mother leaves her children? But the goddess and I worked out an agreement long ago. She saw me through the worst I could imagine, and now it's my turn to do what I can to heal this city and my people. When I am rotting in the ground, I'll pay my debts for what I did to my boys. Until then, I can't worry about my sins. There'll be an eternity for that later."

Gemma found herself admiring the woman's clarity. The world was falling apart around them, but Isbit was willing to do what must be done, even at the risk of her own soul.

"I doubt Tollan will ever speak to me again after tonight." Isbit glanced behind them at Riquin. "I've given him all that I can, though. That ship is . . ." Her voice cracked, and she began to weep quietly.

"You haven't given him everything yet." Gemma shook her head. "You should tell him what you just told me."

Isbit smiled through her tears. "You are young, yet, Regency. Someday you'll see that words mean only so much. It isn't what I've said or what I haven't. I left him. No amount of apology will ever be enough, and no reason will ever suffice."

Gemma wanted to argue, but a cramp took hold of her that shook her like a dog with a rat in its mouth. The edges of her vision faded to starlight and pain. She reached out to support herself on the queen's arm, but the ground embraced her instead.

CHAPTER NINETEEN

THE BELLY UP

After Gemma had stormed out of the tavern, Tollan sat in silence with Elam, Wince and Devery for several long moments. Finally, Devery said, "Well, this is prickling ridiculous." He went behind the counter, poured four mugs of thick ale, and carried them, sloshing, back to the table. He set them down and said, "You gentlemen look as if you could use a drink. It's not every day that you put down a bloody rebellion."

Elam and Wince reached for theirs, immediately, but Tollan waited. Something in the man's words sat sourly in Tollan's stomach. There wouldn't have been a rebellion without Devery Nightsbane. None of this would have happened if it weren't for him and his insane mother and sister, who was sitting in the palace doing goddess knows what to his brother. "It isn't poisoned, is it?"

Wince nearly dropped his cup, coughing ale out onto the table. "Balls," he stammered.

One side of Devery's mouth turned up in a wicked smile. "I've never poisoned anyone in my life, Tollan. I doubt I'd start now when I could have skewered you at any point while we sat here."

"This is your fault," Tollan growled, still staring Devery down. "All of this"—he waved his arms around—"is your fault."

Wince's hand slipped to the hilt of his sword.

"It's been a long night," Elam said gently. "Let's not say things that are—"

"It's all right, Elam. He's right. I've known for a long time that my mother's plan was wrong, but . . ." He shrugged as if in one motion he could indicate all the complexities between mother and son. And maybe he could.

Tollan, goddess knew, had his own complications with Isbit. But it made Tollan's stomach turn that he was even comparing the two of them. What Devery and his family had done was wrong. The pain they'd caused and the damage they'd done to Yigris could not be forgiven. "I should kill you," Tollan said, without thinking.

Beside him, Elam gasped. Wince stood up, shoving his chair back from the table. Devery never moved.

"That's not a good idea," Elam said.

Devery kept smiling, his gaze fixed on Tollan. "Sit back down, Master Quintella," he said softly. "No one is going to do any more killing tonight."

Tollan felt rage roll through him, and his hands began to tremble. How dare this Vagan shit tell him what he could and couldn't do. He slammed his hands down on the tabletop, pushing himself up and sloshing ale over the tops of the mugs. "Prick you, Nightsbane. I'll decide if someone's going to die."

Elam was trying to grab Tollan, Wince's face had taken on the gray pallor of a dead gull, but still, Devery didn't move. Tollan drew his sword.

"Back up, Elam. I don't want anything to happen to you."

"Tollan, please," Elam begged. "Don't do something you'll regret."

There was an edge of emotion in his voice that Tollan had never heard before. It might have been panic.

Every bit of confusion and pain that Tollan had suffered in the last week was boiling within him: his father and mother; his brother, Iven; the fledgling flirtation with Elam; the revelation about the mage women; the fact that his city was still asleep, trapped within burning brambles and that it was no longer his city. He didn't even know who he was anymore, but he knew where the blame lay. He didn't give two pricks right now that he had never wanted the throne to begin with. Right now, he wanted to hurt someone, and the only person he could think to hurt was sitting right in front of him.

Suddenly, like having a bucket of icy water poured over him, he realized why Wince and Elam were so upset. He'd just called out the most capable murderer in the city. He wasn't a poor swordsman, but he wasn't a great one, either. He felt color rise to his cheeks.

"That's a lamb," Devery said, and gestured toward Tollan's chair. "Have a seat, have a drink and let's all sit and pretend we're friends so when Gemma comes back, we don't have to explain our near miss with bloody death, shall we?"

Tollan sat. He took a sip of his ale. Devery took a long pull from his own mug, then said, "Let me make something perfectly clear, sir. You and I can have our differences. You can think me an evil prick, if you like. I don't care. What I care about, right now, is that the woman I love has walked through the Void today, and if you're planning on taking the captaincy that your mama offered, then Gemma is your queen. You will sit down now, drink that ale and put on a happy face. Tomorrow, you can air your grievances, and if the queen believes I should die for my crimes, then so be it. She and Aegos are the only authority I recognize. But tonight, you aren't going to breathe another goddess-damned word about it. Do I make myself clear?"

Tollan nodded, unable to meet the assassin's gaze. Elam leaned against the table as if all the rigidity had gone out of his bones. Wince slipped into his chair and picked up his own mug, draining it before he set it down once more.

"I'm sorry," Tollan mumbled beneath his breath.

Devery grinned broadly. "Mate," he said, laughing, "you've got balls the size of coconuts."

It wasn't more than a minute or two later that they heard footsteps on the ramp. The door swung open and Isbit came inside the tavern supporting Gemma.

Devery was up in a heartbeat, across the room before Tollan

could breathe. Seeing the assassin move with that sort of speed nearly turned Tollan's bowels to water.

Devery took Gemma from Isbit and spoke soft words in her ear as she tried to shrug him off. Tollan turned to Elam, who, he was surprised to find, was still holding his hand. His first instinct—to yank it away before his mother saw—proved ineffective when Isbit slid into the seat that Devery had vacated and eyed the pair of them.

"Well, hello there, young man," she said, nodding politely to Elam. "My name is Isbit, as I am sure you know, and it seems I have missed a great deal in my son's life."

Elam bowed his head, then smiled at her. "I am Elam Bailderas, formerly of the Dalinn," he said, without averting his gaze. "I apologize for our lack of decorum, Your Grace. It has been a most troubling week."

She shook her head and waved her hand. "Think nothing of it, Master Bailderas. I, too, have had a most interesting week, and I'm relieved to find that my son has someone to share his burdens with. I'm very pleased to meet you."

A wave of guilt rolled over Tollan. Here his mother was laying all of his baggage out for Elam to carry, when they hadn't even spoken about, well, about anything, really. She was assuming too much from their casual display. In response, he almost pulled his hand away again. But the idea of losing the warmth and the weight of Elam's hand against his own made him second-guess that decision.

Goddess, he hadn't even known Elam's last name.

And Elam had said he was formerly of the Dalinn. Was he leaving the church? Tollan's mouth went dry with all the imagined implications, but there was no way he could have this conversation with Elam while his mother and Wince sat right beside them. He wasn't sure he could have it even if they were alone. And then the idea of being alone with Elam made his breath hitch in his throat.

"Wincel, it's good to see you, again," Isbit said.

"And you, Your Grace."

Wince had begun to wear a constant expression that was a combination of befuddlement and fear. Tollan couldn't really blame him. He was having a hard time even looking at his mother. Elam, however, made polite conversation, remarking on the beauty of the *Heart's Desire* and his sorrow at hearing of the loss of Jamis Heliata at sea. Isbit responded in kind, pleasantly discussing the weather in Yigris and the beautiful colors of the previous night's sunset.

Everyone ignored the whale in the bath—the fact that his mother had just tortured someone. Nauseated, Tollan looked around the room.

Devery carried Gemma toward the separate dining room. Her skin was strangely pale, her eyes were dull and glassy, and her arms hung limply.

"I ... I need Lian," Devery said to all of them hoarsely. "Will you go find her, please? She'll know what to do." His voice trembled, and his eyes welled with tears. "Please hurry."

Tollan turned to Elam, who was already heading toward the door. "I ... I'll come, too."

As Tollan watched, Elam stopped and turned to Devery. "There were some leaves of something in her satchel. Some tea. It may help." His hands trembled. "We're going for help, Gemma," Elam called out. "Stay strong."

Some moments later, though it felt like hours, Tollan found himself standing outside of the door to the private dining room at the Belly Up. Everywhere he looked—on the floors, on the walls and on one spot on the ceiling—there was blood. He could hear Devery arguing with Lian.

"I'm not leaving!" Devery said, tension thick in his voice.

"Yes, you are." Lian didn't raise her voice, and everything about her tone spoke of calm, but she would not allow for any nonsense. "You can't help her right now, and what I have to do is going to be . . . unpleasant. You will listen to me, boy." Tollan was impressed with the authority in her words as the tiny maid ordered the deadly assassin from the room.

A low sound—part growl, part whimper—escaped Devery before he said, "What do you have to do?"

Tollan heard Lian sigh, then she said, "I think there's a piece of the babe still inside of her. I'm going to try to flush it out, or else she'll keep bleeding. And she can't live through much more bleeding, Dev." There was silence for a long moment before she said, "I'll do what I can to make her safe. You know I love her, too."

There was a muffled sob, and some soft words, before

the door creaked open and a pale-faced, hollow-eyed Devery slipped out of the room. He put his back to the wall beside the door and slid to the floor, his head in his hands. He shook with silent sobs as Elam sat down beside him.

He didn't say anything. Tollan didn't think there was anything to say. He watched as Elam wrapped his arm around Devery's shoulders, and the assassin seemed to flow into his arms. He dampened Elam's shirt with his tears.

Elam began to pray quietly, but as his heart took up the words, he spoke more firmly. All Tollan could do was look on and pray with him.

"Goddess—mother and lover of us all—I beseech you in the name of your daughter, Gemma Antos. If ever there were a woman who embodied your spirit, it is she. She has the mind of a queen and the heart of a mother, the bravery and body of a warrior and the soul of a lover. As your humble servant, I beg of you. I need her. This man needs her. This city needs her. Please, Aegos. Save her."

Devery had stopped crying, though his body still trembled against Elam's. Tollan ached to go to Elam, to comfort him as he comforted Devery. Wince and Isbit stood nearby, faces drawn. The room seemed to hold its breath as they waited.

A trembling scream, weak but expressive, erupted from inside the room, and Elam had to hold Devery back. "Lian will help her, Dev. There's nothing you can do. Trust in the goddess."

Devery looked at him, eyes filled with desperation. "That's a load of horseshit, Elam, and you know it."

Tollan felt like a voyeur. In this moment, the relationships between the team from Under were laid bare, and he and Wince and his mother had no business witnessing it.

Elam smiled. "That may well be, Dev," he said. "But I still have faith in miracles."

Another several silent minutes passed, and then the dining room door opened to reveal Lian, bloodied to her elbows. Her face was streaked with tears. "I've—I've done all that I know to do," she said, her voice quaking. She didn't say anything more. The look on her face made the rest clear.

Wince was standing in a pool of blood. He wasn't sure whose blood it was. There were a number of corpses strewn about the floor. The blood might have belonged to one of the *Amber Mew's* sailors who had stumbled out, wounded but still breathing. The blood might have belonged to the pirate captain himself— Gemma had done a number on him, even before she'd gotten him outside, and Queen Isbit had brought more of him back in with her. And goddess knew that the blood might be Gemma's.

As far as Wince could see, he and Tollan were standing in the middle of the only conscious members of Yigrisian society, every damned one of whom was loyal to the woman bleeding out in the private dining room. If Under took it upon themselves to riot, he had to figure out a way to keep Tollan safe. He wasn't sure that the two of them could sail the *Heart's Desire* on their own, but to Wince's mind, that was the smartest, safest route out of this tinderbox.

He glanced to the side and saw Queen Isbit's eyes glittering with anticipation. He sighed, turning away from the animal desire she exhibited as she waited for Lian's word. It was clear to Wince that no matter what happened to Gemma, Queen Isbit had things positioned right where she wanted them. A shudder ran through him, his hands clammy with nerves.

Out of the corner of his eye, he noticed movement by the inn's front door. He moved toward it just as a heartbroken wail came out from the dining room. The cries of everyone in the room created a song of grief in rounds, and Wince was the only one who saw two things: the look on Isbit's face and the little girl who'd just slipped into the tavern.

She held her hands up in front of her in surrender. "I'm sorry, sir," she said. "I'm looking for my Papa. I'm here to help."

If Gemma never again woke up in a room she didn't recognize, it would be too soon. She rolled onto her side, groggy, and felt wetness upon her legs and thighs. She struggled to sit up, but strong hands were suddenly on her shoulders. "Shhh," Devery whispered into her ear. "Don't move too quickly."

She was finally able to focus on his face, and what she saw there drew her up short. He was pale and haggard, his eyes red rimmed, his face both tear stained and blood spattered. As she met his gaze, a sob slipped from between his lips, and he clutched her to him. "Aegos, Gem. I thought I'd lost you."

Trying to get her bearings, she looked around the room.

She was on a long dining table. Towels and rags and blankets lay beneath her, all soaked in blood. She was naked to the waist, and the hem of her shirt was blood soaked, too. Devery was with her, and against the wall was his daughter, Katya.

"What's going on?" Gemma asked.

Devery sat down on the edge of the table. He looked down at her with so much love that she averted her gaze. "You were dying," he said, "maybe even dead. I don't know. A piece of the baby was lodged in your womb, and you were losing blood. Lian fished it out, but . . ." His shoulders began to tremble.

Gemma looked at the girl who was staring at her own feet. Katya's right hand was stained with blood. Gemma suddenly knew what had happened. Now that she was aware of it, she could feel the mage work running through her. "Come here, Katy," she said softly.

Gemma lifted the bloody hem of her shirt to reveal a small handprint atop her navel, around which lay an intricate mage mark burned into her skin. "You saved me." She couldn't think of the right words to say. Her heart was full of gratitude and awe. Gemma brushed her fingers along the white streak in Katya's hair. "Thank you, mite."

"You're not angry with me?" Katya asked.

Gemma laughed before she could help herself. "Why would I be angry? You saved my life."

"I mean about before. Because of the fires. I was only trying to keep Under safe. Aunt Elsha was going to trap you all and have you killed. I added the fire so she couldn't get to you, but I thought you'd be angry if . . ." Katya stared at her feet.

"You did all that?" Gemma stared at this child of the man she loved. She had always seen the potential in Katya—but this was something different. Suddenly, the idea of a mage queen leading Under struck Gemma like a runaway cart. Katya was a gift she could give Yigris, more than any heir she could produce. "You're perfect, Katy," she said, smiling.

Gemma sighed as she wrapped Katya in a hug. She was sure she was smearing blood all over the girl's pretty dress, but she didn't care. "Now you listen close, mite," she said. "What you did saved people's lives. You saved Yigris, you saved the Guild, and you saved me. So that makes you the heroine of three of my favorite things."

Katya looked up at her and grinned crookedly, but her smile quickly faded. "Aunt Elsha said she's going to kill you and Papa. Grandmother said that you ruined him, and Aunt Elsha's going to have to kill you both so that she can destroy Under forever. Grandmother wants me to go with her to the palace with Aunt Elsha and be queens and make Yigris suffer for what it's done to us. She said Yigris will be a new Vaga with three mage queens. But I…" She looked at Devery. "Papa, I don't want to be a queen, and I don't want to make people suffer. I don't want you to . . ." She started to cry, and Devery picked her up.

"It's all right, Katy. Nothing bad is going to happen to me or to Gemma. I won't let it, and I know you won't, either. You traveled all the way across the city to protect us. You're as brave as the Queen of Under herself." He smiled gently at Gemma, but his eyes were sad.

Katya threw her arms around his neck. Then Devery said, "But I need you to be a little braver, still."

Katya drew away from him.

"I need you to go back to your grandmother before she discovers that you've sneaked away. If she finds out you're gone, she'll tear the city apart looking for you. All of the people you saved will be in danger again. You have to keep pretending just a little longer."

The girl's bottom lip poked out, but then she nodded, trembling. "And then we can be together as a family? You promised. You said that you and me and Gemma would be a family."

Devery's face was awash with emotion as he looked at Gemma and then back at Katya. "That's not up to me, Katy. We need to give Gemma some time to understand everything that's happened."

Katya wriggled free of Devery's grasp and threw her arms around Gemma. "I'll be a good girl!" she said earnestly. "I'll help with chores, and I'll be quiet, and I'll—"

Gemma laughed and kissed her on the cheek, squeezing her tightly. "It's been a pretty full few days, mite. I have a lot to think about, but . . . I love you, and I'd . . ." She looked up at Devery, whose face had gone stark and still. She sighed. "I'd like nothing better than to be a family."

Katya met her gaze with utter seriousness, and a shudder ran through Gemma. She felt as if the little girl were weighing her sincerity. "I love you," Gemma said, putting all of her hopes and fears and weaknesses into those three words. It was the truth, but as with all truths, it was bigger than any words could contain.

Devery stared at her, his blue eyes wide with disbelief. She shrugged. "We'll figure it out," she whispered. Tears streamed down his cheeks as he nodded.

The little girl squealed, wiggled loose from Gemma's grasp and hugged Devery's waist as he stood and tried to hush her. "All right, Katy. You said that Grandmother is planning for you both to go to the palace. When will you go?"

"Tomorrow night," the girl whispered.

Gemma could tell by Devery's expression that he was already planning. "I know you're not going to like this, Gemma, but I want Lian to give you something to help you sleep. We can plan in the morning. You need to go somewhere where you can rest and recover, because goddess knows you're not going to stay behind when we take the palace tomorrow night. Am I right?"

Gemma wanted to argue, but she was battered and exhausted. She felt like a rag that had been used to scrub Guildhall, then was left in the sun to bake. "Will you come, too?" she asked softly.

He squeezed her hand and smiled. "Anywhere and always."

CHAPTER TWENTY

DOCKSIDE

Tollan stared up into the leaden darkness of the storeroom of the Belly Up. Wince's snores echoed against the walls. The air was heavy with the aroma of onions, spices, and cured meats. They'd promised the tavern keep that they'd sleep there tonight to deter any further unrest. But the airflow was clamped off, and Tollan felt like he couldn't breathe. He shrugged down his blanket of thin, itchy wool. He felt tangled up in the night's events, drowning in too much information. His mother had offered her ship—no, his ship—and he regretted declining the opportunity to sleep on the gentle sway of the Hadriak.

But his mind turned another corner as he listened to Wince rolling over on his pallet. Tollan found himself thinking of Elam. He felt himself begin to stiffen involuntarily beneath his blanket, and he shifted uncomfortably. *Aegos. Now isn't the time for . . .*

But it was too late. He rolled onto his side, pressing his cock between his thighs in an effort to dampen the urgency.

Suddenly, the air in the room wasn't oppressive. It was alive with possibility. Elam was sleeping upstairs. They were breathing under the same roof, in the same quarter of Yigris, under the same sky.

Tollan trembled, pulling his blanket tighter around him. In his mind, he heard his father's voice calling him a coward—feeble, impotent, spineless, craven. Calling him a woman, which to his father had been the very worst insult one could give. Tears stung at his eyes. But this was his chance to be brave. All he had to do was get up, pull on his clothes and walk through that door. All he had to do was knock. And hope.

His erection wilted, but his desire to hold Elam in his arms did not. *This may be our only chance. Be brave, you nerveless shit.* Pushing aside any logical thought, his feet found the floor.

Aegos. I knocked. Why the prick did I knock? Tollan turned to slip away, suddenly desperate for the suffocating confines of the storeroom. But it was too late. He heard footsteps. The latch was thrown. He turned back, panic seizing him.

The room was illuminated, too bright for its occupant to have been asleep. Elam stood in the doorway in just his breeches. He was barefoot, and he smiled sheepishly at Tollan. "I was hoping you'd come knocking."

Tollan couldn't help but take in the whole of him. He was slender, muscles not overly defined, but he didn't look soft, either. His skin was honeyed ochre, smooth and unblemished. There was a hint of the old noble Yigrisian blood there, watered down, but stunning in its warmth. A thin trail of dark hair ran from his navel downward, disappearing beneath the lacings of his breeches. When Elam turned to motion him into the room, Tollan saw a crisscrossing of thin scars across his shoulders. Fierce hatred for the person who had tried to mar such beauty settled like hot coal in his belly.

But then Tollan felt the blood rush from his face. How could he think that this perfect man would want to touch him? He was hard and hairy and angular and inexperienced and ... *Oh, goddess. As erect as the palace walls.*

"You weren't sleeping?" Tollan stammered, suddenly aware of his arms and legs, his skin and hair. Every part of his body was singing with hope.

Elam grinned. "The only way men ever respond to the threat of impending death is either with fighting or with pricking. You already tried to start a fight, and, thank the goddess, Devery quashed that urge. So I thought I'd stay up a while, just in case you had a mind for the other. Would you like to come in?" he said, gesturing toward the bedroom he'd claimed for the night. The tavern keep was holed up with one of the Six-Mast girls, enjoying a night paid for by Gemma in reparation for damage done.

Tollan nodded because words were too much for him. He entered cautiously, convinced that at any minute Elam would change his mind.

The only places to sit were a straight-backed chair and the bed. Elam sat down on the bed, leaving Tollan the choice.

Tollan looked at the chair, then the bed. He glanced at Elam and swallowed, urging himself to be brave. Then he sat down beside Elam. Only a breath of space kept the outside of his thigh from pressing against Elam's.

Without giving himself a chance to falter, Tollan turned to Elam and said, "May I kiss you? I'm not sure how you ask in Under. We don't . . . we don't do that kind of thing."

Elam nodded, and Tollan leaned in, tentative and trembling.

Their lips met. It was slow and liquid, each of them feeling out the other. Elam brushed Tollan's lower lip with his tongue, and Tollan shuddered. Their mouths took on a life of their own, dancing the intricate steps of courtship and desire.

After a moment, Tollan retreated, his breath quick. Elam smiled languidly.

"I don't know what to . . . I've never . . ." Tollan stammered his face coloring with shame.

"It's all right," Elam said, taking his hand. "I'll show you." He reached out and started to unbutton the front of Tollan's shirt. He slipped it off his shoulders and looked down at Tollan's dark skin, the thick, unruly hair that covered his chest and belly. Softly, slowly, he reached out. "We don't have to hurry," he said. "Decide if you like the way I look as much as I like the way you do."

Tollan grunted a laugh. It was impossible to believe that Elam could find him half as beautiful as he found Elam. Elam walked his fingers back. But Tollan pulled him closer.

"Tell me to stop, and I will. I promise," Elam said. He ran his hand over the muscles of Tollan's chest, down the expanse of his belly, and downward.

Tollan stared at him, his breathing coming quick, and bit his lip.

Tollan knew about women, but he couldn't possibly understand how they would feel in a moment like this. But as he and Elam lay in a warm heap, their sweat mingling with their breath, he knew exactly how Elam felt. The delicious emptiness, the chilly stickiness, the smile that couldn't be tamed.

Tollan propped himself up on an elbow, untangling himself from Elam's arms. "I'm sorry that I . . . that it was . . ." His gaze drifted, smile slipping. "Fast."

Elam pulled him back down, kissing him with abandon. Then he pushed him back gently and said, "It was your first time, half-wit!"

Tollan blushed. "Well, it's not exactly my first time for that." He grinned sheepishly, waving his hand in the air. "But I guess it makes a difference whose hand it is, huh?"

They laughed until Elam was wheezing, the covers pulled over them, their legs intertwined. Slowly, their giddiness subsided, and soon Tollan could feel the slow rise and fall of Elam's sleepy breath against his neck. He shuttered the lantern and snuggled deeper into the cocoon of Elam's arms. *It could prove dangerously easy to get used to this.* He drifted off to sleep, trying to number the reasons why this was not a good idea, but he kept getting distracted by the soft tickle of Elam's beard against his neck and the sounds of the man sleeping. He'd worry about what Above thought if they managed to survive another night.

"It's not exactly the marriage suite, is it?" Gemma quipped, as she swayed on her feet in front of Devery in an impersonal room in some shit-hole Dockside inn.

"Any room you're in is the best room in town," he said.

She frowned. "You don't have to try so hard, you know. I'm still me." She didn't have the strength to wrestle with all that had happened, tonight.

"I know," he said, just barely above a whisper. "I'm sorry." He reached out, offering his hands to her, and she took them as she bit her lip. "There's no excuse for what I've done," Devery said. "And there's no way I can bring them back. Not Melnora, not Fin. Not the baby. And there's no reason in all the After for you to forgive me. You'd be a half-wit if you did. I won't ask you to."

She pulled her hands from his.

He turned away. "I'll explain it to Katy."

She slapped his face so hard it stung her hand. "You're right," she said. "It would take a prickling half-wit to overlook what you've done. To ignore the hurt you've caused." She looked down at her blood-soaked shirt. "And by the goddess, there has been hurt." Her eyes welled with tears. "I've been called a lot of names before, Devery, but half-wit isn't among them. I can't ignore what you've done, and I can't forget what's been lost. But you don't get to make decisions for me. I might be a madwoman—but I love you." She took his face between her hands. "We'll figure this out. Things will never go back to exactly the way they were, but—"

He kissed her before she could finish speaking. It was the kind of kiss one gives to a priestess in the temple—gentle and dry. Full of reverence.

She didn't speak as he slowly undressed her. He poured water from the pitcher into the basin and knelt before her, sponging the blood from her belly and thighs. Quietly, he began to murmur a prayer of devotion. His hands were his prayer, offering what he could, for however long he could. His tears were his sacrifice, and she let him give it freely.

In Vagan temples, the goddess often enters the body of her priestesses, and when Gemma bent and reached out for him, tipping the basin over and pulling him toward her with all the ferocity of the mother and warrior, she'd have sworn that Devery had found his religion.

It was raining. Gemma could smell it. The fresh water rinsing away the salt and dust and leaving behind a prettied-up Yigris, if only for a few minutes. She drew in a deep breath, enjoying the brief respite.

A counter note to the sweet rain was the clean-sweat smell of Devery snoring softly beside her. She nuzzled against him, still refusing to open her eyes to this day that would bring them to the palace and to his mother. To whatever fate the goddess saw fit for them all.

They must be prickling mad to fight six fully trained mage women. The side of her mouth quirked upward. They could still run away. Make a new life and make babies and . . . but where would they go? Who would they be? She knew in her heart that she couldn't bankrupt the Guild. If she left, she would leave the bank codes with Lian or Elam. Her heart clenched at the thought of leaving him behind. In Yigris, they were important. Respected. Elsewhere—on Far Coast, or in Ladia—who would they be?

She sighed, then opened her eyes. Reality asserted itself. There would be no baby for her. Not for a while, anyway. They had to get Katya away from Brinna. And then Gemma had to punish the woman for what she had taken from them. And despite her discomfort with the idea, Gemma owed Isbit Daghan. The woman had helped her put down Riquin's mutiny. In return, Gemma promised to help Isbit retake her palace.

Without warning, a shameful sob pushed its way out of her, and hot tears streamed down her cheeks. She wasn't even sure why she was crying, but suddenly the world seemed overwhelming. Her life was too much. She felt as if all of her choices had been made for her, as if all her will had been stolen.

Devery's arms snaked around her, pulling her closer. "Are you in pain?"

She shook her head, snuffling. "I'm fine. I just . . ." Another sob raked its way upward.

"What is it, love?" He kissed her temple and wiped her tears.

A quavering wail escaped her lips as she buried her head in his shoulder. "You'll make a terrible farmer!" she howled, before thrusting herself away from him and into the pillows. She pulled the blanket over her head.

He laughed, deep-throated and merry. "Yes, ma'am," he said as his fingers began to wriggle under the edge of the blanket. He pulled it down until he could see her face. "I would be the worst farmer who has ever lived."

She stared up at him, torn between her love for him and

her sudden terror about their future. He bent and kissed her nose. "And you—my beautiful, brave, brilliant woman"—he paused—"would make an awful farmer's wife."

She tensed, anger flowing through her veins. "Well, how hard can it be, Dev? If you're to be out hoeing in the yard all day, I suppose I'll have to mend your socks and raise the children and tend the chickens, or some such horseshit."

"And you would be terrible at nearly all of those things. I suggest that we not take up farming." He wrapped her up in his embrace.

She stopped just shy of pushing him away. Though she felt awful—she didn't want to lose the tenuous thread that connected them to each other. It seemed so fragile. "Well," she sniffed, "what are we going to do, then?"

He sat up, his face suddenly serious. "Gem, I don't see any reason why we have to go anywhere or be anything different from who we are now. But I will go anywhere and be anyone you want me to be."

Her throat grew thick with emotion, and she started to cry again. "I'm just scared that something bad is going to happen. I've already lost . . ." She looked away. "I don't want anyone else to get hurt."

"I'm not going to get hurt," he said.

She glared at his hand that would always bear the scars of his mother and reminded her of the scars he bore elsewhere.

"All right," he sighed, wrapping his arms around her. "I can't promise not to get hurt. But I can promise you that if we come out of the palace alive tonight—I swear to you, by the goddess, that I'm going to be the man you deserve. No more secrets. I'll be the man I always should have been."

She clung to him, crying into his shoulder.

"You have to know that I love you," he said, wiping at his chest with the edge of the blanket. "There isn't another grown woman alive who I'd let snot all over me like that."

A knock sounded on the door as Devery slipped from the bed and pulled on his smallclothes and breeches. He walked as he yanked the laces tight, then tugged on a wrinkled shirt. He unlocked the door and opened it to reveal Lian, damp and wild-haired but grinning.

"Good morning, Devery. Regency." She entered carrying a small basket. "I've come to check Gemma over. Go eat breakfast at the Belly Up," she shooed him away. "I'll bring the queen when I'm done." Her tone left no room for argument. "Put on your boots, lad," she said, turning toward Gemma. "It's blustery, outside."

After Devery kissed Gemma chastely on the forehead and left, Lian went over to the bed and sat down beside her. "Oh, posh," she chortled, "as if that little peck on the head's going to fool anyone. Seems like a little peck is what started this trouble in the first place."

Gemma smiled, though her vision was still cloudy from too many tears and not enough sleep. "It's not like that, Lian. We're in love. We've been..."

"Oh, I know all about what you've been. Me and Master Fin have known for years, but you children think you're so clever. Think you can pull the sails over our heads with your sneaking about. Fin told me two years ago to let you be. He said that once in a while, love is more important than rules. And then he said not to tell Regency Melnora, because she might not see it that way."

Gemma's eye's stung with gratitude for the people who had always taken care of her.

Lian was digging through her basket as she spoke, and she pulled out a small vial. She handed it to Gemma. "That's for later—before you go to the palace. It'll fix up your energy problem in a hurry."

Gemma thanked her.

The maid continued. "Now, I see you've been crying, and I . . . well, I know a thing or two about the wreckage that babes can make of us, you know. When I first had my Tavian and the midwife placed her in my arms, I looked at my child, and I said, 'I don't want this baby. I can barely take care of myself.'" She squeezed Gemma's hand and continued. "Of course, it wasn't true. I wanted that baby more than I wanted air or food or sweet summer wine. But in that moment, I was terrified. All the love and fear I was feeling got tangled up, and I just couldn't think straight. It was the same with all of my children. Somehow the love that they plant within you makes you both stronger and weaker. And it gets your heart and your head all confused.

"So, we cry. We say things we don't mean. We feel alone and broken, as if we have no control over our lives. Then we cry some more."

She leaned over and kissed Gemma on the forehead, just where Devery had. Gemma could feel the paper-thin skin of her lips. She could smell the clean, herbal scent of Lian, and the damp of her woolen shawl. "I've never lost one, sweet girl," she said, drawing Gemma in to her, "but I helped Melnora through it a time or three."

Renewed tears flooded Gemma's eyes. "I feel like such a failure. I wanted the question of an heir out of the way, and I couldn't ... I couldn't do this one simple thing. I couldn't protect the baby I chose to bring into this world. I couldn't ..." A sob shook her.

Lian rocked her, cradling Gemma's head against her chest. "Oh, Gemma. You did the best anyone could have. Some people would say that it was the goddess's will, or some such horseshit. Some people would say that there'll be another babe and not to fret over this one. Some people are full of too much stupid and not enough sense. Nothing is going to make this feel better, not for a long while, and to be totally honest, maybe nothing ever will. But I imagine that gutting the bitch who did it will be a decent start."

Gemma didn't know for sure if that was true—she didn't think that she could spill enough blood to make up for what she'd lost—but she understood Lian. Brinna had to pay for everything. For the baby, for Melnora, for Yigris, for Devery. Brinna had to pay.

Lian reached into her basket and pulled out a flask. "Drink this," she said, passing it to Gemma.

Gemma took the flask and sniffed it. "When Melnora lost her first," Lian said, motioning Gemma to take a sip, "she had terrible grief. Fin was stoic about the whole thing, as even smart men tend to be, but Melnora was rattled by it, and she couldn't make herself get out of bed. I tried everything I knew until Fin sent me to a Balkland herb man. He taught me how to brew this tea. He called it Albatross Tears." Once more, she gestured for Gemma to drink the tea. "It helped Mistress Melnora get through the worst of it, and I assume that you'll be needing to get through the worst of it fairly soon, seeing as how you have an assault to plan."

Gemma took a sip. It tasted like peaches and cinnamon and something exotic and rare, and it tingled in her mouth like magic. Gemma took another long swig and felt the tension in her neck begin to ease.

"Drink it up," Lian said, squeezing Gemma's hand.

A few minutes, and a few swallows, later, Gemma turned to Lian. She felt lighter, as if she could float away from the bed. She hadn't forgotten her grief, but she wasn't doubled over by it any longer. She smiled. "Thank you, Lian. I'm not sure how I would have gotten through today if you hadn't come."

Lian stood, straightening the cover on her basket. "That's what family does, girl. You know that." She bent and gave Gemma a quick hug. "Melnora and Fin would be very proud of you," she said, her own voice cracking with emotion.

Gemma nodded. She wasn't about to let herself fall down the rabbit hole of grief again. She owed Melnora and Fin a bit of revenge. She slipped from the covers and walked Lian to the door, though she wasn't wearing a stitch. "Tell Dev I'll be along shortly," she said, opening the door for the maid. "Tell him to send word to the Ain. Tell Under that tonight we go to war."

"Do you want me to leave some of the men here to escort you?" Lian asked, as she hefted the basket and turned to the door.

Gemma laughed wryly. "I am the Queen of Under. I don't need protection. Our enemies need protection from me."

Tollan opened his eyes to a world filled with more light than he'd ever known. His legs were tangled up with Elam's, his mouth tasted like yesterday's stockings, and he could imagine that his hair was splayed out in an unmanageable cloud, but it didn't matter. A smile spread across his face as he listened to Elam breathing.

Tollan wanted to stay just like this. Maybe forever. Nothing but the two of them and the rain, which he heard pelting the roof of the Belly Up. He felt—for the first time in his life—like a man. The boy he'd been had disappeared sometime during the night. All his fears and guilt and weakness and secrets had been washed away by Elam and the rain, and he was waking up to a new world.

Elam shifted in his sleep, the soft sounds of his breathing changing slightly. "Good morning," he said, without opening his eyes.

Not allowing himself to think about it, Tollan leaned in and kissed him. "Good morning," he said, emotion choking him.

Elam's eyes opened, and he squinted at Tollan. He smiled and moved closer to him, but a brisk knock on the door interrupted the moment.

"Balls," Tollan muttered as Elam slipped lithely from beneath the covers. The sight of him, bare and beautiful, took Tollan's breath away.

Elam fumbled for his spectacles on the bedside table, then he pulled on smallclothes and a pair of breeches, and went to the door. He opened the door to reveal Wince, his pale face haggard in the morning light.

"Have you seen . . . oh," Wince said, seeing Tollan in the bed. A rapid flurry of expressions flitted across Wince's features, ending in a broad grin. "Sorry to bother," he said, bowing exaggeratedly. "I was just worried when I couldn't find you. I . . . umm . . . I'll just go help with breakfast." His eyes met Tollan's and held them, warm and joy filled, for a long moment before he turned to leave.

Elam closed the door and came back to bed. "He's a better man than I'd have given him credit for," he said, as he sat down on the edge of the mattress.

Tollan could only nod. His emotions were too close to the skin to say anything.

Elam fidgeted with the laces of his breeches, tightening them slowly. "When . . . when this is all over," he said, without looking at Tollan. He paused, picking at a piece of lint on the coverlet. "I've never been to sea." He stood, turning his back to Tollan as he pulled on a shirt, then sat and pulled on his stockings. There was tension in the muscles of Elam's shoulders that made Tollan want to wrap him up and never let go. There was vulnerability here that Tollan hadn't known Elam capable of.

"Would you like to, someday?" Tollan croaked.

Elam's amber gaze met Tollan's as a soft smile kissed his lips. He nodded, eyes wide. "I think I might," he said. It was too bad, really, that he'd already wasted so much effort getting dressed.

PART THREE

PERCHANCE TO DREAM

CHAPTER TWENTY-ONE

THE GOLDEN DOOR

A sense of having come full circle overwhelmed Gemma as she stared intently at the Golden Door. Her companions waited restlessly at the mouth of the Black Corridor, and she pushed them out of her mind. It was just her and the door now. Only Gemma's skill could get them through, so she would take her time.

Drawing a deep breath, she approached and laid her hands upon the door, just as she'd done the day Melnora died. It felt like years had passed since that moment, but it had only been little more than a week. She counted the shivers that ran through her, the little telltale pulses of mage work. She held her breath as the number rose higher, each tingle representing a trap that she alone could disarm. *Twenty. Breathe your blessings upon me, Aegos. I'm going to need all the help I can get.*

She started with the gem and mirror she had dealt with on her last trip. Sweat trickled down her back, and she longed for the custom-tailored, tight-fitting clothes that lay trapped inside Guildhouse as the hem of her ill-fitted shirt came untucked and hung loose. *That's one*, she thought as she shoved the shirt back into her breeches.

She closed her eyes and listened. She ignored the shuffling of boot soles behind her and the brief rumble Wince made as he cleared his throat. There, the slightest rushing of air. Another deep breath and she followed the sound to the wall. It appeared to be a blank stretch of black stone, but as she ran her fingers along it, following the sound, she discovered a place where the wall was an illusion. Grinning, she guided her fingers into the hidden space and with infinitesimally careful movements, she felt along its insides.

It wasn't deep—set only about six inches into the wall—but it was wide. Within, she discovered three tubes, each half an inch across. Set inside each of the tubes was a cylindrical shape with a sharp-edged tip. A spear of some sort. Air rushed past the spears from within the tubes, and if she disarmed them improperly, Gemma was sure she would quickly turn into a pincushion. Two pressure switches hung off the bottom of each of the tubes.

She held her breath once more and carefully ran a fingertip along the first switch without exerting any pressure. There was a mark on the switch, some sort of character, though the shape that her fingertip drew in her mind was not any mark she was familiar with. She touched the second switch and found another mark. As she touched it, she saw in her mind's eye the Yigrisian character for the word *disarm*.

These spears were not among the traps she had deactivated

when Melnora had brought her to the door. So far as she knew, these had never been armed. These were made for a special occasion—the sort of occasion when mage women only want Vagans to come calling.

Gemma resisted the urge to look over her shoulder at Devery. He couldn't help her with this. This was the realm of the Queen of Under.

She stepped as far to the side as she could, drew a shuddering breath and pushed the lever that bore the character she did not recognize. There was a loud click, and then the air ceased to blow around that spear. She gripped the spear's shaft in two trembling fingers and slid it from its tube.

As if from nowhere, she pulled two feet of hard steel from within the wall. The spear was tipped in a sharp point that was covered in mage marks.

"Aegos," she heard Tollan mutter behind her, just as Wince said, "Balls! What the . . ." He grunted as someone hushed him.

She easily disarmed the other two, now that she knew what she was feeling for, and laid the spears down next to their brethren on the floor. *That's four.*

She stepped to the center of the hallway once more and listened. There was still more air rushing. This time it seemed to be coming from the other side of the hallway.

With little effort she discovered another panel in the wall hiding another three spears. She disarmed them in the same manner. *That's seven. More than a third of the way done.*

She stepped back to the center of the corridor and listened. No air. The stillness was eerie, as if she had fallen into the Void.

Gemma rolled her neck and approached the door. If there was nothing to hear, then she'd have to use her other senses.

She closed her eyes, and took a deep breath. The oil that lit the lamps was heavily scented, just as it had been every time she'd been here, but there was something odd about it this time—a sharp undercurrent to the fragrant smoke. It was faint, but something in the back of her mind cried out. It was a smell she knew.

"Oh, goddess," she snapped, her eyes flying open. "Light a torch, now!" She moved to the first lamp and saw, to her horror, that she was correct. There, floating in the pot of oil, was a small purple stone. *Farcastian spark stone.* She began to unscrew the glass reservoir that held the oil as she tried to blow out the lamp. "Shit," she grunted, as the stubborn flame simply danced before her breath.

Behind her, she could hear movement, but she had no time. The oil would be gone soon, and if the flame hit the spark stone, every one of them would die. She tried desperately to brush aside that image as she fumbled with the reservoir.

"Prick this," she growled, releasing the glass bowl. She yanked off the leather vest she wore and quickly wrapped her hand and arm in it. She pressed the palm of her hand to the top of the lamp and felt the heat of the flame batter against the leather. The stink of the scorching vest was vile, but she smothered the flame almost immediately.

She moved down the row of lamps, horrified to see that each of them held a spark stone. She rushed, nearly choking on the rancid smoke of her vest as she extinguished the first seven lamps. At the eighth and final one, she watched as the spark stone trembled and rattled within the now dry glass bowl. She swallowed her terror and jammed the tattered remains of her vest atop the flame, throwing out a desperate plea to Aegos.

The rattling ceased half an instant after the corridor went nearly dark. Gemma collapsed as the rush of terror leaked out of her. She drew a trembling breath, then another slower one, commanding her watery limbs to steel themselves. She whispered a silent prayer of gratitude to the goddess and stared up at the dark ceiling of the corridor, which was now only illuminated by the trembling light of the torch someone had lit at the end of the hall.

Staring back at her was a pattern of circular dots that exuded a pale-yellow light. When the room was lit, they would have been impossible to see, but now in the darkness she could see four shapes made of light. They were shapes that made no sense to her though they bore the same curving lines that she associated with mage marks. "Bloody, prickling mage women and their goddess-damned marks!" she snapped.

Sighing, she reached into her pouch and pulled out a notebook and charcoal pencil. Quickly, she copied the shapes, then made her way with utmost care back to the mouth of the corridor. Devery was pacing. Elam sat against the wall, his head in his hands, and Tollan stood over him, watching helplessly. Isbit and Wince seemed to vacillate between being bored and annoyed.

Devery grabbed her and threw his arms around her. "I ... oh, goddess, I can't do this," he groaned into her hair. "I can't just stand here while you put yourself in danger and ..."

"I do it all the time, love. You go off to kill someone, and I don't have the slightest inkling what is happening until you get back. Sometimes it's months. You can do this. I'm almost done." She leaned in, kissing him long and soft on the mouth. "But I need your help."

He looked into her eyes and chuckled. "Thank the goddess."

She showed him the shapes, and he squinted at them, turning the notebook this way and that before his gaze met hers once more. There was a look of honest terror in his eyes as he said, "Elsha did this." He pointed to the shape that was scrawled closest to the mouth of the corridor, "This one is the mage mark for blindness."

Gemma nodded, her mind already whirling ahead.

"This one is the mage mark for fear, and this one is the mark for pain." His gaze was hard and angry.

"What's the last one? What does it mean?" She asked.

The lines around his eyes relaxed, and he swallowed as if he were gathering his courage. "My sister has always been gifted, and . . . and my mother made sure that she used her gifts to become sadistic. When she was younger, Mother encouraged Elsha to create elaborate ways to tease other children. Somehow, my sister invented a mark that linked other magic together, and she would use it to torment the children of our servants. She would link ticklishness with immobility, then add in incontinence, or some such cruelty. She was made to be heartless, but this . . . this is something else entirely."

"I don't understand," Gemma said, turning back to look at the corridor. She could see the four shapes along the ceiling, mocking her. Then her gaze fell upon a fifth shape—tiny and well hidden—at the bottom of the door frame, nearly invisible even from here. She couldn't have seen it had she not been standing so far away from the door.

She pointed at it, but Devery shook his head. "I can't see them. They must've been made especially for you." He handed her the notebook, and she copied down the new tiny mark.

"That's the deactivation mark," he groaned. "If you touch it, the trap will be disarmed." There was a steely edge to his voice that she didn't like.

"So I just have to walk up and touch it?" she asked, disbelieving.

He drew in a deep breath through his nose and said, "No. If it isn't as bright, that means that the last mark will not activate unless you set off the first three. I . . . goddess-damn her, Gem. I'd do it for you in a heartbeat, but the link mark must be coded for you. I don't think I can."

Gemma's heart pounded in her chest, but she nodded. "It's all right," she said softly. "These five, and then we're in." She leaned in and kissed the side of his nose, which was wet with tears. "I'm going to need a lift, though."

Somehow Tollan found himself standing in the center of the Black Corridor with Gemma's right foot on his shoulder. Wince stood next to him, supporting her other foot. Devery stood in front of them, facing her, his arms outstretched to catch her, while Elam and Isbit took up the spaces behind them in case she fell backward.

"This is the worst prickling idea anyone has ever had," Wince growled quietly.

"Goddess, Wince. Thank you for pointing that out. Whatever would I do without you to tell me things I couldn't possibly figure out on my own?" Gemma snipped. Her foot shifted carefully on Tollan's shoulder.

Wince grunted something unintelligible in the shadows as their lone torch guttered precariously on the stone floor.

"All right," she said sharply. "I'm going to touch it now." A wave of tingling mage work rushed over them as Gemma began to curse.

"Mother-prickling mages," she grumbled as she groped around, her hand planting itself firmly on Tollan's head. "Dev, I'm going to hop down."

Devery reached up, touching her hand and giving her something to hold on to as she jumped catlike to the ground.

"Aegos," she hissed, a rising note of fear in her voice. "Keep talking. It's blacker than the Void."

Devery kept up a running commentary of what they were doing as they moved forward to the second mark. When Tollan and Wince were in position, Devery said, "Gem, I'm going to take your blades. All right?"

She hesitated for a second, then nodded. "Yes, I . . . think you should."

Tollan watched as the assassin removed the two blades from their sheaths at her waist, then slipped his hands into her sleeves and removed another two blades from her wrists.

"Do you have on your ankle sheaths?" Devery asked her, and she nodded, coloring slightly.

"Yes. And also the other ones."

A wide grin spread across Devery's face as he removed two small daggers from beneath the cuffs at her ankles. Then he unlaced her breeches and reached down the front of them as he kissed her deeply before removing two more slender blades.

"Sacred goddess," Wince murmured.

"It's a pair of sheaths on my thigh, you prickling pervert," Gemma chuckled.

Tollan took a deep breath as they lifted Gemma into position. This was the fear mark. Tollan had a difficult time imagining Gemma Antos being truly afraid of anything, ever. He just didn't think she had it in her.

But the scream that ripped its way out of her spoke otherwise. She scrambled backward, slipping and clawing her way down his back until she was on all fours like an animal. "Get away from me!" She shrieked, crabbing backward. "I know he's here! I know what he did! Stay away from me, Devery, you murdering shit, or I'll gut you!" Her voice kept rising, both in pitch and volume, as she tried to dash away from them.

Elam grabbed her and wrapped his arms around her shoulders. "Shhh," he whispered. "It's all right. I'm here. Nothing bad is going to happen." Tollan could hear the lie in his words, and so, it seemed, could Gemma.

"You're going to leave me, Elam!" she sobbed, fighting against him. "You're going to run off with King Tollan the

Innocent and never, ever come back! You're going to leave me with Devery and he's going to murder me and I'm going to be all alone when he does."

Tollan watched as Devery moved toward her. His blue eyes were wide with guilt. He motioned to Tollan and Wince, who stepped forward hesitantly. Isbit, Tollan noticed, had backed away, her mouth open but silent.

They manhandled Gemma. There was no other word for it, as the four of them wrestled her forward and thrust her, screaming and sobbing, upward toward the third mark. She flailed, trying to fight against her terror blindly, the sounds of her fear raggedly echoing through the corridor. Then her hand brushed the ceiling and the tenor of her screams changed.

Never had Tollan heard such agony. Even the sounds that Riquin Hawkbeard had made as Isbit had tortured him were dwarfed by the immensity of Gemma's pain. She writhed, falling forward into Devery's arms.

No man should have been able to catch a woman her size falling from that height, but the assassin did. Tears streamed down his face as he strode forward, cradling his lover as she screamed, clawing, writhing and tearing at him.

A moan of misery escaped Elam's lips, though Tollan could barely hear it over the sound of Gemma's pain. As a group, they moved forward. Isbit carried the torch, her green eyes gone cold.

Devery laid Gemma on the ground and kissed her head. "I love you, Gem," he said, as he pressed her hand against the spot that Gemma had shown him.

An enormous wave of magic rolled over them, stealing the

breath from Tollan's lungs. Silence fell as Gemma's head lolled to one side.

This time when Gemma awoke, there was no fog of confusion. She knew exactly where she was and why she was there. She remembered the absolute crushing blackness that had descended as she touched the first mark. She remembered the terror that sunk its claws into her, dragging out every fear that she had. She remembered the things she'd said to Devery and Elam. And she remembered the pain, as if every bone in her body had been pulverized into powder and set aflame. She remembered, and she was furious.

She leaped to her feet. Elam, Tollan, Wince and Isbit shrank back from her, but Devery stepped closer, his hands raised in surrender. "You're all right. The mark is gone."

"I know it's prickling gone," she growled. "I'm ready to go in. Why are we sitting around here with our thumbs up our asses?"

Devery's mouth turned up on one side. He passed her knives to her one at a time. "Aegos, Gem. How much of that brew did Lian give you?"

She winked at him, brushing off the question. He was right. Her blood was singing, but it wasn't the brew. She could taste her revenge. It would all be over very soon. She slid the last of her knives back into its sheath. Then she smiled broadly. "Come here."

He flowed into her arms.

"I'm sorry," she said, burying her face in his shirt.

He reached up, lifting her face until she met his gaze. "No," he said, an edge to his words. "I'm sorry. I gave you a reason to fear me, and I will spend the rest of my life making it up to you. I swear it by the goddess."

She brushed away the tears that threatened, then said, "I like the sound of that."

Moments later, she pressed her hands to the door. She waited, double-checking to be sure there were no more traps. She exhaled loudly, then turned to her friends. "Here goes everything."

She twisted the diamond handle and the door swung open. As the edge of the door passed before her face, she saw a flare of light, an instant before she felt the nerve-tingling wave of mage work. She gasped and tried to shove the door closed, but it opened of its own volition.

Gemma waited for the pain, for fire and poison and death, but none came. Only the almost nauseating shiver of magic rushing against her skin. She turned to look at the group, but her gaze fell on Devery, whose blue eyes had gone wide with fear.

He took a step toward her, and the sound of his footfall echoed in the corridor.

As quickly as the magic had come, it passed. The waves of magery disappeared into nothingness and Devery stood before Gemma with strands of silver at his temples.

She opened her mouth to speak, but he interrupted her. "The mark of unmaking," he said. He reached up to touch her face, and all the sinuous grace he'd possessed slipped away. He was just a man. His mouth curved up in a wry smile. "A gift from my mother."

Her heart hammered in her chest. This man—her man—had just lost a piece of himself. Aspects of him had disappeared, yet he was making jokes. "Are you all right?" she asked.

"I will be," he said calmly. "Let's go get our daughter." She knew there was something he wasn't telling her. Something he wouldn't say in front of the others.

Her tongue grew thick with emotion, and she nodded, unable to speak. Would all of his years catch up with him now? What kind of mother could do that to her son?

Her gaze drifted to Isbit who stood still with hard eyes and the air of a caged beast. Looking at the Queen of Above, Gemma made a promise to herself. *I'm going to be a better mother than Brinna or Isbit.*

She reached up and ran her fingers through Devery's suddenly silvering hair. "Let's go." She kissed him.

CHAPTER TWENTY-TWO

THE PALACE

Tollan was confused. Something had happened between Gemma and Devery. Some change had come over the assassin that he couldn't quite understand, but Elam was clearly distraught. As they shuffled into the palace, Tollan took hold of Elam's arm. "What's going on?"

"I'm not sure, but . . . Devery's not right."

It was clear to everyone that the strangely gifted assassin had disappeared, and in his place was an average, somewhat older man.

"What's happened?" Tollan asked, louder this time.

But Gemma wasn't in the mood for conversation. She flung open the door to the hallway. "If you would be so kind, Your Grace?"

As Isbit pushed past him to take her place at the front of the group, she grabbed Tollan and embraced him awkwardly. "Keep yourself alive," she whispered into his hair. "No one else matters but us."

Tollan opened his mouth to argue with her, but she was already gone. He turned to his friends and saw that both Elam and Wince had heard. He shook his head, hoping that they would see his thoughts. Hoping beyond reason that they had even a spark of the connection that Elam had with his friends from Under.

Tollan's sword trembled in his hand as they followed Isbit through the vacant corridors of the southern wing of the palace. He wished, at the very least, that he had his good sword. The last he'd seen of his sword, it had been dripping with his father's blood, and he'd thought that this was all just a misunderstanding. How stupid and naive he'd been, then. How innocent.

Without warning, Elam reached out and caught his hand. Their eyes met, and Elam winked. *How does he always know just what I need?* Tollan drew a deep breath. *Time to be strong. Time to be brave. Time to be a man.* He squeezed Elam's hand back. He could do this. He could do anything with Elam by his side.

Suddenly, Gemma stopped. Halfway across the hallway, she turned and looked to the right. She held up a hand, motioning them to follow her, then headed quietly down the hall. Tollan caught his mother's tunic in his fingers and she arched an eyebrow before following after Gemma. Her blade quivered in her hand, and the glint of mania in her eyes made Tollan's heart hurt. Promising his mother Above was a mistake—he didn't know why he hadn't realized it before.

They were twenty feet down the hall when Tollan heard the crying, but Gemma was already racing toward the door of the library. Devery drew his sword and followed her. Wince went charging after them.

When Tollan entered, he found Gemma standing over a dark-haired woman in dirty palace livery. Her hair was in tangles, and she leaned protectively over a person lying prone on a chaise. The woman looked up, her eyes wide and terrified.

"Oh, no," she whispered, her voice cracking. "If they find you here, they'll kill you for sure. You need to go. You need to get the king out, or . . ." Her eyes drifted and landed on Tollan. She stiffened. "You're dead," she said. "They . . . they said you were dead. They put the mark on . . ." She looked down, and it was only then that Tollan looked at the chaise.

Madness broke out in the library as Tollan recognized his brother at the same time that Isbit laid eyes on her youngest son. Iven's eyes were open but unseeing, and he wasn't breathing. Every inch of his skin appeared to be mage marked, and many of the marks festered and oozed. He was naked and covered in layers of blood and his own filth. Isbit's howl of grief quickly took on the tone of an angry bear, and she grabbed hold of the maid. "Where are they?" She gripped the maid's chin in her hand. "Where are those bitches?"

A pain that he could not name clenched Tollan's insides—guilt mixed with grief and rage to create a swirling, nauseating hole that threatened to swallow him. At the same time, he suddenly acknowledged his own feelings of terror. He suddenly realized how well and truly pricked they were. If the mage women could do this, he and his companions didn't stand a chance, and their best weapon was starting to look more and more like a middle-aged shopkeeper. He tried not to glance at his brother, tried to ignore the bitter truth. *I should have come sooner. I should have died trying. I should have known . . .*

"They're in the throne room," the maid whimpered. "I've been hiding in here for days, and then they brought him in and dumped him here. I heard them say that they'd wait for the dregs in the throne room."

Wince reached up and gently but firmly removed Isbit's hands from the maid's face. "Where is everyone else?" he asked. "Where are the guards and the servants? Where are the . . ."

"Dead," the maid croaked. "They're all dead. They don't know I'm here, I . . . I was too afraid and I hid."

Tollan couldn't understand the guilt that he heard in her voice. Of course she had hidden. What sane person wouldn't? But then his gaze drifted back to his brother and he understood. Guilt didn't live in the same house as reason and there was a hole in Tollan's mind where logic and reason were supposed to live. He had failed so completely that his brother lay bloodied and maimed by magic, his entire house had been massacred. Everyone he had ever lived with was gone, and the blame lay at his feet. "Dead?" he murmured, confused. "But I . . . I wanted to save him . . . " Tears were starting to well in his eyes and he feared that he would collapse into a pile of his own despair.

But there was no more time for his grief. Isbit rushed out the door, braids flying. His mother would make no time for sorrow. She only desired vengeance and power.

Gemma cursed under her breath and followed after her, and Tollan trailed after Elam and Devery, with Wince supporting the sobbing maid behind him.

The two queens led them through the remainder of the southern wing and into the belly of the palace without slowing down until they reached the enormous mahogany doors that led to the throne room. As Isbit made to push them open, Gemma turned to exchange a glance with Elam and Devery. In unison, they snapped their fingers twice. Then Tollan's mother pushed the doors open and released the Void.

Wince wanted to pull everyone backward—back through the palace, out past the Golden Door, beyond the tunnels and back to Dockside. He wanted a minute to catch his breath and figure out what had happened—what was still happening—and how best to deal with it. He wanted to comfort Tollan, for he knew that the sight of his brother in such a condition must have pained Tollan greatly. But events were moving at breakneck speed, and he had no time to do anything more than make wishes.

Something was wrong with Devery. Something terminal. He was slow and his shoulders were hunched, and Wince was fairly sure that his hair had gone suddenly gray.

Queen Isbit was dragging them ever forward, careening toward the confrontation that he dreaded would destroy them all. She was oblivious to all consequences as she charged headlong toward the throne room and vengeance. Wince had always feared Tollan's mother, but this was something else entirely. And she'd already told Tollan that no one else mattered. He knew without a doubt that she would throw away every last one of them in an attempt to right the wrongs she'd been dealt. He glanced at Tollan and saw actual fear on his face. No mother should instill that kind of terror in her child.

Wince could see the enormous polished wood doors that led to the throne room. It was now or never. He met Elam's gaze and a silent discussion happened in an instant. Elam's hand twitched in his pocket, where Wince knew he kept the reed that held the poisoned needle. Should he use it?

As they neared the doors, Gemma hissed, "Isbit, wait!" but the Queen of Above ignored her. As panic took hold of Wince, he tried to remember what Lian had said when she'd pulled the two of them aside and given Elam the reed just before they left.

"Mistress Melnora always had me keep a few made up," she'd said, *as she carefully dropped the thin reed capped with wax into Elam's hand. "She said you never know when you might have to take out one of your own."* *She'd looked at Wince, then. "And you'll need to serve as Elam's eyes. You know those of the Above better than he does. If it's one of them, you let him know, in whatever way is necessary."* *She had trusted him, and it had felt like an enormous gift to Wince, at the time.*

"Who do you think . . ." *his voice had broken.*

She shrugged. "We eat lies like sweets here in Under, and I suppose Above isn't all that different. It could be anyone. You'll know it when you see it. It won't kill. It'll just . . . take them out of the equation temporarily."

Elam wrapped his hand around the reed, his face showing a mixture of awe and dread. "What if it's me?" he asked.

She'd grinned. "It won't be either of you. It's not how you're built."
She patted his hand thoughtfully. "But, Elam. Don't rule out the
possibility that it could be Gemma."

But it wasn't Gemma. Not this time, anyway. Gemma's rage was fiery and smoldering, but it was the kind of anger you could predict, and it did nothing to blunt the edges of her feelings. Isbit, however, had gone as cold as the depths of the Hadriak, and she no longer bothered to look beyond the borders of her own hatred.

Elam took one more look at Tollan, and Wince saw the moment he made his decision.

The door flew open as he pulled the needle from his pocket. "Isbit!" Elam called, just to grab her attention. They only needed her to hesitate for a heartbeat. He only needed to break the skin.

Wince held his breath and said a silent prayer.

There was no time to think, no time to breathe. Gemma tried to recount their plan. All two hundred of the Ain were in the tunnels, guarding against escape. The dozen sellswords and eight assassins who were still awake were stationed beyond the burning brambles at the front doors of the palace, and Lian was supervising the remaining members of the Guild who surrounded the palace of Yigris.

But Gemma and Dev and Elam and the rest were just as trapped as the mages were now, and Isbit refused to slow down. They needed to gather their wits and come up with an attack plan, but the Queen of Above had gone mad with grief and fury.

Gemma understood. Somewhere beneath the buzzing in her veins and the pounding of adrenaline in her chest, she remembered. Even if they won today, she had lost. Her throat grew thick with pain for an instant, before she smelled peaches and cinnamon, and her breathing eased. She would grieve properly, after. Right now, she had to get Katya back. Right now, she had to protect Devery. Right now, Isbit was flinging open the doors to their doom.

"Isbit!" Elam called as he slipped past Gemma. The Queen of Above paused for just an instant. Elam reached out, his hand brushing Isbit's arm, and the queen slumped to the ground.

"What the prickling Void?" Gemma cursed, gaze darting about as she searched for danger.

Gemma's bowels rumbled. *Goddess, had Elam just killed Isbit?*

Then Elam slipped his hand into his pocket and winked at her. He snapped his fingers, twice, then stood and spread his arms wide. "Regency," he said formally. "If you would."

But she had no time to think. From within the throne room, a voice rang out.

"I had hoped you were dead, you piece of Yigrisian trash. Where is my son?"

Gemma stopped, surveying the room. A young woman with pale flaxen hair sat stiffly on the throne. She wore an immense silver crown, and her eyes were flint and ice. The four captive mage women sat on a bench. Their shoulders were slumped, and their hair hung ragged and dirty around their faces. They did not seem to notice that anyone else was in the room, and they certainly didn't seem as if they'd recently gained their freedom. Gemma had expected them to be aiding Brinna and Elsha, but they sat like statues, and Gemma realized that she was still missing a piece of the puzzle.

She had no time to dwell on it, though, because Brinna held Katya at arm's length, her hand wrapped around the back of the girl's neck. Her other hand burst into flame as Gemma watched. The heat rippled the air around them, and Katya winced, struggling to pull away.

Brinna waved her burning hand in the air. "Ah, there you are," she said, her blue eyes lit with madness. "Now, come here like a good lad so I don't have to hurt Katy. You know it's the last thing I'd want to do."

For an instant, Gemma forgot that Devery wasn't Devery anymore, and she almost smiled, knowing that in a heartbeat he'd cut Brinna to bits for threatening his daughter. But as Gemma heard the plodding footsteps behind her, reality came crashing down around her. "No!" she hissed. He reached out, patting her shoulder as he walked past. It was a half-hearted gesture. He wasn't even looking at her. His gaze remained focused on Katya. But as his hand slipped down her arm, he snapped his fingers. Once. Twice. Three times.

Have patience.

"That's much better, Devery," his mother said, as if she were speaking to a toddler. "Come to Mother so that I don't have to punish you any further. You look terrible, son."

An animal fierceness was building in Gemma. Her legs trembled with pent-up adrenaline, and her mouth was dry. Her hand slipped to the hilt of the blade at her hip.

Devery stopped a few feet in front of his mother. "Let Katya go, Mother, and I'll come willingly. You don't have to hurt her. She's . . . she's a gift, remember. She's just a little girl."

Brinna chuckled. "You've always been soft, Devery. My little experiment with you failed, and I didn't make you nearly hard enough. You were an excellent killer, love, but you still thought you had choices."

The fire in Brinna's hand went out unexpectedly, and a small wave of mage work washed across Gemma's face. Brinna released the girl, who crashed sobbing into Devery's arms. He bent and whispered something into her hair, and she nodded. He hugged her tightly and kissed her on the forehead. Then he released her. She ran toward Gemma with wide, tear-filled eyes.

Gemma caught Katya, and wrapped her in her arms. Brinna turned Devery around and pushed him to his knees. She placed one hand on his head. "I never should have left you with free will," she snarled as she began to trace a character in the air with her fingertip. "I'll give you back all of your gifts just as soon as I have a tighter leash on you."

Gemma stared at Devery, paralyzed. Her heart caught in her throat, terror and pain roaring in her mind for her attention. The blood in her veins pounded so loudly that it was all she could hear, and all she could see was the fear in his eyes. It tore at her soul.

Devery's eyes widened, holding Gemma's gaze with his own. Brinna continued to draw her elaborate mark in the air.

Devery began to snap his fingers.

One.

Two.

Three.

Four.

He stared into her eyes, as if willing her to understand. Gemma shook her head, defiant. It was the code they'd never used.

One meant "run!"

Two meant "I've got your backside."

Three meant "have patience."

And four meant "kill me."

Katya was sobbing into Gemma's shirt, her fingertips running aimlessly along the skin of Gemma's arm. Gemma wanted to push her away. She needed to get to Devery, to save him from whatever evil his mother was going to make him do. She was not going to kill Devery, no matter what he asked her to do.

"No!" Gemma screamed, just as fire raced up her arm, a wave of mage work nearly knocking her from her feet. She looked down, meeting Katya's gaze.

Devery's daughter grinned up at her. Then she stepped aside. She snapped her fingers just once.

Run!

Gemma could feel magic coursing through her. Her body felt capable of anything. She was beside them, blade in hand, before Brinna had any idea that the tide had turned. Gemma reached out, pushing Devery aside. It took no more effort than shooing away a fly. He dropped out of the way, wearing a smile as wide as the room.

Gemma didn't give the woman time to speak. She didn't give her time to draw a last breath. "Prick you, Brinna," she growled as she drove the knife into the mage woman's belly and lifted upward, gutting her just as she'd promised she would. She didn't pause to admire her work. She turned back toward Katya just in time to see the Void break loose.

Tollan had watched Isbit slump over, and he felt as if he was supposed to do something. But in truth, all he'd felt was relief. Her headfirst dive into destruction had been halted, and while he hoped she would be all right, he was glad that she wouldn't be dragging the people he cared about down with her. He ignored the maid's whimpers and moved next to Elam, who knelt beside Isbit.

"Is she all right? What happened?" Tollan asked.

Elam rolled Isbit onto her back and placed his fingers on her throat. He nodded, his brow furrowed. "She'll be fine." Something in his tone made the hair on Tollan's neck stand up, but he didn't have time to analyze it because he heard someone speaking to Gemma.

Whatever was happening, Tollan suddenly knew that it was his responsibility to help them. It was House Daghan that had held the mage women as slaves. His grandfather and great-grandfather had forced them, against their will, to serve the crown. He would not sit idly by while the Under bore the brunt of his family's failings. "We have to help them," he said, meeting Wince's gaze.

To his credit, Wince simply nodded and drew his sword. Tollan stood, looking down at Elam. "I'll be right back," he said softly. And he was grateful that his voice trembled only a little.

They strode into the room with more bravado than Tollan felt. Katya was sobbing against Gemma's chest, and Lady Brinna had Devery on his knees. She was drawing a mage mark in the air, and Gemma was trembling.

Across the room, someone shrieked. Princess Elsha stood before the throne, wearing a crown of silver that he'd never seen before. "You!" she screamed. "You're dead! You're . . . you're ruining everything!" Where once had been the cool, poised princess he saw a woman who had given over to madness. She looked at him with such a particular hatred, as if he had personally done something unforgivable to her, as if he'd murdered all that she loved. The intensity of her gaze sent a shiver through him.

Suddenly, both mage women were scrawling characters in the air. "You have to die," Elsha said, as her mark began to take shape. Her voice had taken on a mechanical quality. "Everything I've done, everything I've given up. You have to die."

Then Gemma shrieked, and he couldn't help but look at her for an instant, even though Elsha was taking aim at him. But it was only an instant. Because suddenly, Gemma was moving toward Lady Brinna with the same awe-inspiring grace and speed that Devery had once possessed. "Balls!" Wince groaned, drawing his attention back to Elsha, who wore an expression of glee.

The mark that she drew was intricate and terrifying. It bore all the characteristics of the other marks he'd seen, but there was something sinister about it as it took shape. The pattern shivered with dark sparks and even his untrained eye could see the menacing nature of it as she made the elaborate swoops and curving lines.

As she finished the mark with a flourish, Elsha stepped back, watching as the writhing black miasma she had made took on a life of its own. It pulsed and throbbed, waiting to be released by its maker. Elsha smiled coldly at him. "Time to die, Tollan. There's nowhere to escape to this time."

Before Tollan could do anything, Wince pushed his way in front of him. He didn't even have his blade up—he just thrust his chest out, waiting to catch the death mark as it raced toward them.

Their friendship flashed through Tollan's mind. The hours they had spent training together, the endless games of tag and Four Fat Fathers. Their rides with Uri and their secret trips into the city. Agony erupted in the pit of Tollan's stomach. He would not let Wince die for him. Wince had accepted him for who he was even when he could not accept himself. He wouldn't let that be stolen from the world.

"I love you, brother," he said, as he pressed his foot into the back of Wince's knee and watched his oldest friend tumble to the floor. It was a damned dirty trick, but one he had played on his friend a dozen times. He stepped over Wince to meet his fate, and as the darkness swallowed him, he felt no pain. He felt pride for the man he'd become.

Wince could see that Tollan was dead, could tell by the vacancy in his eyes. Whatever brightness the goddess had breathed into him upon his birth had gone as the swirling black death mark struck him.

The throne room was silent. Wince tried to breathe but air refused to move in or out of his lungs. He pressed a hand to his mouth and bent over, trying to unsee what he'd seen. Tollan couldn't be dead. He'd only just begun to live.

Wince's field of vision narrowed until all he could see was the gray of Tollan's eyes. He could see in them a history that was now lost—the three of them, Tollan, Wince, and Uri. They had left him alone in a world he didn't want to face without them. A tear slid down from his eye, and as it hit the polished stone floor, sound flooded back into his ears. His gaze widened. Air filled his lungs.

A sound—the keening of the truly brokenhearted—shattered the silence. Elam had run to Tollan's side and collapsed beside him, sobbing into Tollan's stilled chest. "Why did you do that? Why didn't you get out of the way, you stupid, beautiful man?"

Wince thought that perhaps he should go to him, but he couldn't quite wrap his mind around what Elam was saying. Why hadn't they gotten out of the way? Why had he believed that he had to die to protect Tollan?

In Above, he had been raised on stories of knights that battle beasts to save a damsel in distress and men that died to save the ones they loved. He nearly choked on the irony as he realized once again how foolish the things he had learned Above had truly been.

His eyes were drawn to Elsha. Her laughter was like a knife. She looked like Devery. They had the same eyes, though Wince doubted that any warmth had ever touched Elsha's gaze. Her face was split by a smile that spoke of absolute victory. There were no damsels in this room that required rescuing. She had accomplished her goal. The House of Daghan was dead, when they could have simply jumped out of the way.

Suddenly, Gemma crashed into Elsha at inhuman speed. With two flicks of her wrists, Devery's sister was missing both of her drawing fingers.

Elsha hissed at her. "Do you think that will stop me, you sewer rat?" She stuck out her tongue and licked at the stump of her right hand. A mage mark flared on her tongue, and Wince watched in awe and disgust as the severed finger grew back. "You can't win," she said, then licked at the other hand. "Don't you know that, yet? There's nothing you can do that I haven't prepared for. I was born for this. Revenge is my entire purpose."

Gemma had not expected that. Hadn't Devery said that there was no mark to grow body parts back? Apparently, his sister knew something he didn't, but Gemma didn't have time to wonder because a voice behind her drew her attention.

"Stop it!" Katya pleaded. "Please, Aunt Elsha! Stop! You don't have to . . . "

Gemma stared at the little girl, wide-eyed, for the span of a heartbeat. Elsha snapped a mark into existence in front of her, and it came flying toward Gemma, its edges sizzling like acid. At the last instant, Gemma dodged to the side, then launched herself at Elsha. Her blade bit into the Vagan woman's side, leaving a rent in her gown six inches long. The mage mark hit the wall and ate a hole through the paneling.

Katya ran toward them, putting herself too close to the fighting for Gemma's comfort. "Please," she cried, as tears streamed down her face. "Please listen to me! It doesn't have to be like this. The end of this doesn't have to hurt!"

Elsha howled in pain, but then she placed her hand on her side. A visible wave of mage work spread outward from her and she grimaced, "Silly Katy, in the end, everything hurts." She turned her attention back to Gemma. "Do you really think that a knife is going to kill a fully trained mage queen?" She flicked her wrist, and another mark sparked into existence—this time a ball of flame. It catapulted toward Gemma, who ducked, then somersaulted toward Elsha.

"Your mother's dead, Elsha. We'll free the other—" Elsha interrupted her with a mark that turned into a sword. It shot through the air like an arrow directly toward Gemma, who had to dive to the side to avoid being impaled.

As she launched herself out of the way of the flying blade, Gemma caught a glimpse of Katya, who was standing stiffly, her head tilted to the side as if she were listening to something with all her attention. "Mite, get out of the way! She'll kill us both if we're not careful!"

"It just goes to show," said Elsha, her gaze lingering on Gemma's blade, "how little you really understand about anything. I have nothing left to lose. Nothing!" she screamed, her eyes bulging with the effort. "I've lost the only person who ever loved me. I've given up everything for this vendetta, and I..."

"That's not true, Auntie. I know it seems like it is. I... I can hear the pain inside you. You miss him so, but..." Katya's voice was as sincere as Gemma had ever heard her. "You can still have him. He's alive," she said, solemnly. "Cadry is alive."

Gemma couldn't help but glance at her. Katya meant every word that she was saying. The little girl's heart was written across her face and she wanted Gemma to let her aunt live.

Gemma turned to look at Devery. She needed to know what he thought. She didn't know whether she should trust Katya's instincts, but she knew she could trust his. But the man that she loved was collapsed in a heap on the floor, his breathing shaky and shallow. Devery didn't have time for her to waste.

She glanced back at Elsha, whose eyes were wide with shock. "What did you say?" Tears filled her eyes. "Are you sure? Is it true?" Her voice shook.

Just then, Gemma saw Elam stand up behind Elsha. He grabbed the mage woman by the hair and yanked her head backward. "No, Elam!" The words had barely left her lips when Elam slammed the blade of his dagger into Elsha's throat, then yanked it sideways. Gemma could only watch in horror as a gurgling noise bubbled up from the opening in Elsha's throat. Elam spat through his tears, "You're wrong, Princess. You didn't prepare for everything. You didn't prepare for me."

He continued to hold her by the hair as blood spurted down Elsha's regal gown. Her cold blue eyes whirled in panic for a few seconds, and then they just stared fixedly into nothing. After a few more seconds, the blood stopped spurting and Elam tossed Elsha's body to the floor like trash.

"Prick!" he howled, staring down at his bloody hands.

Gemma didn't know who to help first. Wince still sobbed over Tollan's body. Elam, hands bloodstained, stood as if he were lost, his gaze fixed on Elsha's corpse. Katya was huddled on the floor, sobbing into her hands, and Devery was pushing himself to stand.

With a grunt of decision, she moved toward Katya. "Oh, mite, I'm so sorry. That must have been awful for you." She bent over and wrapped her arms around the girl's shoulders. She really was just a spit of a thing, far too small to have seen such horrors.

Katya looked up and met Gemma's gaze. "I . . . I didn't know, until . . . I couldn't hear her, before. But in her mind, she was so sad. She just wanted him back, the boy that Grandmother took from her."

Gemma stared at her. "What do you mean? In her mind? You could . . . you could hear her thoughts?"

Katya nodded. "I can hear everyone's thoughts, if they're loud enough."

"Loud? I don't . . . " Gemma looked to Devery, who had

managed to join them. He glanced sadly at his sister's corpse, then met Gemma's gaze.

"Katy," he said. "How long have you been able to do this?" The look in his eyes told Gemma that this was a revelation to him, as well.

Katya wiped her face on the sleeve of her dress and stood up, forcing Gemma to stand up, too. The three of them stood, ignoring the bodies and the blood around them as Katya replied, "Always, though I didn't know what it meant when I was little. I've always heard thoughts that are strong. Feelings that are pure and true and honest." She blushed, slightly. "That's why I knew to trust you, right away, because my Papa thought so loudly about you."

Devery, silver-haired and wrinkled, winked at Gemma. "It's true. I do have some embarrassingly loud thoughts about you."

Gemma couldn't bring herself to smile. Not after all that had happened. "What did you hear in Aunt Elsha's thoughts, Katy?"

Katya met her gaze with large, sad eyes. "It's so sad. She was in love with a boy at Magehold when she was young, but Grandmother took him away from her. Kept him locked up, so that Auntie would do as she wished. I heard Grandmother think about him often, but I didn't know who he was, until today. Aunt Elsha thought that he was gone forever, and that is why she wouldn't stop. She thought there was nothing left for her in the world."

She glanced at her aunt's body, then said, "I could never hear her thoughts before. She kept everything so quiet and hidden so deep inside of her, I don't know if she even knew it was there.

But something broke inside of her, today. The broken thing exploded within her, slicing through her until she was only rage and ruin." Katya drew in a deep breath. "She said that in her thoughts. 'I am rage. I am ruin.' She kept saying it, over and over, like she was trying to convince herself of it. But the thing that she wanted loudest . . . she just wanted to be loved again."

Devery coughed wetly, and Gemma looked up at him with a rush of panic. If she hadn't known any better, she'd have thought the man standing with his arm around the little girl was Devery's father. He had aged three decades and was getting older before their eyes.

"Hey, beautiful," Devery said, as he reached up to brush a tear from her face. He groaned as if that much movement had pained him. "It's not your fault. Elsha chose her path. We all choose our path." The weight of everything that had ever passed between them—the precious and the painful—was encapsulated in his expression.

She met his gaze, and a sob slipped from between her lips. "You're getting so old." A sad, fearful chuckle escaped her.

"What?" he said, grinning lasciviously. "You don't find older men attractive?"

She wrapped her arms around his fragile frame and breathed in the smell of him, afraid to let him go.

He leaned into her and said, "I chose my path, too. Don't cry for me." She could smell his skin and feel his breath against her neck, and though he didn't look the same, she would know this man anywhere.

"Gemma," Katya interrupted, tugging on Gemma's shirt

sleeve. "Papa . . . I think I can fix it. But I need some help."

The little girl was so full of hope, even now. She still thought that stories came with happy endings. Gemma didn't think that there was such a thing, as she heard another sob force its way out from between Elam's lips. His chance for a happy ending lay dead on the floor, and hers was aging before her eyes. She watched as Elam went to join Wince in mourning what would never be and her heart broke into more pieces than she could count. She cried into Devery's shoulder as he trembled against her, soaking his shirt with tears he'd asked her not to shed.

"Will everyone please listen to me!"

Gemma jerked away from Devery as Katya's voice, amplified by a tiny silver mark that shimmered before her mouth, echoed throughout the throne room. All eyes turned toward the little girl whose hands were on her hips. Her eyes flashed with exasperation in a way that reminded Gemma so much of Devery that her heart ached with love for the child.

"I know you're all sad," she said, staring straight ahead as she continued. "I'm sad, too." Her voice trembled, just a little, as she continued. "Though my grandmother and aunt were wrong in the way they did things, they weren't wrong in why." Her voice dropped a little as she said, "And I loved them, in their own way. They deserved that much." Her gaze shifted to the mage women who had been captive for so long. The mage women that Gemma had completely forgotten about.

Katya looked at Devery and said, "I think they might be able to help you, Papa, but we have to help them, first. They're screaming, inside. They've been screaming for a long time. Since the day I arrived in Yigris, I've been listening to their screams."

The blunt horror of that statement hit Gemma like a punch to the throat.

Katya stepped forward and held her hand out. The silvery mage mark disappeared and her voice returned to normal. "May I have your knife, please, Gemma?"

Gemma handed the knife over to the girl, who seemed to have aged a decade before Gemma's eyes. The day's events would have changed her, left their mark on her in the unpredictable way that tragedy does. Gemma could only hope that Katy had seen the difference between letting love raise you up or allowing it to tear you apart. All she could do was serve as a guidepost. The rest was up to Katya.

"Great-grandmother."

Gemma watched as Katya knelt beside one of the mage women. Gemma thought it was the one she had seen with Tollan in the Black Chamber, the day they'd first met. That day felt like a lifetime ago, and maybe it was. The woman she had been had died that day and she would have to learn what kind of woman she had become.

"My name is Katya Nightsbane. I am the daughter of Devery, son of Brinna. I'm going to free you, now. Please remember that I mean you no harm."

Katya stretched out the mage woman's arm and pointed to a lump near the crook of her elbow. "I need to cut that lump out and remove the gold that's in there. This might hurt a little, Grandmother, but soon it will all be over."

Gemma glanced at Devery, who shook his head in response. Katya sliced through pale, parchment-thin skin, and squeezed out the small lump of gold. It flashed with dozens, if not hundreds, of mage marks. Then they faded and died, leaving only a chunk of pure Yigrisian gold sitting in the palm of her hand. She spat on it and threw it as far away from her as she could.

Then Katya began to draw a mark upon her great-grandmother's skin, and the cut began to heal on its own. Gemma watched as the woman before her began to transform. Katya looked up and met serious indigo eyes that had been nearly colorless a moment before. The mage woman's pale, wrinkled skin grew pink, and her white hair turned a honeyed brown as they all watched in open-mouthed amazement. Thin lips lifted upward into a smile as the mage woman's eyes met Katya's.

"Oh, you are very special, indeed. Aren't you, grandchild?"

CHAPTER TWENTY-THREE

GUILDHOUSE

Gemma stood in front of Guildhouse and watched as the last of the supplies were loaded into the wagon. She was sure her city would sleep more soundly knowing that the foreign mage women were finally free of their borders and it felt something like a happy ending—the mage women finally going home.

Devery rounded the corner of the porch and grinned slyly up at her. He took the stairs two at a time, and even if he wasn't as agile as he had once been, at least he was no longer stooped and rapidly aging. Hannai had refused to replace the mage marks he had once borne, but she and her surviving daughters had guided Katya as she used her magery to make him seem like a man in his twenties once more. He would age at a normal rate and live a long life. He and Gemma would have many years together.

As if he were reading her thoughts, he took her hand and ran his fingertips over the mage mark on her forearm. It was a part of her now, unless Katya undid the mage work. Gemma would remain faster, stronger and with more cunning and stamina than anyone else she knew. She would grow old at a snail's pace.

"I still can't believe she marked you with my name. It's so . . . I don't know. It feels . . . wrong."

Gemma shook her head. "It wasn't wrong to Katy. You told her to help me, and the person she trusted most to do that was you. She wove all of your most endearing qualities into one mark."

Even Hannai could not explain exactly what Katya had done when she'd marked Gemma. The older mage speculated that Katya had never learned the boundaries of her imagination. "If the child believes it can be done, then she can make a mark that makes it true. She believed in her father, and so it was with him that she marked you."

Devery worried that it resembled some sort of mark of ownership, but Gemma didn't see it that way. If anything, she saw the opposite. Katya had given her a piece of Devery to keep inside of her always. That, too, somehow felt right.

It wasn't the first time they'd had this discussion, and she brushed away his discomfort with a kiss. "I don't mind if you claim me just a little," she said.

Gemma could feel the discord coming to Yigris. They weren't out of the storm by a long shot. She knew that Isbit had plans. But here, on the porch of Guildhouse, she felt safe.

Devery kissed her once more, then went inside to collect his grandmother and aunts, just as Elam came out through the front door and stood beside her on the porch. His face was haggard and his eyes were sunken. Even Albatross Tears couldn't seem to lift the fog he'd fallen into, and Gemma hoped that the trip to sea he had planned on the *Heart's Desire* with Wince would help him find peace. But she was also acutely aware that some hurts could only be dulled, never healed. As they stared off into the distance, experiencing two very different emotions, Elam sighed beside her.

"Are you going to be all right?" she asked, squeezing his hand.

"Yes," he whispered.

She didn't call him on it.

They were of Under, and they lied the way most people pissed.

EPILOGUE

The air was musty and cold, and there was no light. Fear gripped his chest, and Tollan had to still himself to calmness. Deep breaths. His hands fumbled around him, but he felt nothing but a stone surface.

He sat up slowly and licked his parched lips. Deep breaths. It felt as if he couldn't get enough air, as if his lungs would never be full again. He ran his hands across his face and down his chest. Something crinkled in his tunic pocket. Clumsily, he pulled it out.

Light flared before his eyes. A swirling silver mark. Mage work. He squinted against the sudden brightness, his heart pounding in his chest as he examined the single folded sheet of parchment. He unfolded it as his eyes adjusted to the light. A letter, written in an unfamiliar hand.

King Tollan,

I do not know if this experiment will work. Perhaps, far in the future, a Yigrisian grave robber will find this letter and wonder.

For more than one hundred fifty years, I was no more than an animal that your family kept as a pet, and that sort of thing is not forgiven lightly.

I do not forgive. However, in all my years within the Yigrisian Palace, only you took the time to learn my name, and so I hope that, perhaps, you are different from the others.

As the greater queen told your great-grandfather, gold absorbs magery, swallowing up the gifts that Aegos gave us. This was how House Daghan controlled me and my daughters for all those years. It is this secret that I hope has saved you as well.

When I placed the cursed mark of the King of Yigris upon your back, I used a gold-dusted blade. If I'm right, then the mage work that Elsha used against you will slowly be absorbed by the gold within your blood, and you will one day awaken as if from a great sleep.

I have given you our greatest secret. Do not prove my trust unwarranted, King Tollan. If I am right and you wake up, do not bring my wrath down upon your city. Use this chance to make Yigris a better place.

It is done now between us. Leave it as such.

Waking up from the dead wasn't a comfortable experience, at least not so far as Tollan could see. The dim light from the mage-marked letter showed him the interior of the Daghan family crypt—stone and hard edges, much like his family. He was sitting upon a stone altar surrounded by the corpses of flowers and the ash of spent incense. Sighing, he ran his hand over the top of his head, then yanked it back in surprise. His head was shaved bald. His heart began to pound in his chest.

Of course I've been shaved. They buried me. They shaved my head and washed my body and sprinkled me with salt and herbs and laid me in the crypt.

He could almost picture his mother, carrying the braid of his hair, twisting it in her grief. The image did little to still his trembling breath.

Air came in gasps as he pushed himself to stand up. Pain ripped through him, fire tracing a line from his lower back down his left leg. He tried to stretch out his leg, hoping to ease the cramp, but even the barest movement sent sharp bolts of pain through his nerves.

Glancing around, he let out a slow moan that built into a sob. On the next altar lay his brother, his body marred by the scars of the mage marks that had killed him, his head shaved of every hair.

Fighting through the pain, Tollan stumbled to his brother's side. Despite the chill of the underground crypt, time had begun to play havoc with Iven's corpse. Tollan tried to ignore it, but his eyes were drawn to the dark spots at the corners of Iven's eyes and mouth, his gaze lingering on the place where his younger brother's cheek had begun to cave inward.

He choked back a wail as he wavered on his weakened legs. The smell of decay lingered near his brother like a courtesan's perfume. Gagging, Tollan clutched at Iven's swollen hand. "I'm sorry, Iven. I'm so sorry I didn't save you. I failed you. I failed…" His voice betrayed him, and he lost his ability to form words or coherent thought.

His back and legs burned in agony, but he pushed himself to stay at his brother's side until his tears ran dry. When he was reduced to sniffling and gagging, he released Iven's hand and looked past him to the next stone bed.

His father's body had fared even worse than Iven's, but Tollan had no tears for King Abram. He felt nothing when he looked at the man—an absence of feeling that only intensified the physical pain. Abram Daghan, King of Above, had been laid to rest with every hair on his head left intact. His own wife had damned him to the Void without regret.

He stumbled away from them, clutching the lighted parchment in front of him like a beacon. Beyond his father lay the body of a woman, petite in stature, her head shorn. She was not shrouded in flowers and herbs, and no ashes lay beside her. Instead, in one hand she clutched a candle to light her way, and in the other, a foot-long dagger.

He silently paid his respects to Melnora before hobbling past her. Seeing her here gave him the briefest whisper of hope. The Queen of Under would not have been carried through the streets to the crypt. That was simply not their way. She'd have come through the tunnels.

He dragged himself to the wall of the crypt, his muscles trembling against the sheer force of the pain in his back and leg. Slowly, painfully, he ran his fingers from the top of the wall downward, moving inch by inch, searching for a hidden entrance to the underground tunnels that crisscrossed Yigris. Bending at all made him cry out, tears streaming down his face, but he forced himself onward, searching. He refused to walk out into the courtyard and face the guard who was undoubtedly outside. He refused to face his mother.

Let her remember him as a child, as the solemn, sad-faced boy she'd left behind. Let her live with her regrets just as he would have to live with his. He was no longer King Tollan the Innocent. Death and rebirth had burned the naivete out of him. He was only Tollan, and he was going to find the man he loved and try to make a life with him.

His fingers slipped into a crevice, and he felt the pressure lever click beneath his touch. He pushed his way into the tunnels and drew in a deep breath.

Despite the pain, despite everything that had happened in the dark of Yigris, Tollan was free.

APPENDIX

The Four Winds: The small island continent that consists of Vaga, the Balklands, Ladia and Yigris. The eastern end of the island is surrounded by the Alabaster Sea and the western end is surrounded by the Hadriak Sea.

It is said that the island was first inhabited by four siblings—Vagal, Balkar, Elladia and Gris—the children of the goddess Aegos herself. The mother wished to grant her four children each a gift so they may create a community that thrived in their own corners of the Four Winds, so she asked them each what they would want most for their people.

Vaga: Vagal was a bright, quiet girl who loved stories, songs and knowledge above all else. When her mother offered her a gift, she simply asked for language—the language of magic—so her people would be able to write down everything that was important to them, so they would never forget their truths and their tales.

It is said that this is where the Vagan mage language came from, and that those who can wield its power are the direct descendants of Vagal herself.

Vaga has been, as a general rule, a peaceful nation throughout its history, but the mage women are known to be fiercely protective of their secrets as well as the land granted to them by Aegos. It was encroachment upon this land that led to the Mage War. Where the lands of the Four Winds were once divided fairly evenly, Vaga now controls its own lands as well as the majority of those that were once controlled by Yigris.

In addition, Vaga controls a small island off its eastern coast called Magehold. It is said that this island was formed completely by mage work and that all the mage women's most important secrets are kept there.

Vaga is ruled by the Council of Queens—one greater queen and seven lesser queens, ranked in power. Socially, they practice polygamy, as one woman may marry several men. Sons of mage women are highly sought as breeding husbands.

The Balklands: Balkar was the eldest of Aegos's children and the strongest. He was born of the mother's tryst with Hadriak, God of the Seas. Like his father, he was smooth skinned and sharp toothed, but like his mother, he was curious and kind. When she offered him a gift for his people, he asked for knowledge of healing and herbs so that he and his people might help each other survive.

Thus was born the Balklander Medicants, who through their brews and herblore are said to be able to raise the dead, cure the incurable, incite love from hate, and bring swift, silent death.

While Balklanders may appear menacing, most are jolly and fun loving. They can be trained in the art of combat but are often more comfortable in more compassionate roles such as caregiver, physician or priest.

The people of the Balklands are ruled by a child ruler who gives up the throne when she or he comes of age. They are advised by a council of twelve, who are chosen at random from all walks of life and all areas of the country to serve for a period of five years. When a child ruler comes of age, she or he is replaced by another child chosen at random from all of those born seventy-two moons earlier.

Ladia: Elladia was Aegos's youngest child, a shy, patient girl who enjoyed tending her gardens more than she enjoyed tending to her lessons. When the mother offered her a gift, Elladia knew immediately that what she wanted for her people was that they should always know peace and never grow hungry.

Her mother was quite proud of her requests, and so she granted her both gifts—the everlasting peace of neutrality and the magic to keep her people fed, no matter their hardships.

The Ladian elders are so secretive that almost nothing is known of their magic. However, the landscape is clear enough. There is sparse vegetation, but their large herds are famous even beyond the shores of the Four Winds. The lands are dry and rocky, yet every year, they supply the rest of the continent with grain, sugar and produce.

Ladians as a people are reclusive and isolationist. Their merchants do trade, but only within their harbors. The Ladian process of government is unknown.

Yigris: The last of Aegos's children, Gris, was shrewd and clever, though selfish and unkind. He watched as his sisters and brother made their requests, and he found them all silly. He wished that his people would always have gold to make others do their bidding. He believed that gold was the solution to all of their needs, and he knew he could always count on his brother and sisters to help, should the need arise. His people would have gold to compensate them, so, of course, they would agree.

It is said that the sigh Aegos released upon hearing his request was loud enough to be heard on Far Coast, but she did as he asked and used her power to fill the earth under his lands with deep, plentiful veins of gold. In her kindness, and even though he had not asked her to, she even gave his people, known as Aurors, the power to draw magic from their gold.

Some time later, Gris grew lonely. He had hordes of gold but no one to share his great golden palace with. One day, he saw a pretty young woman in the street outside his palace selling flowers. He started to watch her every day. He became infatuated with her, but she spurned his advances.

The girl's family was rather poor, despite the prosperity of Yigris, and Gris solved his loneliness by purchasing a marriage contract, against the girl's will, from her father for a pile of gold.

It is said that Aegos was so angered by this that she wiped the memory of the Aurors's magic from their minds, leaving Yigris with a finite amount of gold. In a rage, she turned her back on her selfish son.

The Secret Pact: The secret pact is the document that helped bring about the end of the Mage War by uniting the criminal aspects of Yigris underneath the city with the respectable nobles in the city above. One family, House Daghan, has held the remains of the city-state of Yigris in a peaceful stalemate for over one hundred and fifty years. The document was signed by Jenn Daghan and his sister, Olyn, and it gave her control over the thieves, whores, assassins, pirates and mercenaries of Yigris, while ensuring that Under would pay taxes to the King of Above. By uniting during the Mage War, the two groups were able to keep the Vagan mage women at a distance while they negotiated a cessation of aggressions.

Above: Above is the aboveground portions of Yigris that rise upon hills, leading upward to Palace Hill. It includes Brighthold, Merchant Row and Whitebeach. Unofficially, the term also refers to the noble and merchant class citizens of the city.

Socially, the people in this group are conservative. They do not mingle with other classes, and they follow a strict patriarchal rule.

Under: Under is the aboveground portions of Yigris that sit at sea level, including Dockside and Shadowtown, as well as the entirety of the underground tunnels beneath the city. Unofficially, the term also refers to the peasants and criminal elements within the city of Yigris.

Socially, the people in this group are much more liberal than those in Above. They do not generally wed, and they follow a loosely matriarchal society.

The Church: While most people of the Four Winds worship Aegos, the Yigrisian branch has taken on a more commerce-driven ideal. They cater to the noble and merchant class in Above, while often participating in the dealings of those of Under. Even the temple itself contains hidden depths used for the lesser-known workings of the Holy Aegosian Church.

The Dalinn: The Dalinn are a specially trained elite group of priests and priestesses in the Yigrisian church who serve the goddess through sex acts. They are highly respected and sought after, both for their prowess in the sexual arts and for their closeness to the goddess. A night with a Dalinn can cost a small fortune, and most who've experienced it will say that it was a fortune well spent.

The Ain: The Ain are an elite squadron of two hundred warriors who are trained and maintained by the Holy Aegosian Church.

Housed within the depths of the Slit, they guard the secret banks of the church. The last time they were called into active battle was during the Mage War, when nearly two-thirds of their number died at the hands of only a handful of mage women.

The Shadow Guild: The Shadow Guild is the business aspect of Under, falling under the direction of the Queen of Under. It includes all business dealings of whores, thieves, mercenaries, pirates and assassins of Yigris. All those who fall under the Shadow Guild's rule must pay their dues, but in return they are protected by the might of the Queen of Under, as well as given shelter, food and clothing. Those who provide for the queen are in turn provided for.

The Guild Council: The Guild Council consists of the public heads of the different factions of Under, which include the pirates, thieves, whores, sellswords, and assassins. They report directly to the Queen of Under.

Riquin Hawkbeard: Riquin is the head of pirates. Born the son of a Yigrisian merchant sailor, he joined the Guild when his father lost his ship to pay his gambling debts. Bright and brutal, Riquin climbed the ranks quickly and became captain of his own ship, the *Amber Mew*, by the time he was thirty.

Dalia One-Eye: Dalia is the leader of thieves. Dalia was raised in Under and was picking noblemen's pockets by the time she was four. She lost an eye at eighteen, when she had the choice between saving her eye or stealing a diamond-studded bracelet. Though she is the leader of thieves and must spend most of her time with bureaucracy, she still occasionally goes out on the hunt, simply to keep up her skills. She is currently seventy-three years old.

Madam Yimur: Yimur is the mistress of whores and paramours. The daughter and granddaughter of a whore, Yimur was raised in the Six-Mast surrounded by sex workers her entire life. Woefully flat-chested, she made it her goal to become so sought after that she would have to turn men away. The tales of Yimur's kisses spread far and wide, and men (and women) came from as far away as the Balklands to spend a night with her. In the end, she married a merchant sailor and turned them all away, choosing to spend her time overseeing those who worked for her instead.

Gellen Brightblade: Gellen is the captain of sellswords. Little is known of him. It is believed that he may be Ladian, though he denies it. He is a vicious fighter, a shrewd tactician and a merciless drinker. He and Riquin despise each other, while he and Dalia are close friends.

Devery Nightsbane: Devery is the master of assassins. The youngest member of the council, he is the son of a Farcastian noblewoman who immigrated to Yigris several years ago. He is unnaturally fast, and his name strikes fear in the hearts of those in the know throughout the Four Winds.

ACKNOWLEDGMENTS

Accomplishing anything worth doing never happens in a vacuum. They say it takes a village to raise a child, but it took a small island nation to raise this book. Without the help of friends, family, acquaintances and one very helpful stranger, this story would still be just a pile of words on a hard drive, and that is all it ever would have become.

First and foremost, I must uphold a promise that I made almost four years ago. Two-thirds of the way through writing the first draft of *The Queen Underneath*, my computer crashed, and I lost the document. I had saved it to the cloud, but the program I was using wasn't compatible (note to Scrivener users—this is a real thing), and I spent about six hours howling and sobbing until a stranger—a man named Hutch who worked for Google— helped me find my book floating in the ether of the internet. I promised him that if I were to ever see that book published,

275

he would be the first name mentioned in the acknowledgments. So here it is, Hutch from Google. Without your help, this book would never even have been finished. You made this possible, and my gratitude can't be expressed with only a few words on this page.

Second, but nearly as important to the finished product of this novel as Hutch finding my book, is my amazing agent, Rena Rossner. I don't really even have the words to say, publicly, how much your belief in me and my work has meant to me, but let me just say that if we were together at a pub, after a few glasses, I'd be weeping and possibly getting down on one knee to propose to you. Your advice, your editorial notes, your listening ear when I was falling apart have made you invaluable, but your kind heart has made you my friend. You are a rock star, and I can never thank you enough.

Thank you to my fantastic editors, Alyssa Raymond and Lauren Knowles, who have guided this story in such a brilliant, beautiful way. Thank you for believing in Gemma and her ragtag crew. To Ruth, my copyeditor, to Rosie Gutmann who designed the final product, to Will and everyone else at Page Street who had a hand in bringing Yigris to life, I salute you and am so grateful for all your hard work.

To the Ozzies—my poet friends who put up with my sword-waving, beheading, blood-letting ways, I can't tell you how much your friendship, support and words have meant to me. Bryan—you're a huge part of why I'm here. Thanks for making me go to that first meeting. Debbie—I love you with all my heart, tiny preacher woman. Thank you for brushing off my tarnished soul every once in while. John R.—your words set my creative heart aflame. Your classes are a cathedral. And Susan— dear encyclopedia of wisdom and wit—thank you for everything but especially for playing matchmaker. To Judy, who is too smart by half and too kind by three-quarters—you are the sister of my heart and the critique partner of my dreams.

To my dear friends who have suffered through beta readings—Doug, Liana, Wendy, Earl, and Kevin—you guys are the real MVPs. The finished product is so much better because of the sludge you waded through. To all my agent sibs—I'm so glad to be on this journey with you guys. Thanks for making me laugh with your GIFs, your wit and your love of avocados.

This book is about found family, which was important for me because I didn't find a good portion of my family until I was a grown woman. Ric and Carolyn—you add to every story I'll ever tell. We don't share blood, but you are my team. Thank all the gods that the dice shook out the way they did, because I don't want to live in a world where you aren't my family.

And to my blood family. You know who you are. Thank you for everything—I don't have enough pages to write all the ways that you helped shape me into the woman who finally grew up to be an author, but thank you, Mom, for stories at bedtime and overlooking the fact that I was still reading at 2:00 a.m. Thank you Jo and Cassy, Jen, Jon and Bill for hours of pretend, for always being there and for growing up to not just be my siblings, but also my friends. To Grandma H.—thank you for always giving me books for Christmas and for being a wonderful storyteller. Grandma and Grandpa M. and Grandpa H.—I so wish you were here to see this. I love you and will miss you always. And to my daddy—thank you for *Beastmaster* and *Star Wars*, *Star Trek*, and *Johnny Quest*. I only ever wanted to make you proud.

Thank you most of all, Isabella, Grayson, Willow, and Duncan for putting up with microwave dinners and a daydreaming mom. For loving me despite my flaws, and for teaching me that all the best books have maps, and every story is made better with magic. I used to think that my dream was to be an author, but in fact my dream job is being your mom. Publishing this book is just a bonus. And to Clay, who saved me from myself, thank you for believing in me enough for the both of us. Thank you for being you.

ABOUT THE AUTHOR

Stacey Filak is an unabashed Chicago Bears fan, a die-hard tabletop role player, a partially recovered Pinterest addict, and a born-again Viking princess. She lives in Michigan with her husband and four children, as well as a menagerie of pop-culture-named pets. She can be found haunting Twitter (@staceyfilak) when she's not busy crafting worlds, daydreaming about recipes she'll never make, or plotting her enemies' demise. *The Queen Underneath* is her first book.